FALLEN ANGELS

Terence West

FALLEN ANGELS

DOUBLE DRAGON

Dedication

This novel is dedicated to my beloved wife Shannon. Without her, none of this would be possible. Thank you.

Thanks

I really owe this book to the assistance of a lot of people. First and foremost, my wife Shannon, my mother and father, Donna and Herman, and my sister, Danae, of whom without this book probably wouldn't have been finished. They were kind enough to read through the first few drafts and keep a smile on their faces. Thanks guys!

CHAPTER ONE

Shades of brown and yellow painted the desolate landscape as the Great Pyramid rose magnificently from the Giza plateau. Two smaller pyramids on both sides guarded it. A large crowd had gathered in front of the massive stone paws of the sphinx.

The Sphinx, according to Egyptian mythology, was a creature of mythical proportions. It had the body of a lion with the head of a man. Towering above the crowd, the head shadowed them from the burning sun of the Egyptian desert. Excitement was thick in the air.

A tall brunette woman wearing a cotton t-shirt and a pair of khaki shorts stood in front of the sphinx. She was speaking to several workers holding pry bars. She was beautiful, but not by popular standards. Her hair was long and curly with curves at the bottom rolling in toward her neck. Her eyes were a deep green which showed her intelligence, but also displayed her youthful excitement. She would turn thirty next year, but for now, she still enjoyed being in her twenties.

Trying to explain what she wanted the workers to do, she demonstrated the technique with her hands. The workers began to understand and went quickly to work. They slammed their pry bars into the edges of a massive stone door they had located in the front of the Sphinx and began to loosen it. The door was flush with the surrounding surface. It was a very large stone, close to ten feet tall and eight feet wide.

An older man emerged from one of the tents

that stood near the Sphinx. He was close to six feet tall, but very overweight. He had a full gray beard matching his shoulder length hair. Adjusting his thick black-rimmed glasses, he looked down into the dig site and was mortified to see what was unfolding. Yelling at the top of his lungs, he tried to warn the men off. Knowing his pleas were going unheard, he mustered all his stamina and started to run toward the Sphinx.

The brunette woman heard his pleas, but ignored them. She had worked too hard and too long to be stopped, especially when she was this close. She barked commands at the workers, pushing them harder toward her goal.

The stout man made his way through the group. "Alex!" He pushed his way to the front. "Alex, you can't do this."

She turned and shot him an icy glance. "Freddie, I'm not going to stop now." "You have to." He pulled her away from the group. "Alex, I just got off the phone with the Egyptian Government and they've pulled the plug. They want us out." Doctor Alex Robinson turned away from him. "Dammit. What happened?" Freddie placed his hand on her shoulder. "They called the Chicago Museum of Natural History and discovered you lied about your credentials."

"I was wondering how long that story was going to hold water." She turned to look at her workers. They had almost pried the stone loose. She smiled. "We have to finish, Freddie."

"I can't let you do that!" He was motioning emphatically. "The Egyptian Government is sending several military units down here to see that we are escorted out and turned over to them. They want our heads, Alex!"

"Then they're going to have to drag me kicking and screaming out of here because I'm not going to quit. Not when I'm this close!" She turned and began to walk back to the Sphinx. "You can leave if you want, Freddie," she smiled at him, "but I'm staying."

Shaking his head, he followed her back to the Sphinx. The workers had pulled the stone about three inches out of the surface. Far enough so they could get a grip on it and begin to pull. Alex stood behind them watching in excitement.

Freddie took his place by her side. "What do you expect to find?"

She looked at him and shrugged. "I'm not sure. The carbon dating on this place proves that it predates the Pyramids and everything else built here. We've also used sonar equipment and discovered a large room hidden beneath the Sphinx. This stone obviously hides the entrance to that room. What we find there could validate all my work."

"What work, Alex? You've been running around the world since you were eighteen looking for signs of extra-terrestrial involvement on our planet. What makes you think you'll find it here in Egypt?"

"Many researchers have theorized that these incredible monuments were actually built by aliens."

Freddie lowered his head. "I've funded your work since you started, but I had no idea you were going to take it this far. The Egyptian Government isn't happy with us and they're going to be here very soon."

"I know, I know—"

She stopped as the mighty stone fell away from the door throwing up a huge cloud of dust. The workers scattered. As the dust began to clear, a lone figure stood in front of the doorway. It was Alex.

"Finally." Stepping toward the door, she peered into a long, dark hallway. "Freddie," she turned to look behind her. "Hand me a flashlight."

Curiosity overwhelmed him. Reaching into a worn out tan bag slung over his shoulder, he removed two silver flashlights. Handing one to Alex, he flipped his on and followed her into the doorway. Looking behind them, they saw all the workers standing in a semicircle around the door.

"They think this place is cursed."

"That's absurd, Freddie. It's been proven that none of the tombs have been cursed. Everyone who died has done so from ancient bacteria found inside them."

Both looked at each other. Removing two filter masks from his bag, they quickly slipped them over their mouths. Stepping further into the hall, they found themselves standing in front of a large staircase.

"I wonder how far it goes down?"

Freddie shook his head. "What did the sonar show?" "We estimated it was about forty feet down."

"Well, let's find out."

The two slowly made their way down the ancient staircase. Shining her light on the wall, Alex saw thousands of Egyptian Hieroglyphs.

Freddie reached over and ran his hand across the wall. "What do they say?" Alex stepped near the wall and gave it a quick once-over. "I have no idea." "Some researcher you are." He let out a small nervous chuckle, trying to lighten the mood.

She smiled and began to make her way down the stairs again. Finally reaching the bottom, they found themselves confronted with another long hallway. At its end, they could see light filtering out onto the floor and walls. "Do you see that?" Alex asked anxiously. Freddie nodded. "What do you think it is?"

"I'm not sure, but I want to find out," she replied.

The two quickened their pace as they proceeded. Stopping short, they found themselves confronted with a beam of bright light that crossed the hall in front of them. "Looks like a trap."

Freddie examined the beam. "How ingenious. It seems rather like one of those laser alarm systems. When you break the beam, an alarm goes off."

"But in our case, something bad happens." Freddie nodded in agreement.

Alex stared at the beam and snapped her fingers. "I've got an idea!" Removing a small round compact from her back pocket she flipped it open revealing a mirror in the top. Snapping it in two, she dropped the bottom half. After pulling a piece of gum out of her mouth, she stuck it to the top of the mirror.

"What are you doing?"

"I think I saw this on an episode of 'MacGyver' once. I'm going to try and reflect the beam back into itself. All we have to do is decide which side the beam is emanating from." The two examined both sides. "They look identical."

"Well, you've got two choices and one of them is wrong."

"That's very reassuring, Freddie." Looking at both ends, she decided to just pick one. "I've got a fifty-fifty chance. Here goes." Moving to the right side, she readied herself. Counting to three, she quickly passed the mirror into the beam. Slowly moving it to the right, she attached it to the wall with the piece of gum. She let out a sigh of relief. Turning to Freddie, she motioned for him to keep moving.

The light appeared to grow brighter as they approached the end of the hall. Rounding the corner, they were confronted by a blinding white glare. Raising their hands to shield their eyes, they both pulled on their sunglasses.

"Oh my God," Alex muttered nervously under her breath.

Moving into the room, they stared at the object in the center. "Alex...what is it?" Freddie was awestruck.

"It's not Egyptian. That's for sure."

Stepping toward the object, they both tried to get a good look at it through the harsh light. It seemed to be a long cylinder with a glowing orb on top. It was standing upright thanks to four legs that extended down from its midsection. On the front of the device was an odd-shaped control panel. It was pentagon-shaped with what seemed to be a recessed handprint in the center.

Alex neared the panel to get a better look at it. Something about the handprint struck her as odd.

"Look at this, Freddie."

Freddie knelt down beside it. "It has four fingers just like a normal hand, but look at that! It has what appear to be two thumbs. One on each side."

"Definitely not Egyptian," Alex was transfixed on the device, "or human for that matter." The two were startled by the sound of footsteps behind them. Twirling around, Alex found herself confronted by several armed guards. "Oh shit," she muttered.

The guards shouted at them in a foreign language much too quickly for Freddie and Alex to understand. They motioned for the two to slowly step away from the object. Nodding to each other, Alex and Freddie raised their hands as the two guards escorted them out of the room at gunpoint.

Alex leaned over and whispered to Freddie. "We need to get out of here." Simultaneously, they glanced over at the mirror Alex had attached to the wall. "Are you thinking what I'm thinking?"

Freddie nodded. "This will be very dangerous." Alex agreed. "When I say so, run like hell."

She let out a loud moan and doubled over. She leaned her left hand against the wall near the mirror and wrapped the other around her stomach. Freddie immediately moved to her side and laid a hand on her back. Turning back to the soldiers, he motioned frantically. "She's sick! We need help!"

The soldiers looked at each other. "Sick," they repeated in broken English. Alex looked up at Freddie. "Run!" Quickly snapping her arm across the mirror, the light beam shot across the hall. The two took off, breaking the beam. The soldiers began to take aim when several wooden spikes shot out of the wall impaling them. Alex watched in horror as they hung awkwardly from the spikes as their bodies twitched.

Alex and Freddie were almost to the top of the stairs when another soldier dashed out of the room, his machine gun blazing. Freddie screamed as a bullet ripped through his back dropping him instantly to his knees.

Alex reached the top of the stairs and flattened to the ground. "Freddie!"

Waving with his hand, he motioned for her to run. "Go! I can't walk!" He moaned. "Save yourself!"

"No!"

"Do it!" he shouted.

She looked at him with tears in her eyes. "I'll never forget you, Freddie!" Jumping to her feet, she ran out the doorway. Breaching the entrance, Alex was quickly blinded by the bright sun. She had inadvertently left her sunglasses inside the lower chamber. Taking several steps forward, she bumped into something.

"Ma'am, I'm going to have to ask you to come with us."

"Who...?" She trailed off in midsentence. Looking up, she was standing in front of a large man dressed in Air Force blue.

He grabbed Alex's arm. Twisting it behind her back, he handcuffed her hands together. Guiding her toward his jeep, he forced her inside. Sitting on either side of her were two heavily armed soldiers in desert camouflage. The man in the US Air Force uniform climbed into the driver's seat and cranked the ignition.

"Where am I being taken?" Alex asked.

"You are to be taken directly to the airport, where you will be shipped back to the States," the driver answered. "For what reason?"

The man was silent. Putting the jeep in gear, he turned the car around and began to drive out of the desert.

***

Living in Las Vegas isn't all it's cracked up to be. Christina Anderson played with the ballpoint pen in her hand as she stared aimlessly off into space. Brushing an errant lock of blonde hair out of her blue eyes, she began to doodle in her notebook. Her bright red nail polish looked good with her black sweater, she thought.

The room had a bit of a musty smell mingled with the scents of perfume and cologne from the other students. She glanced around at the various objects dealing with history in the room. Her eyes caught on a painting of Washington crossing the Delaware. She wondered how he managed not to fall out of the boat standing up like that.

"Are you with us, Christina?"

Snapping herself out of a daze, she sat up in her chair and stared at her third hour history teacher. "Yes, Mr. Matthews."

"Then you can answer the question I just asked the class." Nick Matthews hated teaching senior History. He remembered a time when the students brought the teachers apples instead of packing guns in their backpacks. He was a man in his fifties with gray hair and a neatly trimmed beard. The gray suit he wore was one he had owned for years, but he liked it.

"What was the question again?" Christina asked sheepishly.

"Can you tell me what the Magna Carta is?" He stared at her impatiently. "From the chapter you read last night in your history book!" He stepped closer to her.

She could feel all the eyes of her fellow students burning into her. Christina's mind was frantic as she searched for the answer. She hadn't read the assigned chapter last night, instead, opting to go hang out with a couple friends. She decided to make a guess. "The Magna Carta was—" She was cut off by the bell.

"Well, well, Ms. Anderson. Saved by the bell." The kids started to gather up their notebooks and get up to go to the next class. "Before you leave, don't forget to read chapters five and six tonight and finish the questions at the end of each chapter."

Christina hurriedly began to pull her papers together and throw them into her bag. She rushed out of the room so as to avoid facing the wrath of Mr. Matthews. "Hold on there, Tina!" She spun around to see her friend Libby standing behind her.

"Oh, hey, Libby." She was relieved to discover it wasn't Mr. Matthews following her.

"Man, Matthews came down kind of hard on you in there." Libby was the same age as Christina. She was close to the same height, but had short brown hair and brown eyes. "He is such an asshole sometimes."

"Yeah, really."

The two girls started to walk down the crowded hall toward their lockers. Libby was about a step behind Christina. She had stopped to admire one of the many boys she liked in school. Catching up quickly, she grabbed Christina's arm. "How about we skip fourth period and get an early lunch?"

"I don't know. This will be the third time we've missed English this week." She fumbled with the combination on her locker. Opening the door, she lifted her backpack off and placed it in her locker. "All right. Let's go." Both girls checked themselves in her mirror, and then slammed the locker door closed.

The school was open campus, so it was generally known that if a student wanted to leave early or show up late, they could. It was a policy the school board was desperately trying to change. The two girls strode through the metal detectors in the lobby and out the front doors.

"Come on, we'll take my car," Libby began to walk in the direction of the parking lot.

"What are we gonna do if we get caught, Libby?" Christina had always been the good girl in school. She always tried to get good grades and had never missed a day of class until her senior year.

"We'll be fine. We'll just tell them we have senior priv this hour." Libby, on the other hand, was known as many things in school, none of them good. "That always works for me."

Arriving at the parking lot next to the school, they weaved their way through until they found Libby's car. Both girls climbed into Libby's red convertible Volkswagen Bug.

Immediately rolling down her window, Libby lit a cigarette she'd pulled out of her purse. "Want one, Tina?"

"No thanks." She watched Libby take a long

drag off the cigarette and slowly exhale the smoke. "How can you stand the smell of those things?"

"You get used to it." Putting the car into gear, she pulled out of the parking lot. "Where do you want to go for lunch?"

"Wherever. You're driving, and I'm not really that hungry." Christina rolled down her window to try and get some fresh air. "Just somewhere we can talk."

"I know just the place. Trust me." With that, Libby piloted the car out into traffic and headed downtown.

The two didn't talk on the way. Libby had turned up her car stereo and was dancing and singing along to her favorite song on the radio. Christina stared out the window at the many casinos they passed. The signs on the casinos advertised everything from a ninety-nine cent buffet to topless waitresses, obviously geared to pull in tourists.

Christina had only lived in Las Vegas for about a year now. She'd moved out here when her dad had taken an important government job. Prior to this, her father was a captain in the Air Force. She had never really asked many questions about his new job, mostly because she really didn't care and didn't want to be living in what she referred to as 'the sin capitol of the world'. She missed living in Colorado. It had been a culture shock moving here. She was used to living in the mountains with all the trees and snow. Every time she looked at the Nevada landscape, she cringed. She hated the sagebrush and the one hundred and fifteen degree temperatures in the summer. *Oh, well. In a couple months, I'll be eighteen and graduated from school and I'll finally leave this god-forsaken state.*

"We're here." Libby pulled the car up to the curb and shut off the engine. Both girls got out of the car and into the dry heat of the Nevada summer. "Louigi's Pizza Palace."

"Louigi's Pizza Palace? Why here?"

"I was in the mood for a slice of pie, and there's a really cute waiter that works here."

Christina sighed and followed Libby into the restaurant. It was decorated in what seemed to be a mobster motif of the late twenties. All the tables had red and white checkered tablecloths, and the room was dimly lit with green light fixtures that hung from the ceiling. Along the left wall were several booths, and at the very back, she could see the white tiled kitchen through the service window. Several ceiling fans whirred nosily above their heads. In the far corner, a group of men sat at a table laughing and drinking beer. They all turned to look at the two teenage girls as they entered.

"Come on, let's get a booth." Libby grabbed Christina's hand and led her over to the first empty booth. Sitting down, Libby immediately grabbed a menu and began to look it over. "I'm in the mood for pepperoni, how about you?"

Christina nodded in response. She was feeling a little guilty for skipping class, and a little uncomfortable in this place. "Can I tell you something, Libby?"

Libby looked up from her menu just long enough to answer. "Yeah, sure. What is it, girlfriend?"

Christina began to fidget a little bit. She hadn't wanted to say anything to anyone, but at the same

19

time, she wanted to make sure she wasn't losing her mind. She started off slowly. "I haven't been sleeping well."

"Well that's not too uncommon," Libby answered from behind her menu.

Grabbing the menu away from Libby, she set it on the table next to her. "I haven't been sleeping well ever since I moved to this state." She hesitated, "I've been having the worst nightmares."

"Probably just the shock from moving here. I've heard of people dying when they move to a different state because it's so different." Libby's voice was heavy with sarcasm.

"Get serious, Libby." Christina was now regretting bringing up the subject. "I keep having the same recurring nightmare."

Libby's interest had now been piqued. "Tell me about it."

Just thinking about the nightmare brought vivid flashes of it into her mind. Christina cringed. "Okay." She composed herself. "They all start the same way. I'm lying in bed, then suddenly—"

"A gorgeous man walks into your room, right?" Libby began to snicker to herself. "Actually, that sounds more like one of my dreams."

Christina just glared at her.

"I'm sorry." Libby declared, unnerved by Christina's stare.

"Anyway," Christina paused momentarily to see if she would be interrupted again, "I'm lying in bed, then suddenly, I see a bright flash of blue light outside my bedroom window." The small hairs on the back of her neck began to stand up. "Then I'm somewhere else."

"Where?"

"I don't know. I've never seen this place before. The walls seem to be made of some kind of metal, because they're really shiny."

"Do you remember anything else about the dream?"

Christina nodded. "There's something else." She felt her throat get tight. "It feels like a hospital because I always end up lying on some kind of table." Libby moved her hand onto Christina's. She could see that Christina was visibly shaking now.

"You don't have to go on," Libby comforted her.

"The worst part is always at the very end. I'm lying naked on the table and I can't move. I can hear things moving around me, but I can't turn my head to look. Even if I could, it's very dark in the room and I can hardly see anything." Christina bit her lip to try not to cry. "Then I feel something touch my leg and slowly move its way up my body." Libby's mouth was now agape as she listened to emotion fill Christina's voice. "I don't know what's touching me, but I don't like it. As it nears my chest, a very bright white light begins to shine in my eyes." Christina stopped. It was the last part she always hated the worst. "I start to feel like I'm drifting off to sleep. My eyelids get heavy and I have a hard time keeping them open. But just before they close, I see this...this thing." The tears began to roll down her face smearing her mascara into long, black streaks on her cheeks. "It's not human, Libby. Just for a moment, I see it's large head and it's big black eyes!"

Libby was shocked at how traumatic this dream

21

was to Christina. She searched for an explanation to ease her friend's pain. "Maybe it is a person. You're just seeing them through the glare of the bright light making their face shadowed, or—"

Christina cut her off. "No, that's not it. Don't you think I thought of that? I know what I see in my dreams sounds crazy, but that's what happens!" She was crying heavily now. Lifting her hands up, she placed them over her face. Both girls sat there silently for what seemed an eternity until the waitress interrupted them.

"Is everything all right here, girls?"

Libby looked up. "Yeah. We're just fine, and just leaving." Standing, she reached down and put her hand on Christina's shoulder. "Come on, girl. I'm gonna take you home."

Christina looked at Libby and nodded.

The car ride home seemed to take forever. Libby had turned off the radio and the only sound they could hear was the tires riding on the pavement. They arrived at Christina's house about ten minutes later. Christina's house was a tall light blue three- story house. The yard was always freshly cut and the hedges neatly trimmed. It was in a nice neighborhood, but all the houses tended to look alike. All the yards had tall trees along the front and back of the property, but the browns of the Nevada desert were visible looming behind them. Her house was on the very edge of a new subdivision.

Libby was the first to get out of the car. She walked around to the passenger side and reached in to help Christina out. Slowly, she guided her up the stairs to her front door. Christina dug her hand into the right pocket of her jeans and fished out a set of keys. Finding the front door key, she tried to push it into the lock, but her hands were still shaking badly. Libby took the keys from her and easily unlocked the door.

Stepping inside, Libby closed the door behind them. She had been in Christina's house many times, but every time she saw it, she felt like a poor girl walking into a palace. Christina's house was lavishly decorated. The floors were all a deep brown shade of hardwood. The furniture was cream colored and perfectly complimented the white interior walls of the house. Pictures of all shapes and sizes hung on the walls showing the many members of Christina's family at various stages of their lives. The front wall of the house was a gigantic picture window with light white curtains that filtered the sunlight as it flowed in, giving the living room a kind of ethereal feel.

Taking a right into the hallway, Libby moved Christina past the master bedroom and up the stairs to the second floor where her bedroom was located. This floor was very similar to the first, except the wood floors had been replaced by a light colored carpet. Libby swiftly guided Christina into her bedroom.

Entering her room, she quickly sat Christina down on the edge of her king-size bed. "Stay here for a sec, okay, Tina? I'll go get you a cold rag."

She walked swiftly through the room, past hordes of stuffed animals that occupied every corner, and into Christina's bathroom. Opening one of the cupboards on the left, she retrieved a small washcloth and quickly wetted it down with cold water in the sink. Walking back, she found Christina now lying down on her bed.

Handing the cold rag to Christina, she sat down on the edge of the bed next to her, "You okay, Tina?"

Christina shook her head. "I'm tired of the dreams, Libby. I don't think I can handle them anymore." She placed the cold rag over her eyes and lay back on the bed.

"Yes you can. You're stronger than that."

Christina shook her head in a mocking gesture. "Yeah right."

Libby slid back onto the bed next to Christina. Looking up at the ceiling, she noticed for the first time a poster of Brad Pitt with his shirt off. "What do we have here?"

"What?" Christina asked innocently.

"The poster on your ceiling. Isn't that Brad Pitt? No wonder you're having bad dreams." Libby began to giggle.

For the first time all day, Christina tuned to Libby and smiled. "Some people have no taste I guess." The two girls laughed. It felt good.

"Sorry to run out on you, but I've got to get back to school. If I miss anthropology one more time, Mrs. Jenkins is going to fail me." Libby sat up and turned around to face Christina. "Are you gonna be all right?"

"Yeah, I'm gonna be okay."

Libby stood and headed for the door. She stopped just outside of it and turned around. "I'll call you tonight to check on you, okay?"

"Okay." Christina smiled at Libby.

Libby walked out the door, only to peek back

24

in. "And by the way, I'll bring over my poster of Ricky Martin. You'll definitely have better dreams with him watching over you at night." She snickered and left.

Christina lay on the bed for a long time, just allowing her mind to drift off into space. She tried not to think of anything as she held the cool damp rag to her face. The images from her dreams kept flashing in her mind no matter how hard she tried to keep them out. *I have to do something to keep myself occupied.*

Looking around her room, she decided to turn on her stereo and listen to some music. It always had a way of calming her down. Reaching over to her nightstand, she grabbed the remote and hit the power button, then the play button. The music rolled out of the speakers filling her mind with nothing but images of the band performing. Lying back on the bed, she slowly began to drift off to sleep. She knew she couldn't face the dreams again, but she was so tired...

***

Christina's mind was screaming. Her lungs and body felt as if they were on fire, but she forced herself to keep running. The crunch of the hard dirt under her feet was being drowned out by the sound of her heart pounding in her ears. The warm summer wind blew across her body giving her some relief from the hot sweat running down her face and chest. Her long blond hair was waving in the wind as she ran and her deep blue eyes were filled with terror. The night sky was empty and silent. The moon stared down unforgivingly, as if it knew what was about to happen.

25

Running hard across the desert, she spotted a highway in the distance. *I need to get out of here.* She couldn't remember how she had gotten here, but she knew she hadn't walked. Christina wore only a nightgown and she wasn't prone to sleepwalking. She didn't know why she was running, only that she was very scared, more scared than she had ever been in her life.

Just before she reached the highway, her bare foot caught on a rock knocking her sprawling to the ground. Her body hit hard against the pavement. She started to lift herself up, when she felt a trickle of blood drip down from her nose. She looked at her bare foot that had caught the rock. It had a jagged cut all the way across the top and was bleeding heavily. Wiping the blood away from her nose with her sleeve, she slowly turned to look behind her.

The landscape was barren except for a few jagged rocks and several patches of sagebrush. A few mounds of dirt filled her vision. She couldn't help remembering how much these looked like the sand dunes of the Sahara Desert she had seen in her schoolbooks. Then she saw it. She felt as if all her nightmares had come to life. Slowly rising above one of the mounds, she saw an ominous glowing blue light.

Lifting herself off the ground, she forced herself to start running again. The cut on her foot was getting worse and the pavement was chewing up the soles of her feet. She turned to look behind her just in time to see the ball of light streak past her in the sky. Instantly stopping, she gasped as the ball of light hovered silently in front of her.

The light looked tiny when she had first seen it.

Now with it not more than ten feet in front of her, she could see how enormous it actually was. It was slowly changing from a light blue to a crisp white, then back again. She could see it slowly rotate from left to right.

Her heart felt as if it was going to jump out of her chest, it was beating so hard. Trying to take in a deep breath, she lifted her arms in front of her in an effort to guard herself from the ball of light. Although no sound was coming from the object, Christina could feel an intense heat emanating from it.

Her eyes were trying to adjust to the blue light in front of her when it slowly began to brighten. A wave of fear washed over her. Her mind was telling her to run, but her body wasn't responding. Quickly, she began to feel tired. Her muscles ached from the run through the desert. Her eyelids became heavy and finally shut. She felt her pulse slowing and it was becoming harder and harder to take a deep breath. It became too much. She gave up fighting. Her body crumpled to the ground, her head crashing onto the highway.

Christina's mind was drifting on the edge of consciousness when she began to hear a voice inside her head. "You will not be harmed," it asserted calmly. The voice sounded as if three distinctly different voices had said the same thing in unison, but she could tell this was only one voice. Calmness washed over her body as she finally succumbed to sleep. "You will not be harmed."

***

Jake Silver had moved to Lake Tahoe, Nevada to get away from it all. He didn't go far enough,

27

though. He lifted his feet up onto his desk. The worn leather chair creaked in protest as he leaned back in it. Reaching to the left side of his desk, he opened his top drawer and extracted a cigar out of the humidor inside. From the pocket of his faded leather jacket, he retrieved a gold colored lighter and snapped it open. "Where did you say they found her?" He lit his cigar.

Two clients, a man and woman both in their fifties, sat in chairs opposite Jake's. They had introduced themselves as the Andersons, Jonathan and Susan Anderson. They were well dressed, but not extravagant. The man wore a gray suit with a blue tie. He had dark hair with gray streaks and was starting to go bald on top. A full beard also graying graced his face.

The woman was first to speak. "On a highway about ten miles outside Las Vegas." She was a little overweight for her height, but it was barely noticeable. Wearing a black skirt with a white blouse, her blond hair was pulled up with a clip. She felt her voice fill with emotion. She had promised herself she would be strong. "She...she was apparently beaten," she placed her hand over her mouth, trying to hold back the tears. "And raped," she hissed.

Jake brought his cigar to his mouth and took a long puff. "How long ago did this happen?"

"About a week ago."

"And you've already come to a private investigator?" The couple looked at each other in silence. Jake dismissed the question. "Why me? Isn't this the sort of case the police usually handle?"

"Yes." The man spoke up for the first time

since entering Jake's office. "We tried it their way. We went through all the standard police methods, which turned up nothing. Mr. Silver," he glanced at his wife, then back again, "we're tired of all the red tape and bureaucratic bullshit. We want someone who isn't afraid to cross some lines to get what we want."

"And what exactly is it you want?" Jake asked.

Sitting forward in his chair, Jonathan kept his voice low as he answered the question. "We want to find the son of a bitch who raped our daughter and make him pay." Leaning back in his chair, he continued. "We must know, Mr. Silver." He paused as he began to lose his composure. Reaching over, his wife placed her hand on his shoulder and gave him a look of courage. "Christina must know."

"Christina being your daughter?"

"Yes." Susan began to answer questions again. "She'll turn eighteen this October. She's a senior in high school. We just want her to have a normal life. We want her to grow up knowing her parents love her very much and would do anything for her." Jake nodded in understanding. "Can you help us, Mr. Silver?"

Jake leaned over on his desk crossing both arms, cigar still smoldering in his left hand. He rolled it between his fingers and thumb before returning the cigar to his mouth. "I'm going to take this case, Mr. and Mrs. Anderson." He saw a smile light up both their faces. "Don't get excited yet, we still have to talk about my fee. I want my usual four hundred dollar fee. That's non-negotiable. Plus, you put me up in a hotel for the entire time I'm in Vegas, and—"

29

Jonathan cut him off, "That's fine, Mr. Silver. Whatever you want. We just want to help our daughter."

Jake nodded. "Then it's a deal." The three stood up and shook hands. Jonathan and Susan moved toward his office door. Susan stopped and turned around, "When will you be able to start?"

"One, two days, tops. I have some loose ends to take care of here before I leave. I'll fax over the necessary paperwork later this afternoon." Susan smiled at Jake again, and then walked out the door closing it behind her.

Jake leaned back in his chair putting his feet back up on the desk. He was wearing blue denim jeans with a white T-shirt, a faded leather jacket and a pair of hiking boots. He rubbed his hands through his short blondish hair and closed his eyes for a moment.

Glancing down at the calendar on his desk, he noticed today's date had a large red circle around it. *Damn, it's Samantha's birthday.*

Picking up the phone, he quickly dialed her number from memory. He didn't like the fact she lived so far away from him in Baltimore, but when the divorce was finalized, she had chosen to go with her mother to Maryland. He listened as it rang on the other end and finally picked up.

"Hi!" A young woman's voice answered on the other end. "Hey, Samantha! Happy birth—"

The rest of the recording quickly cut him off. "This is Samantha Silver. I can't come to the phone right now, but if you leave me a message, I'll get back to you!"

He waited for the beep. "Hey, Samantha, it's

your dad. I just wanted to call and wish you a happy twenty-first birthday," he hated talking to answering machines. "I've got to go out of town for a couple days, but I'll try and get a hold of you when I get back. I love you, Sammy. Take care."

He slowly hung up the phone. He felt like a heel for forgetting his daughter's birthday. He knew he would have to pick up a present for her when he got back.

Laying the remainder of his cigar in the ashtray, he stood and walked around his desk to his office door. He looked at his office. It was a disaster. He hadn't had time to buy a filing cabinet yet, so all his files and papers were strewn across the floor along the back wall. Jake's desk was a large metal one he had picked up at a yard sale. It always reminded him of the ones teachers sat behind when he was in high school.

Out the two windows behind his desk, he could see Lake Tahoe. It was a calm day, despite the rain that had been falling intermittently throughout the past few hours. He turned to glance at his office door. It had an opaque window with the words 'Jake Silver—Private Investigator', stenciled sloppily on it. He recalled, vaguely, a dispute over a sum of money with the artist he had hired to professionally do it. He also recalled punching the artist in the mouth and buying a cheap set of markers. He told himself to be more patient next time.

Opening the door, he was greeted by a cool breeze blowing in off the lake. Locking the door behind him, he strode out into the crisp air. All around him were the mountains and trees of Lake Tahoe. He liked it here. It was very different from

New Orleans where he had been an FBI agent for twelve years. He had steadily gotten used to the mountains instead of the flatness of Louisiana the longer he spent here.

He had also grown to like his new life. He did miss the day to day action of being an agent sometimes.

Walking briskly across the street, he spotted a familiar face inside one of the local coffee shops. Pushing open the door, a cowbell clanged above his head. *I hate that damn bell.* Jake groaned.

The store's sweet smell reminded him of his grandmother's kitchen when he was a child. She always had cookies, or brownies or some treat fit for kids, cooking in her oven. He remembered spending a lot of time there as a child. He also recalled spending a summer at fat camp because of all that.

A young woman of about thirty emerged from behind the counter. "What brings you here, Jake?"

Rachel Wills moved to Tahoe shortly after Jake had. She had taken the job at the coffee shop to help pay her way back into college. She was shorter than Jake, but not by much. Her reddish hair hung in curls above her shoulders while her light green eyes sparkled in the summer light. Her smile could always brighten up a room. She was what Jake referred to as a 'people person'.

Jake walked around the end of the counter toward Rachel. "Would you mind keeping an eye on my house for a while?"

"What's in it for me?" Rachel quipped.

"You already live next door, so it shouldn't be any trouble," Jake thought for a moment, "and I'll return the favor sometime."

She smiled. "You twisted my arm. I'll do it." She began to arrange a batch of pastries on the shelf in front of her. "Where are you off to this time?"

"Las Vegas. I'll only be a couple days at most. Jake reached down to grab a cinnamon roll out of the display case. Rachel immediately slapped his hand away.

"Are you gonna pay for that?"

"Are you gonna watch my house?"

"I hate it when you answer a question with a question." She picked up the roll and handed it to Jake. "You better get going before I change my mind."

"I appreciate this, Rachel. I'll be leaving tomorrow morning. I've got a long drive ahead of me, so I want to get started early." Rachel nodded as Jake began to walk toward the door. He opened it with his free hand. He had taken one step out the door, when he turned and looked back. "Thanks again, Rachel," he smiled, "and for the roll."

Walking out of the shop, he pulled off an edge of the pastry and popped it into his mouth. He hadn't eaten all day. The light rain that had been falling was gradually turning into a small storm. Realizing he better get inside before it got any worse, Jake ran back across the street to where his car was parked. He hopped into his blue Taurus and started the engine.

He had always wanted something bigger like a truck or an SUV, but the first rule of private investigators kept him from that. P.I.'s usually tried to drive a very unassuming car in an effort not to be seen when tailing someone. This was about as unassuming as it got. His house was a couple miles down the road from his office. Pulling onto the street, he flipped on the windshield wipers to try and wipe away the endless stream of rain.

Taking the last bite of the cinnamon roll, he licked his fingers to get the extra frosting off them. "Rachel sure can bake," Jake laughed to himself.

***

"Christina, lie down and try to relax." Doctor Bill Monroe was trying to be as calm as possible. He had done many such physicals, but never one on an alleged 'alien abductee'.

"I'm trying." Her voice was still a little rough from all the screaming she had done several nights before during the 'incident', as it had now become known. She was wearing the standard light blue hospital gown loosely tied around her back. She was very familiar with this room. She had been here many times since her family had moved to Las Vegas. She suffered from a touch of asthma, a disease of the lungs. Christina's condition required her to see a doctor for a check-up at least once a month. She knew the sink in the far corner where he always washed his hands before and after an examination, the yellow flowered wallpaper, and the black padded examination table where she now sat. She usually liked seeing Doctor Monroe, but she didn't want to be here today.

"I'm gonna take a look at some of your abrasions now, okay?" Monroe tried to be as gentle as he could. He had always heard that people who claimed to have an abduction experience were a little on the strange side, and he didn't want to set her off. He started by examining the foot she had caught on the rock. "You have a really nasty cut on your foot, Christina. How did you say you got it again?"

"I told you." Her tone was firm, but full of exasperation. She was tired of all the endless questions. "I tripped on a rock and cut my foot."

"I see." He leaned in for a closer look. "You're going to need a few stitches in this foot. We can take care of that right here in the office. " He stood and pulled off his rubber gloves. "Let me go get the nurse and we'll stitch you right up, okay?" He smiled. "Maybe we'll even give you one of those *cool* Flintstone Band Aids." He was trying to lighten the mood.

"I'm not a child. I don't want a fucking Flintstone Band Aid, okay? I just want to go home."

Monroe nodded, then left the room. Walking down the hallway, he entered the waiting room. It was full of people, but he easily spotted Christina's parents. "Susan, Jonathan!" He motioned for them to join him.

Both parents looked up and then quickly walked across the room to meet him.

"What is it, Bill?" Sarah asked first. "Is there a problem with Tina? "No, no," he assured them, "it's just that..."

"What is it, Doc?" Jonathan asked.

"It's just that I've never had Christina treat me this way."

"What way, Bill?" Susan was like all mothers. She never wanted to acknowledge that her baby was growing up.

"I've been your family doctor ever since you moved to Vegas," he steadied himself. "She's treating me like an enemy."

"She's been that way ever since the 'incident'." Susan confessed, embarrassed by her daughter. "She's always been such a good girl."

Jonathan cut in, "Is there anything wrong with her, Doc?"

"Besides the cuts and bruises and a mild concussion, no. Nothing. She seems to be perfectly healthy." He knew what he wanted to advise the couple, but he didn't want to hurt their feelings. Sometimes being friends with patients is the hardest thing. "I think," he fumbled the words around in his mouth, "maybe she should see a—"

"What, Bill? A specialist?" Susan was hoping, but she knew what was coming.

Bill shook his head. "I think she should see a psychiatrist." That word shook Susan deeply.

"Really? A psychiatrist?" Jonathan was a little rattled by the word, too.

"I think it would be in her best interests. She doesn't seem to have any physical problems. Maybe her problem is psychological." He seemed apologetic for even suggesting it. "That's the only thing I can think of."

Suddenly, the door burst open "Doctor! We need you right now!" It was one of Monroe's nurses.

"What is it, Janice?"

"Something is wrong with the Anderson girl!" Bill looked at Jonathan and Susan very quickly, then dashed off. As he neared the room, he could hear Christina's panicked screams. Throwing open the door, he found two nurses trying to hold her down on the examination table.

"What's going on here?" Monroe shouted.

"We don't know! I was ready to begin putting in the sutures—"

Christina screamed again as the tears rolled down her face, "Let me go, let me go, let me go, let me fucking go!" Fragments of hidden memories flashed inside her mind's eye. Images of beings with large black eyes...the black eyes...those terrible, soulless black eyes...

The nurse began again, shouting above Christina's screams. "I brought out the lamp so I could get more light. I accidentally flashed it in her eyes and she went berserk!"

"Hold her down, I'll give her a sedative!" Moving over to his table in the examining room, he yanked open one of the drawers and quickly pulled out a syringe. Setting the syringe on the table, he quickly opened another drawer and pulled out a small bottle of clear liquid.

Christina let loose with another blood-curdling scream. She couldn't see the doctor, or the two nurses. Her eyes were filled with images of another examination room, of horrible beings with large black almond-shaped eyes.

"All right. I'm ready. Keep her still!"

"We're trying, Doctor," the nurses exclaimed.

Using all his skill, he swabbed an area on her upper arm with alcohol. Taking a final deep breath, he tossed the cotton swab aside and plunged the syringe into the soft flesh of her upper arm. Christina wailed again in agony, but slowly began to quiet down. "All right, you can let her go now. She's gonna be all right."

"Doctor, she's saying something..." The three

37

leaned carefully over her.

She was mumbling incoherently, "I just want to go home," Christina moaned. "...Please, don't hurt me... the eyes... the black eyes... no, they're not human..."

***

Jake arrived home minutes later. He turned into his driveway and glanced at his house. The rain was giving everything a very tranquil look. The sprawling pine trees behind it dwarfed his small two-bedroom home. From his driveway, he could see Rachel's house. Hers was very similar to his in design and area. Pulling his car into the garage, he shut off the engine and got out. Walking to the front of the garage, he leaned up against the edge of the door and just watched it rain for a while. Pulling the door closed, he walked inside.

His house was loosely decorated. The entire place was painted a dull tan with brown highlights for the door and window frames. His walls were bare, except for a few scattered remnants from his past. His living room was filled with a green flowered couch against the far wall and a small nineteen inch television sitting on a milk crate opposite. Two other milk crates sat in front of the couch with a piece of plywood on top to form a table, on top of which was a small red lamp. The final piece of furniture was a bookshelf in the corner of the room. *Home.*

Walking over to the television, he clicked it on to the news. It made a crackling noise as it slowly sputtered to life. He clicked on the lamp, which barely gave off enough light to illuminate the room. Pulling off his coat, he dumped it on the floor.

Heading around the corner, he found himself in his kitchen. It was a disaster, looking as if a small tropical hurricane had hit it. Pots lay piled on top of each other atop the stove, and his glasses, plates and silverware lay heaped in the kitchen sink. "Probably time to invest in a dishwasher," he pulled a plate out of the sink that seemed to have something growing on it, "or some new dishes." He smiled to himself as he dropped the plate back into the sink. He ransacked the kitchen for a clean, or partially clean, glass. After searching for several minutes without much luck, he decided he wasn't thirsty anymore.

Leaving the kitchen, he walked down the hall into his bedroom. This was the only room in the house even partially clean. Mostly because he still hadn't unpacked most of his clothes. The floor was scattered with brown cardboard boxes still full of clothes and decorations. On the far wall next to the window was a tall wooden dresser. In the middle of the room was his bed, which was rarely used. Jake usually fell asleep on the couch.

Pulling off his white T-shirt, he tossed it on the top of a stack of clothes that had been accumulating for about two weeks now. He paused for a moment. His house seemed unusually still this evening. He decided it was probably due to the rain outside. Moving to his closet, he dug out an old gray sweater very close to falling apart at the seams. Slipping it on, he returned to the living room and sat on his couch to watch the news.

"...Plane crash today in Los Angeles. The 747 apparently couldn't put down her landing gear. Officials say the pilot was advised to try a belly landing. The plane hit the runway and skidded to

the end, where it capsized and burst into flames. The fire caused massive structural damage to the plane...” The woman reporting the gruesome story was your average blonde broadcaster. Her lips were a dull shade of red and her teeth were pearly white.

“The news is so dammed depressing. I should really stop watching it,” but Jake didn’t.

“Twenty-seven reported fatalities along with the pilot. Rescue workers arrived on the scene within minutes to save the remainder of the crew and passengers. This...” A knock at the door startled him. Standing, he walked over to the TV and clicked it off. “Hold on. I’m coming, “ he shouted. He walked to his front door. Opening it, he found a very wet Rachel Wills standing there.

“What brings you over tonight, Rachel?”

“You forgot to give me a key to your house, Jake,” Rachel said as she walked in the door.

“Oh, yeah. Sorry.” Closing the door behind her, he followed her into his living room. “Go ahead and grab yourself a beer out of the fridge. I’ll get you a towel.”

“Thanks.” She moved around the corner of the living room into the kitchen and let out an audible gasp. “Jesus, Jake. What the hell happened in here?”

He handed her a towel as he peeked around the corner. “What can I say, Rachel, I’m a bachelor.” The pair moved into the living room and sat down on the couch.

“Wow, Jake. Did you decorate this place yourself?” “Yeah, why?”

She began to giggle. “A red lamp, brown carpet, a green couch, a table made out of milk crates and plywood?”

"I like it."

Rachel set her beer on the plywood table watching it for a moment hoping the table wouldn't tip over. "Tell me about your job."

"It's a long story."

"I have plenty of time."

"I don't." Getting up, he walked over to the bookshelf in the corner of the living room. Reaching up on the top shelf, he produced a small silver key. "Here's the key to my house, Rachel. I don't mean to be rude, but I have to get some sleep. It's going to be a long day tomorrow."

"I understand. I just was wondering." She stood and took the key from Jake.

"Tell, you what. As soon as I get back, we'll go out for drinks and I'll tell you about my job, okay?"

"Sounds good to me." She started to make her way towards the front door. "How long are you going to be gone again?"

"Shouldn't be more than a couple days."

"Okay." Opening the front door, Rachel stepped out into the rain. "You be careful, Jake."

"I will, Rachel." Closing the door behind him, he walked into his bedroom. Pulling off his sweater and jeans, he slipped into his bed. Reaching over to his nightstand, he set his alarm for seven. The display read ten forty-five. Clicking off the light, he laid back thinking about the case he was about to begin the next morning. He felt more and more confident about his chances of solving the case the longer he thought about it. Eleven o'clock rolled around and he was fast asleep.

CHAPTER TWO

Christina couldn't sleep. Ever since the incident, she had gotten little rest. Even though she was allowed to come home, she hadn't been able to relax. Every time she closed her eyes, she saw the hovering blue light, but there was something else...something elusive. It nagged at her like a splinter in her mind, coming so close to remembering, yet it felt as if something was blocking her.

Burying her face in her pillows, she began to cry out of frustration. Waves of fear and anger washed over her body just as a light knock on her door caught her attention.

Christina quickly sat up and watched as the door began to creep open. She felt a burst of fear grip her body as those long, gray, fingers slipped around the door.

"Honey? Are you okay?"

It was only her father. Relief flowed over her as she answered, "Yeah, I just can't sleep." Christina pulled herself into a sitting position.

"Doctor Monroe said you might be experiencing some sleepless nights due to your concussion, but you really should try and get some rest." Sitting down on the edge of the bed, he placed his hand on her shaking knee.

"Every time I close my eyes, I see the light, Dad." She closed her eyes and leaned forward placing her head in her hands.

"What about the light, Tina?" He paused for a

moment. He didn't want to push her. "Can you describe it to me?" He had asked this question many times before, but had never gotten a satisfying answer.

"It kind of floated." She lifted her head to look at him. "It scorched the sage brush like it was on fire. Then they came after me."

Jonathan looked puzzled for a moment. "Who's 'they'?"

"I don't know who they are," she leaned her head over on his broad shoulders. "I don't even know *what* they are."

He was worried. Maybe Doctor Monroe was right. Maybe she did need to see a psychiatrist. One thing still troubled him though. "How did you get into the desert in the first place? You were about ten miles out of town with no shoes on."

"I don't know." She was visibly shaking now. "Dad, I don't want to talk about it anymore, okay?"

"I understand, sweetheart. I'll leave so you can get some rest." He stood up and walked toward the door.

"Dad?" Her voice was soft and quiet. "Yeah, Tina?"

"Could you leave the light on?"

He smiled. "No problem. Goodnight, sweetie." He left the room closing the door behind him.

She listened as the sounds of his footsteps slowly faded away. The light did little to ease her nerves. Lying back down in bed, she pulled the covers tightly up to her neck. She lay there, motionless, watching the shadows of the tree branches just outside her window dance on the ceiling.

She felt as if hours had passed as she lay there, but when she looked at the clock, she saw only a few minutes had elapsed. Pulling the covers up over her head, she lay there cowering. The fear was paralyzing her body.

***

It took four strong men dressed in yellow jumpsuits to carry in the large wooden crate. The device had looked deceptively light sitting underneath the Sphinx. They carefully set the crate down in front of several men dressed in long white lab coats, then exited the room.

The small room had highly polished silver floors and the walls were covered with several banks of computers. Tables occupied several spots in the room. They were filled with high-tech computer equipment and tools of all shapes and sizes.

One of the men lifted a crow bar off a nearby table and jammed it between the lid of the box and the body of the crate. With several swift cranks on the handle, the box's lid separated and fell to the floor.

The men marveled at the artifact inside. "Where did they say they recovered this?"

"On the Giza Plateau. Some researcher uncovered it beneath the Sphinx." "This is an incredible find. Do we have any idea what it does?"

"No, but it's been under the Sphinx for thousands of years and still registers incredible amounts of energy."

"Well, let's get to work." The men started to carefully pull the strange looking device out of the crate.

The morning light poured in through Jake's window. From under the covers, he removed his hands and began rubbing his eyes. He lifted himself into a sitting position and set his feet on the floor. Dragging his hands down his face, he tried to rub away the sleep. Still groggy, he glanced over at the clock on his nightstand. It was seven fourteen in the morning.

Fighting his body's urge to fall back to sleep, he stood and made his way into the bathroom. Turning on the faucet, he splashed some warm water on his face. *I am definitely not a morning person.*

He reached into the shower and turned it on. While waiting for it to warm up, he glanced across the hall into his room. His eyes caught the red glare of his digital clock. It read seven twenty-three. Jake walked over and shut the bathroom door. Something didn't feel right, but he couldn't place it. Pulling off his shorts, he checked the shower. Stepping in, he let the warm water flow over his body and wash away the sleep. He reached across to the shelves that held the soap and grabbed his shampoo. Squeezing a generous helping into his hand, he closed his eyes and began to wash his hair.

Suddenly, Jake began to feel very uncomfortable. He opened his eyes just as soap washed into both. His vision blurred and his eyes stung, but he saw a dark shape in the shower with him. Momentarily forgetting the pain, he concentrated on the dark blur. Just as he began to get the soap out of his eyes, he saw a long spindly arm reach for him. He panicked. Trying to move

45

back, he slipped on the floor banging his head on the edge of the bathtub. He sank slowly to the floor, his head throbbing. He felt himself begin to lose consciousness. The last thing he remembered was the large dark object looming over him.

Jake awoke in the same place he had fallen. The shower was turned off and there was no steam on the mirror. *How long was I out?* He began to stand up, but an intense burst of pain shot through his head knocking him back to the floor. When he finally managed to step out of the shower, he clamped both hands to the side of his head. He staggered out of the bathroom and into his room. He was shocked to realize the display on his alarm clock read ten. *I was out for three hours?* Running his hand down his face, his mind jumped to something more insidious. *What the hell was that thing in the shower?*

Trying to shake the cobwebs from his mind, he ran over to his dresser and pulled out a pair of sweats and put them on. He rushed to his front door. It was still locked. *What's going on here?* He ran to his back door and checked it. Still locked. Jake's nerves were running wild. At every noise in the house, a shiver of anxiety ran through him.

"The hell with this. I'm getting out of here!" Running back to his room, he yanked his suitcase out of the closet and tossed it on the bed. Moving over to his dresser, he began removing clothes and tossing them haphazardly into his suitcase. Out of the corner of his eye, he saw a dark form streak in front of his bedroom door. Slowly, he stopped what he was doing and watched the intruder with his peripheral vision. Moments passed as the dark form stood frozen in the doorway.

He knew it was now or never. Snapping his head around, he drew a bead on the object and began to squeeze the trigger, but it was gone.

A loud buzzing noise cut through his thoughts arousing him from a deep sleep. Immediately sitting up, he wiped the sweat off his face. *Just a damned dream. I've got to stop watching those late night horror movies.*

Jake quickly got out of bed and walked over to the closet and pulled on an old pair of blue jeans and a shirt. He moved to his dresser and began to rummage through his sock drawer trying to find a pair that resembled each other. He began to pack up a week's worth of clothes in his suitcase. He reached up to the top shelf in his closet and removed a box of expensive cigars. Taking one from the box, he deposited the rest in his luggage. Popping the cigar into his mouth, he stepped over to his dresser and removed his handgun and a box of shells and placed them in his suitcase. He flipped the lid closed and zipped up his bag. He quickly grabbed it off his bed and left the bedroom.

Double-checking the living room, Jake made sure everything was in order for Rachel while she housesat. He gave the place a cursory glance and decided it was good enough. Grabbing his coat off the floor where he'd deposited it last night, he slung it over his shoulder. With his suitcase in hand, he walked out into the garage.

Opening the trunk of his car, he tossed in his suitcase. Closing it, he made his way to the driver's side and got in. Hitting the button on his visor, the garage door began to open. Jake pulled the keys out of his coat pocket and started up the car and pulled out.

It was a beautiful day in Lake Tahoe. The sun glistened off the morning dew that still clung to the trees and plants in his yard. It was just above the tops of the mountains casting an orange glow across the landscape. He took a deep breath of the fresh morning air. He loved the smell of pine trees in the morning. Pulling the car out of his driveway, he maneuvered into traffic and made his way to his office.

Stopping next to the curb in front of his place of business, he shut off the engine and got out of the car. Using his keys to unlock his office door, he opened it and walked inside. Quickly moving to his desk, he slid opened one of his drawers and removed a small gray laptop computer. After plugging it in and turning it on, he keyed in to initialize his modem. Logging on to the FBI's site, he accessed their database of criminals. Being a former FBI agent, he knew how to circumvent their security measures, and easily slipped into the database.

"Let's see here. I want to take a look at the Anderson family." Typing his query into the search field, he tapped the enter key with his finger and began the search. "Nothing on a Susan Anderson. Let's try Jonathan." Re-entering his information, he again started the search. This time, it came up with a very interesting find. "Restricted? Why would it be restricted?" He sat there for a moment, planning his next move. "We'll come back to Jonathan. Let's see what we have on Christina Anderson." The computer whirred to life once again. The search took only seconds and returned nothing. "Well, Mister Anderson, you seem to be the only one with any kind of record. Why is it restricted?" He clicked off the computer.

"I think it's time I called in an old favor." Picking up his office phone, he dialed a New Orleans number. The phone rang several times before someone answered "FBI, New Orleans field office. How can I help you?" It was a pleasant female voice on the other end.

"Hi, I need to speak with Special Agent Connor, please."

A moment passed. Jake knew she was obviously initiating some sort of recording device on her end. This had become common practice since every nut case who wants to blow up a building calls the FBI to tell them about it first. "One moment, please." Jake waited on the phone patiently. Connor owed him a favor.

"Special Agent Connor." He answered the phone with a very stern, no nonsense kind of voice.

"Hey, Sam! How the hell are you? This is your old partner, Jake!"

"Well, I'll be damned. How are you, Silver?" Instantly, his voice lightened into a more playful tone.

"I'm doing good. How's life in the Bureau?"

"Same as ever. What made you to decide to call me?" Jake hesitated, "I need to ask you a favor, Sam."

"Somehow, I knew this was coming. You know I can't help you out anymore, Jake. I could get in a lot of trouble if my AD found out."

Jake took on an apologetic tone. "I know, I

know. I wouldn't call you if it weren't important. Besides, you still owe me one."

"For what?"

Jake could hear Connor roll his eyes on the other end. "That time I saved your life."

"What?"

"You know what I'm talking about. That time I took a bullet for you in that warehouse shootout." Jake had the scar to prove it.

"Okay, okay. I remember." He lowered his voice. "What can I help you with, Jake?"

"I was looking up some information on a client of mine in the database—"

"You were in the database?" Sam asked angrily. "You know you're not supposed to be in there anymore!"

"I know. I just needed a little background." Jake began to feel a little impatient. "Are you gonna help me or not?"

"All right. Hold on. Let me fire up my computer." It took a few seconds. Jake could hear the clacking of keys on the other end of the phone, then the familiar beep of the hard drive. "Okay I'm ready. Give me the name."

"The name is Jonathan Anderson." Jake waited a moment. "When I pulled it up, it was marked 'restricted'."

Over the phone, he heard his friend typing the information into his computer. "Okay, the name is coming up now. Well, looks like you were right, Jake. It's restricted."

"Yeah, but what does that mean?"

"I don't run across this kind of thing very often, but usually, it means he's some sort of high-level government employee."

Jake ran that information through his mind for a moment. It didn't mean anything to him at present. "Thanks, Sam. I appreciate it."

"No problem. Hey, by the way, you take care out there in Nevada. Don't you go playing in any toxic waste or anything," Sam smiled.

"Very funny," Jake said with a forced laugh. "Take it easy, Sam." Jake slowly returned the phone to its base, toying with his new information for a moment. *Jonathan Anderson is a government employee. What does that mean, and does it have anything to do with this case?*

Standing, Jake decided he would have the whole drive to Vegas to think about it and was really eager to get started. He grabbed his laptop off his desk and walked out the front door hastily locking it behind him. Jumping into his car, he carefully stowed the laptop on the back seat, then started the vehicle.

Jake retrieved a cigar and his lighter from his pocket. Flipping the lighter open, he ran his thumb over the switch and lit the flame. He held the flame to the end of the cigar and took a couple of long puffs. As smoke began to roll out of the cigar, he snapped shut the lighter. *This case is getting more interesting by the minute.*

CHAPTER THREE

The southern Nevada desert streaked past. It was a strange place at night. Shadows fell in odd directions, and patches of sagebrush created entire sections that somehow, seemed to swallow the light.

The crew of the helicopter was bathed in an unnatural red light used only for night-time combat missions. The four members worked their controls diligently as the pilot skimmed across the desert. This was an average reconnaissance mission and all the men knew it. The pilots had taken to calling this patrol the "snooze cruise", because nothing ever happened on this watch. None of the men knew now, but this night would be very different.

"Radar, what's the word, Red?"

Lieutenant Gary 'Red' Jansen was manning the radar controls. Checking his screens, he flipped several switches. "Nothing to report, sir. All scopes clear." Keying in a command, he changed the settings on his screens.

"Very well," Captain John Pike said with a sigh. "Let's put this flight to bed. Heading back to Dreamland." Swiftly and skillfully, he turned the helicopter toward the south. The chopper smoothly answered the controls.

Looking hard at the screens, Red noticed something. Moving several dials, he recalibrated his controls to make sure he was getting a true reading. "We've got something on radar, sir!" He was understandably excited.

"What is it?"

"Don't know, sir, but it's moving fast, and right toward us."

"All right, let's see what it is. Bearing?" *Finally, some action,* he thought with a wicked smile. Even if it was a stray kite drifting into their airspace, it was something to do.

"Bearing is due north of us. It's still heading our way." Altering his course, he turned the helicopter to the north.

"Bogey is still bearing down on us. ETA," he rechecked his computations, "three minutes. It definitely has size and mass, sir. The object could be an aircraft."

"Good. Let's see what we can see." He turned and nodded to his co-pilot, "Lock and load."

The co-pilot nodded and swiftly began to carry out the order. He toggled the switch on his radio to the 'on' position. "Dreamland, this is Red Bird. Do you copy?"

His radio crackled to life, "Dreamland. Go ahead, Red Bird."

"Dreamland, we have a radar contact directly north of us and heading our way. Its ETA is about two minutes now. Please advise."

***

Turning away from his screen, Colonel Rick Hunter swiveled around in his chair. He was a tall and slender man with dark skin and hair. He wore his blue Air Force uniform well. "General Davis, could you come take a look at this?"

The command center was buzzing with activity. The bare metal walls were filled with banks of controls and video screens. Men moved chaotically across the room trying to finish their tasks in a timely fashion. This was the central brain of Area 51, deep in the Nevada desert. Every radio communication went through this room. The base, mostly built underground, was safely hidden from wandering eyes and satellite photos.

General Tom Davis was sitting in the command chair at the center of the room. He was a tall, broad man in his early sixties. The four stars on each shoulder sparkled in the lights of the control room. "Yes, Colonel? What is it?" His gray hair was crisply combed and his rugged face neatly shaved.

"Sir, Red Bird has just reported in. They have an object on radar due north of their location, and quickly bearing down on them."

"What is it, Colonel?"

"We don't know that yet, sir."

"Well, find out, Colonel." His voice was hard and stern.

"Yes, sir." Spinning around in his chair, Hunter keyed his mic. "Red Bird, this is Dreamland."

Pike breathed a sigh of relief. The bogey was now less than a minute away from contact. "Red Bird here, Dreamland. Awaiting instructions."

"Red Bird, permission to investigate bogey granted."

"Yes, sir." Clicking off the mic, Pike turned to his co-pilot. "We have orders to intercept and investigate the bogey."

"Roger that."

"Red, what's the status of the bogey?"

"Still closing, sir. ETA is now about thirty seconds."

Pike flipped on the mic again. "Flight one-three-four to unauthorized aircraft. You are entering

54

restricted airspace. Repeat, you are entering restricted airspace. Turn your craft around." Nothing. Static filled the speaker.

"Captain, bogey is continuing on its present course."

Pike tried again. "Flight one-three-four to unauthorized craft. You are in restricted airspace. Be advised, deadly force is authorized. Repeat, deadly force is auth—" A sharp high-pitched squeal erupted from his headset. Just as quickly as it began, the noise stopped. "Jesus Christ!"

"Captain, what the hell was that?"

"Beats the hell out of me." Searching the sky with his eyes, Pike couldn't see the intruder yet. "Do we have a visual on the target yet?" He felt his crew tighten up. This was strange. Even for working at Area 51. "Stay loose. We're just here to take a look around—"

Red interrupted. "Sorry, sir, but I've got a visual. It's dead ahead of us."

Staring directly in front of him, Pike spotted the object. It appeared spherical, and was emanating a blue glare. "Are those it's running lights? They're damn bright." The bogey was casting an odd glare on the ground around it.

"Sir, the object has stopped. It's hovering directly ahead of us."

"Bringing us into a hover. Gunner, target your weapons on the bogey." Seconds went by. The crew watched intently as the object just hovered in front of them. Slowly, the gunner activated his controls bringing his guns to bear.

"Weapons locked, sir." Suddenly, the object shot out of its hovering position toward them. A beam of bright white light slammed into the helicopter, rocking it back and forth. In a matter of seconds, the object was right on top of them. Seeing the object right in front of them, the men gasped at its sheer size.

Pike panicked and quickly started to bark orders. "Evasive maneuvers! Fire all weapons!" The gunner squeezed the triggers and in an instant, the sky lit up with gunfire. The yellow glow of the tracer bullets slid past the object as it quickly jumped to the left. "What the hell is going on?" Grabbing the controls, he pushed the helicopter to the right just as the object headed straight for them. "Fire missiles! I want that son of a bitch out of my sky!"

Smoke and flame ejected from the firing tubes as two missiles headed straight for the object. Shifting right, the object easily avoided the first missile, but was caught by the second one. Sparks and debris erupted from the object as it began to violently shake.

Pulling the helicopter back from the object, Pike tried to avoid the wildly spinning craft, but it was too late. The object careened into the side of the helicopter, hitting the rotor blades first. Shards from the blades became projectiles that shot in all directions. Several large chunks of the rotors ripped into the cabin, cleaving the metal in two. Smoke erupted from the gash and quickly began to fill the cockpit. The two craft quickly began to fall to the earth engulfed in a giant ball of flame.

"Dreamland! Mayday, mayday! We are going down!" Pike was frantic. He knew his chances of survival were slim. "Repeat: we are going down!

Object is hostile! Mayday!"

The two vehicles rocketed into the ground, gaining velocity with every inch. The helicopter hit first and was instantly transformed into fragments of burning steel and rubble. The object hit next. Its nose slammed into the ground and dug in. The rear of the craft whipped around, slinging the entire ship away from the helicopter. Seconds later, it was over.

***

"Red Bird, do you copy?" Hunter keyed the mic again. "Red bird, do you copy?" Only static replied on the channel. "General Davis, Red Bird just sent out a mayday and both crafts have disappeared off our radar."

Davis stood and paced around the room. Turning in Hunter's direction, he stepped forward. "Damn." Rubbing his chin, he leaned over Hunter's shoulder. "Colonel, send out a search team for survivors and see what the hell it was that brought Red Bird down."

"Yes, sir."

Moving away from Hunter's console, Davis walked toward the side exit. Reaching into his jacket pocket, he removed a flat, rectangular piece of plastic resembling a credit card. Flipping over the key card in his hand, he slid it through the lock on the door. The lock was a silver box with a slit down the middle to slide the card through. It had two red lights on the left side and two green lights on the right. Immediately, the red lights switched to green and the door unlocked. Stepping out of the room, General Davis felt the cool regulated air blowing against his neck. The control room was regulated, but due to the staff inside, it stayed very warm.

Standing in the long corridor outside the control room, he leaned against one of the walls. The corridor was one of the few areas in the facility yet finished. The walls were still bare rock.

It had been a long week for Davis. It seemed to him that his week had been one botched mission after another. He had been posted at Area 51 for over fifteen years now. He was getting old and tired. He knew this would probably be the year he retired. But retiring from a position like this wasn't like any other job. Davis had seen things most people could never even imagine. This made it very difficult to return to civilian life. Rubbing his hand through his gray hair, he closed his eyes and exhaled a long, deep breath.

Several hours from now, Air Force Chief of Operations, General Perry, would be visiting the facilities at Area 51. Davis was dreading this. Perry was a five star general, whereas Davis only had four stars. Perry's visit was to decide if funding was still necessary for the project. It had been over fifty years since Area 51 had been put into service, and Davis was only the second man ever to be in charge here. He had taken over from an Army general when the base switched over to Air Force hands. The President, at the time of the switch, had made the change to Air Force control after the Army had failed to show any progress in the operation. That decision had been a huge turning point in base operations.

General Perry would surely be bringing several of the President's advisors along with him. Davis hoped his scientific minds would stack up to the

President's.

***

The drive from Lake Tahoe to Las Vegas was harder than Jake had expected. About an hour out of Tahoe, he'd left behind the tall pine trees and the greens and blues of the lake for the plain browns of the Nevada desert. Day was slowly fading into night. Looking out the window of his blue Taurus, it seemed to him like he had traveled into another world. The Sierra Nevada mountains had gradually faded into the hills of southern Nevada. The trees had shrunk and sprouted into bushes of sagebrush. He had his air conditioner cranked up, but was still sweating. Over the horizon, Jake began to see the bright lights of Las Vegas. He flicked a switch on the dashboard. Gusts of cool air began to flow out of the dark vents in front of him. Rolling down his passenger side window slightly, he retrieved a long brown cigar and lighter from his pocket. Lighting the cigar, he took a long puff and slowly exhaled it out the window.

Random thoughts were shooting through Jake's mind, most of them dealing with his newest case. The one piece of the puzzle that didn't fit was the hovering blue light. *What does that mean?*

As he took another long puff off his cigar, his gaze began to wander away from the road. There was one thing he could say for the desert, it had the most beautiful sunsets he had ever seen. As the sun dipped down behind the horizon, shades of orange, red, purple and blue mixed together to paint a wondrous picture across the western sky.

It was about forty-five minutes later when he crossed over a hill and began to gradually descend into Vegas. The lights of the casinos lit up the night in all the vibrant colors of the rainbow. Pulling a small piece of paper out of his pocket, he checked the name and address of his hotel. "'The Tikki Hotel and Casino'," a smile crossed his face, "Nice."

He decided to take the long way, through casino central. Cruising down the strip, he saw all sizes and shapes of humanity. The streets were packed with people on their way to dinner, or to catch a show, or just simply to go gambling. This had never appealed to Jake. In New Orleans, they had gambling on all the riverboats, and in Nevada, they had gambling everywhere. Every time you walked into a supermarket or gas station, you had to pass right by a ringing wall of one-armed bandits.

In front of one of the many casinos, a group of showgirls stood trying to draw people into the theater. They were swathed in sparkling costumes made out of strands of rhinestones and pink feathers. They all looked very similar with long pink gloves that reached up to their elbows and glittering silver stiletto heels. The extravagant headpieces they wore were crafted out of the same material as their costumes. Tall plumes of feathers shot out of the top standing at least a foot off their heads. Jake roughly estimated that about ninety percent of their body was uncovered. One of the girls noticed Jake's stare, so she gave him a little wiggle of her hips and blew him a kiss. *Maybe I could get used to this town.*

Leaving the strip behind, he drove deep into the heart of the city, finally arriving at his destination after several wrong turns. A foreign tourist had even shouted at him in another language when he managed to find himself driving the wrong way on a one-way street. Pulling into the casino parking lot, Jake tuned off his lights and got out of the car. Looking at the casino, he noticed its bright neon sign for the first time. It was a picture of a man in surf trunks with a large rounded wooden mask breathing fire. Yellow neon words flashed above it: "Tikki Hotel and Casino".

Walking through the front door, he was greeted by a menagerie of slot machines and gaming tables. The room was decorated with various stuffed aquatic animals on the walls and small groves of palm trees in every corner. The ceiling was painted black and had hundreds of small bulbs in it simulating the night sky. The gaming tables were made out of old surfboards with the fins taken off.

Two girls dressed in grass skirts met him at the door. "Welcome to the Tikki Hotel and Casino," they smiled broadly. "My name is Drew, and this is Jennifer." Drew's grass skirt hung just past her knees. She was wearing a tight blue Hawaiian shirt with a yellow floral print that she had tied in a knot at her waist showing off her trim stomach. She had Asian features as well as straight black hair and sparkling blue eyes. Jennifer was similarly dressed, except she had two flowers tucked in her short brown hair. Both girls produced a plastic Hawaiian lei from behind their backs, leaned forward and slid them around Jake's neck. "We're here to help our guests. What can we do for you tonight?"

"I'm staying here in the hotel. I have reservations. Can you girls point me to the reservation desk?" Jake was enjoying the attention from two very attractive women.

The two girls looked at each other seemingly disappointed he wasn't there to gamble. Drew pointed across the casino. "Walk straight that way," she said, the sexy tones gone from her voice. "There's a big sign. You can't miss it."

Before he could say thanks, the two girls had already turned and were talking to another couple that had just entered the casino. *What a strange city.* Lifting up his suitcase, Jake began to walk across the room. Weaving his way through the various people and tables, he finally arrived at the registration desk. Walking up to one of the receptionists, he immediately set his bag down and waited for service.

"How can I help you?" the young man behind the desk asked. He didn't seem old enough to drive, let alone be in a casino.

"My name is Jake Silver. I have a reservation," he handed the man his identification.

"Okay, let me check my computer real quick." Jake watched as the boy's fingers flew over the keys. It was only seconds before the information was being displayed on the screen, "Ah, yes, Mr. Silver. I have you right here. You will be staying in room two- twelve." Tearing off a sheet of paper that had been printing next to him, he handed it to Jake with a pen. "I'll just need your signature and we'll be ready to go."

Jake lifted the pen and hastily signed his name. He was eager to make it to his room and rest. "There you go." He handed the piece of paper back to the clerk.

"Okay, here's your key." He handed Jake what

looked like a credit card. "All you have to do is slide it through—"

"I know how to use a key card," Jake interrupted rudely. He resented the fact that every teenager who saw him assumed he didn't know how to program his VCR, let alone use a key card.

"Okay. Then let me tell you about the continental breakfast and the swimming pool."

"No thanks," Jake cut in. "Which way to the elevators?" The clerk pointed to his right.

"Thanks." Heading straight for the elevators, he punched the 'up' button and waited for it to slide down. He watched the glowing lights above the doors quickly count down, and the doors finally slide open. Stepping in, Jake jabbed the button for the second floor and watched as the door began to whisk shut.

"Hold the elevator please!"

He quickly pressed his hand against the door to keep it open. Peering outside, he saw a tall brunette woman running toward him.

She jumped into the elevator just as Jake closed the door. "Thanks. Most people wouldn't hold the door." Her long brown hair was streaked with blonde highlights that accented her green eyes. She was dressed in a pair of blue jeans and a dark gray shirt. The two stood in the elevator for a moment in silence. Turning, she held her hand out to Jake, "Hi. My name is Anne."

Jake took her hand and shook it. "Mine's Jake."

"Where you headed, Jake?" She had a smooth and soft voice.

"Just up to my room to catch a little nap. Been a long day." He lifted his head to watch the display above the doors count up to the second floor.

"I hear that. I've been on my feet all day long." A small bell chimed and the elevator doors began to slide open.

Jake extended his hand. "It was nice meeting you, Anne. I hope we see each other again."

Shaking his hand she gave him a smile, "Me too, Jake."

Jake stepped out just as the elevator doors began to close. Shaking the stupid grin off his face, he turned and looked down the long hall in front of him. The walls were decorated in much the same way as the casino. Turning to his right, he walked down the hall until he came across his room number. Sliding his key card into the lock, he heard the dead bolt slide out. Opening the door, he stepped in and shut it.

***

It was raining the day Christina decided to return to school. She had been gone for over two weeks now. Her mom had offered to give her a ride, so she wouldn't have to take the bus. Walking out the front door of their house, Christina looked up at the dark gray skies as she felt the raindrops pelt her. *I can't do this.* "Mom, I don't want to do this."

Susan Anderson had her long gray trench coat on as she came out of the house. She gave her daughter a quick glance. "Yes you can, honey. I know you're stronger than this." The two huddled together in the doorway. It provided a little shelter from the rain.

Christina was dressed entirely in black, against her mother's wishes. The black sweater she wore with her black jeans was the same one she had worn the day of the incident. She didn't know why she insisted on wearing that particular outfit. Maybe it was psychological, but more likely, it was just a coincidence. Pulling her black leather jacket a little tighter around her shoulders, she stared at her mother. "The other kids are going to say things about me. Libby's already told me about some of the rumors circulating about me at school. I'm not ready. I need more time." She stuck her hands in her pockets.

"Christina Dee Anderson. I don't believe what I'm hearing."

Christina was shocked. Her mother hadn't used that tone with her since she was a little girl.

"Never in your life have you backed down from something," Susan continued, "don't let this be the first." She looked up into the rain as she considered her next line. "As for those kids," she shrugged, "who cares what they think? Only you and God know what really happened."

Christina knew her mother didn't believe her story about the glowing blue object. She needed more of an Earthly answer to satisfy her. She needed to see someone pay for this. "I know, Mom. I'm just scared, I guess."

Wrapping her arms around Christina, she gave her a big hug. "You're gonna be just fine."

"Yeah, you're probably right," Christina conceded. She didn't know how, but mothers always had a way of making problems seem a lot smaller than they actually were.

"All right. On the count of three, we run for the car, okay?" Christina smiled. "Ready."

"Okay." Both women leaned over like sprinters

in the one hundred meter dash. "One...two...three!"

They took off toward the car parked in the driveway. Stepping in a puddle along the way, Christina accidentally splashed her mom. Christina stopped and laughed as her mom tried vainly to wipe the water off her coat.

"Now you did it, girl!"

With a big smile, the two began to splash each other with water. Finally climbing into the car, the two were soaked to the bone. This was the first time they had laughed together since the "incident". Both realized it, and knew they should cherish this moment. A bond between a mother and a daughter is a very special and unique thing.

Leaning over, Christina hugged her mom. "I love you, Mom."

"I know, sweetie. I love you too." She ran her hand over her daughter's wet hair trying to comfort her, "Everything's going to be all right."

***

Jake woke in the same place he had fallen asleep. Face down on the bed with all his clothes still on. Sitting up, he glanced at the clock on the nightstand. It was closing in on nine in the morning. Finally deciding to get up, he pulled off his leather jacket and laid it on the bed next to him. He hadn't really had a chance to look around his room last night. Taking a quick glance around, he surmised that his room could double as a surf shop. The headboard of the bed was made out of three interlocking surfboards. Two that stood vertically, and one that ran horizontally across the other two. A small shelf had been drilled out of the board. The rest of the bed frame was made out of faux bamboo poles. The room had a queen-size bed in the middle with much of the same Hawaiian floral print on the sheets and bedspread he had seen yesterday in the lobby. Across from the bed was a small dresser designed to make it look like it was built out of bamboo and leaves. In the corner was the door to the bathroom, and on the other side of the room was a small round table with a lamp and a phone on it. A small chair sat beside it. On the far wall, there was a small window with the air conditioning unit right below it.

Tossing his suitcase on the bed, he unzipped the top and began to pull out clothes, looking for his box of cigars. Pushing a dark green shirt to the left, he saw the box. Lifting it out, he opened the top drawer of the bamboo dresser and placed them inside. Turning back to the suitcase, he dipped his hand in again and pulled out his .45 and a case of shells. Placing them next to the cigars, he slid the drawer closed.

Turning his attention to his laptop, he unzipped its carrying case and pulled it out. Looking for a good spot to set it up, he decided the table in the corner would be ideal.

He plugged it in and began powering it up as he set it on the table. He reached over to the phone and removed the cord. Clicking it into the jack on the laptop, he opened the icon on his screen that gave him access to the internet. He heard the familiar sounds of the computer dialing the number and logging on to his network. "Let's see if I've got any e-mail." He hated to admit it, but he had become a bit of an e-mail junky. He loved getting mail, no matter who sent it. Typing in his password, a small gray box popped up. Clicking on the box, he moved into his inbox. "One piece of mail," he muttered to himself.

He clicked the button to open the new mail. There was no return address, or subject line. Now, he was curious. It read:

Mr. Silver,
For the time being, I must remain unidentified, but be assured that I am a friend. I have taken an interest in the case you are working on right now. I have facts you may find very interesting.
She was not raped.
I am sure you will come to the correct answer of this mystery. That's all I can say for now, but I will contact you again.
Keep digging, Mr. Silver.

Strange. No one that has my e-mail address knows I'm working on this case. Standing, he turned to look out the small window. Not much of a view. All he could see were the dark storm clouds looming over the city.

CHAPTER FOUR

The helicopter rested in a mangled heap on the desert floor. Getting out of the white Jeep Cherokee he had driven to the crash site, Hunter instructed his men to comb the area for bodies. Eight men dressed in black fatigues split up into two teams of four and began to search. Stepping closer to the wreckage, he immediately saw what looked like the charred remains of one of the chopper's crew.

Rubbing his hand across his forehead to wipe off the sweat, Hunter knelt down next to the corpse. Reaching over a piece of metal imbedded in the man's chest, he lifted the dog tags to read them. "Gary Jansen." Dropping them in the sand, he stood. "Major Griggs, front and center," Hunter barked.

A tall man dressed in black fatigues emerged from behind the wreckage. Walking up to Hunter, he saluted. "Yes, Colonel?" Jason Griggs was fairly new to the base. He was a hulking blonde-haired man, with broad muscular shoulders. He had been recommended for this detail after he had shown great tactical skills in a battle he had been involved with a few years back.

"Get this man's body wrapped for removal," pointing down to what was left of Jansen. "I want all missiles that were on this bird accounted for and loaded on the truck before we leave."

"Yes, sir." Griggs saluted again and moved off to fulfill his orders.

Walking away from the wreckage, Hunter

adjusted his uniform. Reaching the Jeep, he turned around to watch his men. They were moving in a precise fashion over the wreckage. Letting his eyes wander, he caught sight of something strange. Taking off his sunglasses, he squinted in the bright light to see what looked like an impact crater. "What the hell is that?" Climbing into the Jeep, he grabbed the CB receiver off the dash and keyed it on. "Rescue team to base. Rescue team to base."

The CB's speaker crackled to life. "Rescue team, this is base, go ahead." It was the unmistakable voice of General Davis.

"General, this is Hunter. Requesting air support for our location." "Why do you need air support, Colonel?"

Hunter glanced out the front windshield of the Jeep at the crater. "To locate possible crash site of bogey."

"You mean they brought it down with them?"

"I'm not sure yet, General." Letting go of the send button on the CB, he waited for Davis' reply.

"Request granted. I'll have a chopper out there ASAP."

Hunter looked at the crater. *What the hell was that thing?* He knew most planes and helicopters, even traveling at maximum speed, wouldn't make a crater that large upon impact. A cold chill ran down his spine.

***

"Mom, I really don't want to do this." Christina stared at the brick facade of her school through the passenger window of her mother's car. Even in the car, she could feel the stares of the other kids burning into her. The rain was coming down even

70

harder now. A quick flash of lightning tore through the sky followed by a loud crack of thunder. Unconsciously, she realized she was biting her nails.

"Come on, honey. You need to go back to school." Her mother leaned over and placed her hand on Christina's shoulder. "It's your senior year. You don't want to miss any more than you have to."

"Yeah, I know, but—"

"No 'buts'. You've got to go. Show everyone how strong you really are." Turning to her mom, Christina wrapped her arms around the woman and gave her a big hug. "You're right, Mom. This is something I've got to do for myself."

"Good girl. I knew you could do it." Her mom smiled brightly at her. She knew her daughter was strong. Christina had been all her life.

Mustering all her confidence, Christina opened the car door and got out into the pouring rain. She stared at the building for a moment, then turned back. "I'll call if I need anything." Her mother nodded. Shutting the door behind her, she began to walk away.

Hearing the window roll down behind her, she paused momentarily. "Christina!" Turning back to look at the car, she saw her mother leaning over toward the passenger window. "Yeah, Mom?" "I love you."

"You too." She stayed and watched as her mom rolled up the window and drove off.

This is it, the moment of truth. Walking briskly toward the school, Christina felt a knot of fear well up in her throat as she reached for the door handles. Pushing the doors open, she stepped inside.

The halls were crowded and hot. Usually, all the students were lounging around the schoolyard, but since it was raining, most of them had decided to go inside. Faces stared at her as she began to walk down the hall. Keeping her gaze straight ahead, she walked slowly and carefully. The crowd seemed to part for her as she continued on her way. From the crowds of teenagers, she could hear the laughter and some of what they were saying about her.

"She's making it all up. What a liar."

"Little green men came down and had their way with her. What a joke." "I can't believe she came back. If I was her, I wouldn't."

"She has a lot of nerve showing her face here again."

The words cut her like a knife. Moving quicker now, she threw herself at her locker. Hurriedly working the combination, she opened her locker and removed her books for her first hour class. Out of nowhere, a hand landed on her shoulder.

"Seen any aliens lately, Tina?" It was Buzz, the captain of the football team, accompanied by several of his friends. They were all laughing at his childish joke. He was of medium height with dark curly hair and brown eyes. Like most other jocks Christina knew, Buzz wore his letterman's jacket like a badge of honor. At any other time, Christina would love to talk to him, but she was not in the mood or the right mind.

"Take off, Buzz. I've gotta get to class." She turned to walk away.

Slamming his hand against the locker in front of her, he leaned in close. "I want to know the real

72

story. You didn't see any aliens, did ya, Tina?" His tone was light, but still had an element of animosity in it.

"Buzz, leave me alone, okay? I don't want to talk about it." Turning the other way, she began to leave, only to be stopped by one of the other jocks.

"I don't think so, Tina. Either you tell us what really happened, or—"

She snapped. "Or what, Buzz? You'll kick my ass? You'll spread rumors about me?" She felt a tear roll down her cheek. "What, Buzz? What the fuck are you gonna do to me?"

Just then, she heard a familiar voice stand up for her. "Get out of here, Buzz. We don't need that bullshit around here." Libby pushed her way into the group to stand beside Christina. Pushing Buzz hard, she stood toe-to-toe with him.

"You need to leave, Libby. Or you'll regret it."

"Are you gonna hit me, Buzz? Are you so tough, you can beat up a girl? Yeah, that'll show everyone!" Libby wasn't moving.

Neither was Buzz. "You dumb bitch." Lifting his hand, he opened his palm to slap her. Libby knew it was coming, but she stood firm. She wasn't giving up any ground. Not for anything.

Out of nowhere, a hand reached into the crowd and grabbed Buzz's arm before he had a chance to slap her. "I don't think so, Buzz."

"Who the—?" Spinning around, Buzz found himself standing face-to-face with Coach Fox.

"What do you think you're doing, Buzz? Slapping girls doesn't look good for the team." Coach Fox was a tall man with broad shoulders. His was in his early thirties and rumored to be built like

73

a tank. In addition to being the head of the athletics department at the school, he was also the head coach of the football team.

"Sorry, Coach. I—"

"I don't want to hear it, Buzz." He moved his steely blue eyes over the predicament that had erupted. "Buzz, you get your boys the hell out of here. I don't want to see your sorry faces until practice tonight. Do you understand?"

Buzz nodded. Motioning to his entourage, the group quickly turned to leave. They all knew Coach Fox wouldn't send them to detention, or to the principal. He had his own brand of justice. They were called wind sprints, and you did them until you puked or passed out, whichever came first.

Coach Fox turned his attention to Libby and Christina, "And as for you two, get your butts to class."

Christina took a step closer to Coach Fox. "Thanks, Coach. I appreciate—" "Look, I don't care what did or did not happen." His blue eyes remained fixed on Christina, "I wasn't here to take sides, just keep the peace." He quickly turned and began to walk off, all the while shaking his head.

Jumping in front of Christina, Libby shot her a big smile. "Hey, girlfriend! How are you? I've been worried about you. You haven't been returning my calls."

Turning, Christina began to walk to class. "I know, Libby. I'm sorry."

"That's it? 'I'm sorry'? You're gonna have to do a lot better than that for your best friend."

"I really am sorry, Libby. I just haven't been feeling like myself lately." Taking a right turn into a

74

classroom, she was gone.

"Didn't even say goodbye." Shrugging, Libby turned and began to walk toward her first hour class.

Avoiding her usual seat in the middle of the room, Christina decided to sit in the back row. Sliding into the desk, she pulled off her backpack and set it on the floor next to her. She knew everyone was staring at her as she walked in. Trying to avoid eye contact, she reached over to her pack and unzipped it. Pulling out a blue notebook and a blue pen, she laid them on the desk and began to doodle. Looking up for a moment, she watched her teacher walk into the room. He seemed to do a double take when he saw Christina there. Walter Jones was a short, stocky man wearing a pair of black slacks and a red polo shirt. His dark hair was slicked back to his head and his black beard was showing some signs of graying. Laying his briefcase on his brown wooden desk, he clicked open the locks and opened it. The bell sounded over the intercom system.

"Good morning, class. If you'll take out your anthropology books and open them to chapter seven, we'll begin." His voice was slightly nasal, but very easy to listen to.

Opening her book to the correct chapter, Christina began to feel a little more at ease. She had always been able to immerse herself in her studies.

"Today, we're going to begin studying the magnificent culture of the Egyptians," Mr. Jones announced.

Christina began to skim ahead in the chapter. Looking at the pictures on each page, she saw familiar shapes. The Great Pyramids of Giza loomed above the Valley of the Kings. It was a place she had always wanted to visit. She was in awe of their majesty and beauty, and somehow, she felt strangely drawn to them. Flipping the page, she came across a picture of a wall of Egyptian hieroglyphs. Studying the picture, she ran across something interesting. In the corner of the picture was a statue of what seemed to be a cat. She knew from her studies that the Ancient Egyptians held cats in high regard.

She stared at the cat intently while she listened to Mr. Jones talk. Looking closely at the statue of the cat, she began to feel strange. Turning the page, she came across a drawing of a young Pharaoh holding a black cat. Running her hand across the picture, she smoothed out the wrinkles on the page. The cat seemed to be staring at her. She felt like she was losing her mind, but those eyes... The cat's eyes were drawn out of proportion with the rest of its body. They were large and almond-shaped. Sitting back in her chair to get away from the book, Christina began to feel as if it was indeed watching her, almost tormenting her. She felt a cold sweat running down her forehead. The eyes...where had she seen them before? Slamming the book closed, she folded her arms and lowered her head to her desk. Even now she could see the eyes in her mind, just staring at her. Nausea clawed at her stomach. *What's wrong with me?* In her mind's eye, she saw the yellow eyes of the cat morph into big black soulless eyes. She began to see a long spindly gray arm reach for her. On the hand were four fingers and two thumbs and she knew whatever it was, it wasn't human. Panic set in as the hand neared her face. She could see the huge black eyes examining her, staring at her. Suddenly, it lurched toward her and grabbed her.

Sitting straight up in her chair, she screamed at the top of her lungs. Looking around, she saw all the students staring at her. Turning to her left, she saw Mr. Jones standing above her. "What's wrong, Christina? You were sleeping, I just came to wake you up."

She looked bewildered. "I was sleeping?"

"Yeah, the class is almost over." Mr. Jones' voice was soft and comforting, not scolding. He had heard what she had been going through and was trying not to be judgmental.

Looking up at the clock on the wall, she found that Mr. Jones was right. She had been asleep for almost half an hour. Tears again began rolling down her face. "I'm sorry, I didn't mean to." Standing up, she pushed Mr. Jones aside and began to run out of the room. From behind her, she could hear his voice calling for her to stop.

Christina ran down the hall for what seemed an eternity. Her mind was swimming and her eyes were filled with tears. Hitting the front doors, she flung them open as she ran out into the pouring rain. Running down the stairs, she tripped on the bottom step and fell hard. Her body hit the concrete sidewalk with a resounding thud.

Charging out the door behind her was a puffing Mr. Jones. "Oh, my God!" Turning back to one of the students who followed him, he yelled for them to get the nurse and the principal. Kneeling beside Christina, he tried to shelter her from the rain with his body. "Oh, God. Christina? Are you all right, Christina?"

***

The restaurant of the Tikki Hotel and Casino was crowded. The Hawaiian decor was beginning to get tiresome to Jake. Everywhere he looked, he saw palm trees and bamboo decorated tables and chairs. Even the bar in the middle of the room looked as if it was made of sticks and coconut shells. Sitting in a booth near the door, he was reading the morning paper and enjoying a cigar. Taking a long drag off the cigar, he slowly blew out the smoke, savoring the taste. "There's nothing better in the morning than a good cigar."

"Is that so?"

Jake was startled. Turning around, he found a familiar face standing in front of his booth. His memory raced trying to remember her name. "Hi," he couldn't, "how are you?"

"You don't remember me, do you?" Her brown hair was up this time. Her eyes reminded Jake of the ocean. So green and deep, one could almost see forever. She had on a blue blouse with black jeans.

"I haven't forgotten you." He motioned with his hand. "Please, sit down. I was just about to order breakfast, would you like some?"

She smiled at Jake. Reaching out with her hand, she offered it as a greeting. "Hi, my name is Anne. We met in the elevator last night. You seemed pretty tired at the time, so I don't blame you for not remembering."

He smiled at her. "I'm sorry, Anne." Folding up his newspaper, he leaned forward and placed his elbows on the table.

"So what do you do for a living, Jake?" Reaching over to the edge of the table, she grabbed a white coffee mug and flipped it over.

"I'm a private investigator. How about you?"

"I'm in between jobs right now."

A waitress arrived carrying a pot of coffee. "Anyone for coffee?" Both nodded. The waitress filled up the white porcelain cups. "We'll have your breakfast out real quick." Turning to Anne, the waitress asked if she wanted to order. Anne shook her head no and the waitress left.

"Listen, Jake, we've got to talk." "What about?"

"The case you're working on."

Jake became hesitant. "What are you talking about?"

"I have inside information on a lot of things," Anne replied with a crooked smile. Sitting back in his chair, Jake took a long drag off his cigar. "Look. I don't even know who you are, or what you want, but I've got a case to work on here and I don't need any crank tips. Now if you'll excuse me," he began to get up to leave.

"Jake, wait." She reached up and snatched his arm. "I need to talk to you about this case." She let go of his arm. "I know what's going on with Christina Anderson."

Jake stopped. "How do you know her name?"

"I told you. I have information about what's going on."

Leaning over, he placed his hands on the table in front of Anne. "All right. I'll listen, but not right now." He checked his watch. "Meet me in front of my room at about seven thirty tonight. Right now,

79

I've got to get over and meet my clients."

"All right. Seven thirty in front of your room."

"Room two-twelve."

She nodded and stood up. "You think I'm crazy, don't you?"

Jake nodded and smiled, "Yeah." Lifting his cigar out of the ashtray, he began to walk out the restaurant.

***

Christina regained consciousness in a stark white room. Setting up in the bed, she looked around. Reaching up, she wiped her hands across her face. "Where am I?

What happened?" she blurted out.

Sitting in the chair beside Christina's bed, Susan Anderson felt relieved. "Christina, honey, are you okay?"

Looking over at her mother, she had that faraway look in her eyes. "What happened to me, Mom?"

Reaching over to the bed, Susan grabbed Christina's hand. "You fell and hit your head, dear. You've got to be more careful." She took a long breath. "Your teacher said you just started screaming in the middle of class, then you ran out the room. Mr. Jones tried to stop you, but you just ran out the front door."

"I remember now. I tripped on the steps and fell down." She reached up and felt a bump on her head. Closing her eyes, she leaned back against the wall. "It has been a long week."

"I know, honey." She was trying to be comforting. "You lay down and try and get some rest. I've got to get home."

"Why do you have to go, Mom? Can't you just stay with me?" Christina had always hated hospitals. She always felt queasy in them.

"I'm sorry, but I can't. I'm meeting someone a little later." "Who?"

Susan paused. They hadn't told her about the private investigator yet. "A man named Jake Silver...he's a private investigator."

"A private investigator? Why do you need one?"

"Your father and I felt we needed more results than the police were giving us." She felt as if she was apologizing to her daughter. "We did it for you, so you could have some kind of closure. So you could know what happened to you."

"I told you what happened, Mom." She turned away. "I knew nobody would believe me."

"That's not true. You know we—"

She was sobbing heavily. "It is true, Mom. You all think I'm crazy! I'm talking about hovering blue lights and little green men. No wonder no one believes me."

"We believe you, Christina. That's why we hired a private eye." She was pleading now. "We want to believe you."

Turning her head to look at her mom, she smiled. "Thanks."

Standing, Susan leaned over the bed and kissed Christina on the forehead. "Everything's going be all right. You try and get some rest and I'll be back soon." Pulling up the sheets, she kissed her daughter again and walked out the room.

***

"Alpha One to Reconnaissance Team, come in,

81

Recon." "Recon Team here. Go ahead, Alpha One."
"We'll be in range in three minutes."
"Understood."

"Alpha One out." Colonel Hunter stood on a small hill above the wreckage of Red Bird. The warm wind whipped through his hair. It was a hot and dry day in the desert. For miles around, all he could see was light brown. Light brown dirt and light brown sagebrush. Adjusting his sunglasses, he tapped the mic on his walkie-talkie. "Major Griggs, do you copy?"

"Yes, sir."

"Air support will be in the area in three minutes. Get your men out of the way when they do their sweep. Copy?"

"Affirmative."

Stepping around in front of the white Jeep, Hunter stared at the crater. It was immense. All vegetation within one hundred fifty feet around it had been charred. The search team had found shards of glass mixed in with the sand. Whatever had hit, it had been hot enough to sear sand into glass, and left a hole big enough to land a plane in.

He began to hear the tell-tale sounds of rotor blades. Turning around, he saw a helicopter approaching from the south. It was similar in shape and size to Red Bird, and also carried the same crew compliment.

The speaker on his walkie-talkie sputtered to life. "Alpha One to Recon team." "Recon here," Hunter answered. "Go ahead, Alpha One."

"We're ready to begin the search."

"Acknowledged, Alpha One. Begin search directly above crater and radiate outward."

"Copy." There was only static for a moment. "Colonel, what are we looking for?"

"A second crash site."

***

Jake knocked on the front door. He was impressed with the Andersons' house as soon as he pulled into their driveway. The three-story dwelling dwarfed Jake's own in comparison. Knocking again, he heard a voice inside telling him that she was coming.

Opening the door, Susan Anderson stood in the threshold. "Hello, Mr. Silver. Come in." Jake walked into the house. He was impressed at its lavish decorations. Susan walked past him and stopped at the door leading into the kitchen. "Please, make yourself comfortable. Let me just finish up in the kitchen and I'll be right with you."

Jake nodded and seated himself on the nearest couch. He looked down at the hardwood floors. *This stuff looks better on TV.* Moments later, Susan emerged from the kitchen. "Nice place."

Walking into the living room, she seated herself on a couch opposite Jake. "Thank you." Susan gave him a modest smile, "It's home."

Sitting up, Jake pulled a small notepad and pen out of his jacket pocket. "I'm ready to start if you are."

Shifting in her chair, Susan crossed her legs. "Okay, where do you want to start?" "Christina's friends. Tell me about them." His voice was matter-of-fact.

She felt bad about what she was about to say. "She doesn't have many. She has a best friend named Libby Jacobs. They're always together. She was the one who brought her home from school the day it happened."

"Tell me about Libby. How much do you know about her?" He was taking notes as she talked.

"She's a nice girl. She's had dinner with us many times, but Christina told me Libby has a bit of a wild side." Susan felt like she was gossiping about her daughter's life.

Jake could see this was making her uncomfortable. "I'm sorry if this is bothering you, Susan, but it is information I need."

"I understand, this just feels so," she searched for the right word, "awkward." Jake nodded. "I don't know how I would feel if a total stranger came into my house and started asking me questions about my daughter."

She smiled, "Let's go on."

"Have there been any signs at home that Christina may be changing?" "In what way?"

"Altered sleeping pattern, loss of appetite, strange mood swings," Jake answered quickly. "Things like that."

Susan thought for a moment. "No, she seems the same. She's always been a good student, and she always respects our wishes. She's a very good girl, Mr. Silver."

"Please, call me Jake." He made several notes on his pad before continuing, "How would you describe Christina's sex life?"

The question horrified Susan. She had never thought of her daughter that way. "I'm not sure what you're asking."

"Is she sexually active?" Jake had always found the best result in asking these types of questions was to get to the point, not skirt around the subject.

"Not that I know of. I mean, she's had a couple dates, but..."

"So you're not sure?" Shifting in his chair, he tried to find a more comfortable position. "A lot of parents really don't know if their kids are sexually active. I know when I was a kid, the last people I wanted to tell I was having sex were my parents."

Susan tried to force a smile.

Jake knew this was making her extremely uncomfortable. "Let's continue," Jake made a quick note on his pad. "What do you and your husband do for a living?"

Susan perked up at the relative ease of the question. "I'm a housewife, and Jon works for the military."

"So your husband makes enough money to support the family and lavishly decorate this house?"

"Oh, no," Susan laughed. "We're renting this house. Jon makes enough money to support the three of us, but not enough money to buy a beautiful house like this." She was a little more at ease now.

"You said your husband works for the military. Is he an enlisted man?"

"No. He's a researcher. Back when we lived in Colorado, he worked at a firm that developed gene therapy for people suffering from diseases. He's doing good work trying to help people."

"What does he do now?"

"The same thing, I think," Susan answered honestly. "We don't talk about his work."

"Does he work at Nellis Air Force Base?"

"All I know is he drives to the airport every

morning and takes a plane to work. Where he goes, I don't know."

"How did he get this job?"

"He told me he was approached by some military personnel who were interested in his work. They offered him the job." She leaned forward in her chair. "Look, Mr. Silver, I don't understand what this has to do with our daughter."

"You never know, Susan. I'm just trying to be thorough." Closing his notepad, he tucked it back into his jacket pocket. "Sometimes, even the smallest detail can have the biggest effect on a case." Standing, Jake turned and began to walk toward the door. Susan stood and followed him. "When is the soonest I can speak with your daughter?"

Susan stepped in front of him and opened the front door. "She's in the hospital right now, but when she—"

"She's in the hospital?" Jake cut her off, "For what?"

"She fell today at school and hit her head pretty hard. They had to rush her to the hospital. She has exacerbated her concussion."

"What hospital is she at?"

Susan paused. "She's at the University Hospital." "You mean UNLV's hospital?"

"That's right."

"Do you mind if I stop in and see her?"

Susan was hesitant. "I'm not sure that's such a—"

"It's very important I hear her side of the story, Susan." "All right. If it will help."

"It will." Jake smiled politely, "Thanks for your

time. If you have any questions, here's my card. It has my cell phone number, along with my hotel's phone number and my room number on it."

"Thank you, Jake. We really appreciate this."

Jake shook her hand and walked out the door. Stepping onto the walkway, he became very aware it was still raining.

"Does it usually rain like this?"

Susan shook her head. "From what our neighbors tell us, it hardly ever rains this much in Vegas."

Jake nodded. "Thanks again." The rain pounded down on his head and shoulders. Pulling his jacket up over his head, he began to run toward his car parked in the driveway. Grabbing the door handle, he pulled it open and jumped inside. Shaking the rain out of his hair, he leaned back in his seat.

"This case is getting more and more interesting." Pulling the keys out of his pocket, he started the engine and put the car in gear. *I think I'm going to pay a visit to Christina, but first I need to head down to the police department and see if I can take a look at the police report.*

CHAPTER FIVE

General Perry prominently displayed his five stars on the shoulders of his dark blue Air Force uniform. He was slightly taller than General Davis and several years younger. His hair was brown and beginning to recede slightly. He had a wide face with a thick brown beard. His eyes were like black lumps of coal staring out from under thick eyebrows. He was a hardened man. Being the President's chief advisor on Area 51, he worked closely with him and made most of the decisions regarding the facility and operations. He had attained the job shortly after being promoted to a five star general.

It had always annoyed Davis that Perry had made five star general before he had. Davis had been in the service a full ten years longer than Perry and had been passed up for promotion several times, while Perry had gotten a promotion the first time he came up for it.

They were standing in the main hangar of Area 51. It was a cavernous room carved straight out of the mountain behind it. The walls were layered with thick steel plates that blocked out prying eyes and satellite photos. Every surface was polished to a high glossy shine.

Several men in expensive business suits accompanied General Perry. These were the Air Force's, Army's, Navy's, and President's chief advisors. "What are we looking at, General Davis?" Perry asked gruffly after a moment.

General Davis tuned to the men and began to give the standard tour. "This hangar, as well as most of the base, is carved deep inside the mountain and could, in the event of war, survive a direct nuclear assault. Plus, we have the longest landing strip in the world. Area 51 was originally designed in the 1930's to study the effects of an atomic attack. We had six hundred twenty-five square miles to detonate the bombs. This area became known as the 'Tonopah Test Range'." Davis led the advisors deeper into the hangar. "Back then, we were just considered part of the Nellis Complex. We didn't even have an official name of our own. We were often referred to as the 'Red Triangle', or 'Dreamland'.

"The Atomic Energy Commission formally dubbed us 'Area 51' back in 1958. By then, most of the super powers of the world were beginning to express concern about the growing UFO phenomenon." Davis began moving through the hangar with the other men accompanying him. "So the US Government deemed it necessary to have a Top Secret facility to research and study these events and The Groom Lake Complex was born."

One of the advisors stepped forward. "Pardon me, General Davis, but we all know the history of this facility. What we're here to talk about is your progress."

"My apologies, gentlemen, I'm usually giving this tour to Washington bureaucrats who don't know their asses from holes in the ground." Davis began to laugh, but stopped quickly when no one else did.

General Perry was standing silently at the rear

of the group, observing Davis' every move.

Davis began to feel slightly uncomfortable. "If you'll follow me, gentlemen." Walking toward the rear of the enormous hangar, Davis led the men to a giant steel door. It was close to fifteen feet high and sixty feet wide. Moving to its right side, Davis stopped in front of a waist-high rectangular table, which had several computer screens and controls built into the top of it. Removing his identification card from his jacket pocket, he slid it through a slot on the left side of the control panel. A door slid open revealing another screen with an outline of a hand on it.

A cold, metallic voice sprang from the control box. "Please place hand on the screen for identification."

"These are the latest in security devices, gentlemen." Placing his right hand on the screen, a white bar of light scanned it. "These devices are fool proof. Anyone can duplicate the key cards we use, but no one can get in unless they have the correct handprint, no two of which are exactly alike."

The metallic voice sounded again. "Thank you, General Davis." Turning to look at the men behind him, he saw the blank expressions on their faces. They were obviously not impressed.

The huge door began to slowly slide open revealing another enormous room. The men were in awe as the objects inside came into full view. The room was full of activity. Men and women in white body suits with respirators were working on several strange crafts. Davis spread his arms like a ringmaster in the center ring of a circus.

"Welcome to our main research facility."

The room was filled with five saucer-shaped crafts. Three were completely intact, and the other two had been taken partially apart. They all had highly polished silver shells, with a transparent dome in the center of the flat top and bottom. Each one was about forty feet wide at the center. They were all docked on individual platforms with three struts leading up to the front and sides of the objects. "These are all the crafts we have recovered since 1947."

The Presidential advisor stepped up front. "Have we ascertained if these craft are, or will be, operational once repaired?"

"Our boys over at S-4 have repaired three of the crafts. Once they were brought here, they were tested."

"What were the test conditions?" General Perry asked abruptly.

"We tested the hover and flying capabilities." The group walked closer to the first craft so they could inspect it. "The first test was here on the base. We wanted to find out if these things still worked, so for each ship, we did five separate hovering tests, each varying from one minute up to fifteen. All of them passed the tests."

The Navy's advisor began to run his hand across the front of the craft. "Its skin is rough, and rather warm to the touch."

"The design of the covering is very ingenious." Davis smiled. "Have you ever seen a shark chase after its prey in the water? They're faster than greased lightning and they have rough, sandpaper like skin, which is made up of millions of tiny teeth-like structures called 'denticles'."

The Navy's advisor was losing interest. "I fail to see—"

"Now just hold on a minute while I explain. It has been found that a rough surface, rather than one completely smooth, moves better. It allows the air stream to flow along it, not off it like a smooth surface." Davis ran his hand across the ship, "and as for the warmth, we have no idea what causes that."

"What about the metal itself. What is it?" The Army's advisor was now inspecting the ship.

"We're not sure what it is, yet. It's lightweight, flame-resistant and ultrathin. A one inch thick piece of this material can stand up to steel approximately a foot thick." The men were completely in awe of the craft.

"Where were these craft recovered from?"

"The very first craft was recovered from Roswell, New Mexico in 1947. The other four were recovered at various crash sites around the country since then. Until this base became fully operational in 1960, they were all were kept at a Top Secret hangar at Wright-Patterson Air Force Base." Turning away from the ships, Davis began to walk toward the door. "Now, if there are no more questions, let's continue the tour through the rest of the base."

The group of men began walking toward the massive doorway which led back into the main hangar. Making sure he was the last one out, Davis slid his card through the control panel again. The massive doors slowly sealed shut.

***

The Las Vegas Police Headquarters was

nothing like Jake had expected. Originally from New Orleans, he was used to crumbling brick buildings with tall steel fences all the way around them. Here, the police headquarters was a four story building with white stucco siding. It was very clean in appearance and was surrounded by various shrubs and trees.

Walking inside, he almost expected to see slot machines lining the walls. The lobby was a large room with tiled floors and benches on both sides. Potted trees lined the walls while two translucent glass doors stood at the end of the room. *Looks more like a library than a police station.*

Moving through the doors, Jake was surprised to see a flood of activity. Behind the long reception desk sat a multitude of small wooden desks. Police officers were hustling people in and out of the main office, while plainclothes detectives sat at their desks making calls and questioning suspects. Stepping up to the front desk, Jake found himself looking down at a young dark-haired officer who didn't look old enough to be an officer of the law. *Perfect.*

"Good afternoon. My name is Jake Silver and I'm a private investigator out of Lake Tahoe. I'm here to see the captain."

The officer adjusted his wire-framed glasses and seemed to look through Jake. "I'm sorry, sir, but Captain Morgan is very busy today. If you'd like to make an appointment—"

"Excuse me, but it was Captain Morgan who called me down here."

The young officer looked confused. "Let me check with his secretary." He began to pick up the phone and dial the Captain's secretary.

Slamming his hand down on the phone, Jake leaned in close to the young officer. "Listen, Officer, I don't have time to screw around. Captain Morgan is expecting me and I don't want to make him wait. Do you?" The young officer was obviously at a loss about what to do. "Why don't I just head back to the captain's office while you straighten this out?" Jake began to walk around the edge of the desk.

"Well, why don't you head on back to the captain's office while I straighten this out?" the officer declared meekly.

Turning his head back, Jake looked at the officer. "Thank you."

Making his way through the office, he came to an open door at the rear. Stepping inside, he found himself in a long hallway. Looking in both directions, he needed to take a guess. Deciding to go right, he walked past several offices and storage rooms. Knowing the officer would quickly figure out he was lying about his appointment with the captain, Jake picked up his pace. Passing several officers in the hall, he nodded and kept on his way so as not to arouse any suspicion. Taking a turn down an adjoining hallway, he stopped in front of a door marked 'Records'. *Being a PI was ten percent intuition and ninety percent luck.*

Slowly opening the door, Jake found the room empty except for several tall black filing cabinets. Stepping inside, he carefully shut the door behind him. He began to move further into the room when he heard several footsteps running down the hall. Immediately flattening himself against the wall, he listened as the footsteps moved away.

"Damn, they're on to me. Gotta be quick about this." Hurriedly moving over to the files, he hastily began to scan the labels on the cabinets. Finding the 'A' drawer, he pulled it open and began to thumb through the files. "Anderson...Anderson. Where are you?" His fingers flew furiously over the files.

Finally finding the one he wanted, Jake immediately pulled out the file and tucked it under his coat. Closing the drawer, he crept back to the door. Listening for a few seconds, he carefully opened it and scanned the hallway. Seeing it empty, he slowly moved into the hallway and began to progress down it. Stopping at the end, he peeked around the corner. He saw that the hall led to more offices, but to the right, he spotted an exit sign.

Turning the corner, Jake began to walk toward the exit. The sound of footsteps behind him startled him. Making a quick decision, he ducked into a nearby office. It was small with only a desk near the back wall. Jake decided it was apparently empty due to the lack of personal belongings and decorations. Hearing the footsteps nearing, Jake ducked under the desk. From under the desk, he could hear the door to the office creak open.

A few tense moments went by in the silence. "Nothing in here."

Hearing the door close, Jake waited several minutes to get out from behind the desk. Once out, he listened at the door for any signs of people in the hallway. Nothing. Opening the door, Jake checked the hallway. Seeing it was once again empty, he broke into a dead run toward the exit. Slamming through the door, he stopped to catch his breath.

"That was easier than I thought."

Walking away from the police station, he pulled his car keys out of his pocket. He had parked his car around the corner from the station anticipating this kind of situation. Turning the corner, he walked by several other cars before reaching his own. Quickly unlocking the door, he slid into the driver's seat. He pulled the file out of his jacket and began to leaf through it. "Let's see what the police have on Christina Anderson."

Setting the file on the seat next to him, he pushed the key into the ignition and started up the engine. He felt it was best to get as far away from the police headquarters as possible since every cop inside was looking for him. "Time to pay a hospital visit to Christina." Putting the car in gear, he pulled away from the curb and into traffic.

**

"He agreed. He's meeting me tonight at seven thirty in his room." Anne held the sleek black receiver up to her ear, twisting the cord around the fingers of her right hand. She was sitting at a small round table in her hotel room at the Tikki. The slender black phone base was sitting in the middle of the table with several sheets of paper scattered around it.

"Very good. Don't forget what your mission is." "Yes, sir. Misinform the subject."

"Very good, Anne. You're doing very well. Did you get the bio sheets I faxed you?"

She looked at the paper on her table. "Yes I did. This will be extremely helpful." Hanging up the receiver, Anne leaned back in her chair and crossed her legs.

Her hair was still wet from the shower she had just taken. She was wrapped in a white bathrobe. Reaching over to her nightstand, she grabbed her reading glasses and put them on.

Picking up one of the sheets of paper, she began to read it. "Who you are, Jake Silver?" Scanning down the page, she ran over his history. "Let's see here." Starting at the top, she began to read. "A ten year veteran of the FBI, formerly attached to the Violent Crimes Division. Very interesting." She moved further down the page, her eyes widened. She unconsciously started to read out loud. "During an especially trying case dealing with a child molester, he was relieved of duty after nearly killing the suspect. He left the FBI shortly after that. Too bad, it says here he had a very promising career ahead of him."

Laying down the copy, she sorted through the piles of paper and pulled out another sheet. Reading it, she suddenly stopped. "Well, Mr. Silver, you appear to be in the same boat as Christina."

***

Christina wiggled the IV needle in her hand. She watched as the long silver needle moved back and forth in her vein. *Gross.* A thin white plastic curtain was the only thing separating her from the other side of the room. Pulling the white linen sheets up to her chest, she stared at her bleak surroundings. She was so bored. Lying back in her hospital bed, she grabbed the remote for the television and clicked it on. She surfed through the channels trying to find something to watch. After flipping through the three channels the TV offered, she decided to turn it off. She slid down into the bed to take a nap.

A knock on her door startled her. "Hello?" she called out.

Opening the door, Jake stepped in. "Christina Anderson?" "Yes?"

Closing the door behind him, he walked toward her bed. "My name is Jake Silver. I'm a private investigator hired by your parents to look into what happened to you. Do you mind if we talk for a moment?"

She looked away. "Yeah, whatever."

Jake turned around and reached for the chair behind him. Pulling it near her bed, Jake sat down. "Christina, I'm here to help. But in order for me to help you, you've gotta help me."

"Look, Mr. Silver, if that's even your real name, I've answered all the questions that I'm going to. So you can save your breath," Christina's voice was filled with cynicism.

Jake leaned back in his chair and crossed his legs. "I am being paid a lot of money to find out what happened to you. I don't want to let you or your parents down. I will find whoever did this to you."

"I doubt even you're that good." "Why's that, Christina?"

She sat up and looked at Jake with disdain. "Because the person who did this to me isn't a person!"

Jake leaned forward. "Come again?"

Christina continued to glare at Jake. "You heard what I said." "Yes I did," Jake admitted, "but I didn't quite understand."

Pulling her legs off the bed, she sat facing Jake.

"I don't know what happened to me. All I know is that one minute I'm getting ready for bed, then suddenly, I'm running through the desert being chased by a glowing blue light." She ran her hand through her hair. "Whatever it was, it wasn't man-made."

"How do you know that?"

"Because the fucking thing shot past me like a rocket, then stopped and hovered right in front of me. It was a giant floating ball of blue light!"

"Tell me exactly what happened on that night, Christina."

She was shaking now. "I was having these dreams, then they came true."

"Dreams about what, Christina?" "About *them*."

"Who?"

"The things that took me away!" Christina was flailing her arms wildly. "I saw them in my dreams, then they fucking came after me!"

She jerked her arm around in front of her accidentally ripping the IV needle out of her hand. She screamed in pain as the open wound began to bleed. Jake stood up and grabbed the button off her bed that called the nurse. He began pressing the button frantically. He watched as her eyes began to roll back and she began to wobble. He reached out his arms as she began to fall forward off the bed. Catching her in his arms, he laid her back down on the bed.

Two nurses ran in the door to the room and immediately began to tend to Christina. "What happened to her?"

Jake stepped back from the bed. "She got really

upset and accidentally pulled the IV needle out of her hand, then her eyes began to roll back!"

"Are you family?"

"No, I'm not. I'm a private investigator hired by the family to—"

One of the nurses turned to Jake. "Unless you're family, I'm going to have to ask you to leave, sir."

Jake began to walk to the door. Before he left, he took one of his business cards out of his pocket and laid it on the table next to the phone. " Is there anything I can do?"

The nurses were ignoring Jake as they frantically tried to get the IV needle back into Christina's hand. One of the nurses ran past him muttering about getting the doctor.

Jake walked out the door and into the hallway. He began to walk slowly away, but was immediately passed by a nurse and doctor running toward Christina's room. Stopping in front of the nurse's station, he noticed Christina's chart lying open on the curved desk. Lifting it up, he quickly slid it under his jacket. Taking a left down the hall, he found a room marked "Staff Only". Peeking inside, he could see no one in the room. Slipping inside, he strode past the round coffee table to the copy machine near the back wall. Pulling the chart out of his jacket, he began to make several copies of it. Calmly, he pulled the last page off the copier. Spinning around, he heard footsteps approaching.

Surveying his options, he spotted a utility closet on the far side of the room, just beyond the coffee table. Grabbing his copies, he bolted for the closet. The footsteps came closer. Stealthily opening the closet door, he jumped inside and quietly pulled it shut behind him.

Jake listened as the door to the room creaked open. Two people entered, a man and a woman. They were talking about a patient suffering from diabetes. Apparently, they were having some difficulty treating him. The conversation slowly turned from work into pleasure as the two began talking about recent movies they had seen. Jake looked down at his watch in the dark room. Pushing the light, he noticed he had been in the closet for over ten minutes now. Leaning back against the rear wall, he tried to make himself comfortable. He knew he could be here for a while.

He suddenly heard a page come over the loudspeaker. The two people in the room both muttered under their breath. Setting down their coffee mugs on the table, they both stood and walked out of the staff room. Hearing the door shut, Jake cautiously stepped out of the closet. Checking to ensure that the room was once again empty, he swiftly made his way out into the hallway. Walking past the nurse's station, he slyly pulled the chart out of his jacket and laid it back on the desk where he had found it. Checking around, he was sure no one had seen him.

Making his way to the elevator, he pressed the down button. The doors slid apart and Jake began to get on as another man walked off. The two men stood face to face for a moment before they got out of each other's way. The man was about Jake's height and weight, but a little older. He had brown, shortly cropped hair and an odd scar on his left cheek. He was dressed nicely in a black suit with a crisp white shirt and black tie.

Stepping into the elevator, Jake stared as the man began to walk down the hall. Jake felt something strange and familiar about that man. He couldn't quite place it, though. He shook his head and stepped to the side of the elevator allowing the doors to slide shut. Reaching over, he hit the button labeled 'Lobby'. Feeling the elevator jerk to life, he stood quietly thinking about what had just happened. Rubbing his hand over his face, he let out a long sigh.

"This case is getting out way out of hand."

CHAPTER SIX

Colonel Hunter watched his men as they went about their business. Looking into the distance, he saw a helicopter circling around. He was second-in-command at Are a 51. His place was at the control center of the base. What the hell was he doing out in the blazing hot desert commanding a bunch of grunts when he could be meeting General Perry? He kept asking himself that question over and over.

His radio crackled to life cutting through his thoughts. "Alpha One to Recon Team."

Walking back to his Jeep, he pulled out his radio. "Recon. This is Hunter, go ahead, Alpha One." He lifted the radio to his ear.

"Sir, we've got something here." "What is it, Alpha One?"

"We plotted the trajectory the bogey may have taken after hitting the ground and we hit the jackpot, sir. We found the second crash site."

"Copy that. Distance from us?"

"About three miles due south of your location, sir." "Good job, Alpha One. Head home."

"Thank you, sir. Alpha One out."

Lowering the radio to his side, Hunter watched as the helicopter faded off into the distance. Walking back to his Jeep, he deposited his radio on the passenger seat. Moving back to the top of the hill, he cupped his hands around his mouth. "Major Griggs, front and center!" He watched as Griggs ran out from behind the wreckage of Red Bird and up the hill toward Hunter.

He stopped directly in front of Hunter. "Yes, sir?"

"Alpha One has located the second crash site. We will be abandoning Red Bird. Are the charges set?"

"Yes, sir. All the detonators are set and primed."

"Good. Set them for remote detonation and round up your men."

"Yes, sir." Griggs made his way down the hill toward the wreckage of Red Bird. Hunter watched as Griggs called all his men together and gave them their instructions.

The men then scattered quickly to complete the mission.

Walking back to his Jeep, he grabbed the radio off the seat and lifted it to his mouth. He pressed the send button. "Recon to Dreamland."

"Dreamland here. Go ahead, Recon."

"Inform General Davis the second crash site has been located by Alpha One. We're just finishing up here, then we're heading to the site, over."

"What is the site's location, Recon?"

"Site is about three miles south of here. It's rough terrain to cross, but we should be there in about twenty minutes."

The radio was silent for a moment. "Recon, you have just received new orders from General Davis. You are to complete your task there and return to base for debriefing."

Hunter dropped the radio to his side. *What are they doing? I'm so close!* Hesitantly, he lifted the radio again. "Orders understood. Recon out." Hunter returned the radio to its place in the Jeep. He turned around to see Griggs running up the hill to him.

"Sir, remote detonation set."

"Good job, Major. There has been a change in orders. After we finish here, we are to report back to base for debriefing."

Griggs nodded. "Understood, sir."

"Round up your men and let's get the hell out of here."

Moments later, all the men were back in their vehicles and driving away from the crash site. Close to three hundred yards away, both vehicles screeched to a stop.

In the first vehicle, Hunter turned to Griggs, "Press the button so we can go home."

Griggs pulled a small black remote from his jacket, he extended the silver antenna and flipped the switch to turn it on. Seeing the red LED lights on the remote flicker to life, he informed Hunter the remote was ready.

"Then push the damn button, Major." Griggs pressed the center red button. About a second elapsed before it happened. Just above the horizon, the men watched a red, black and yellow cloud of smoke and fire rise up into the sky. Turning the vehicles around, the men began to make their way back to the base.

***

"Ms. Anderson, may I have a word with you?" The man in the black suit strode into Christina's room.

Christina laid facing away from the door in her bed. "I don't care who you are or what you want, but I want you to get the hell out of my room and

105

leave me alone."

"I think you'll find it very important to speak with me, Ms. Anderson." He spoke with a proper British accent.

Rolling over, Christina prepared to unleash on whoever was bothering her this time. Her hand still throbbed from having her IV needle reinserted. "Look, you son of a bitch, I want—" She stopped herself when she saw the menacing figure standing next to her. "Who are you?"

"That is not as important as what I have to tell you." She watched as he reached into his jacket pocket and pulled out a pair of black leather gloves and proceeded to pull them on. Walking over to the side of the room, he peered up at the lone surveillance camera on the wall. Reaching up, he grabbed the power cord connecting the camera to the outlet and yanked it out. Feeling satisfied he was well protected, he turned to face Christina. "It has come to my attention that you have had a bit of a strange experience."

She stared at him for a long time before answering. "I've heard about you. You're one of those 'men in black', aren't you?"

"Yes I am."

Her eyes widened. "I didn't think you'd just admit that kind of thing."

"The main point here is that no one believes your story, so no one will believe you that a 'man in black' came to visit you in the hospital." Adjusting his gloves, he leaned over her and placed his hand on the back of the bed.

"What do you want from me?"

He wasted no time getting to his point. "I want

106

you to tell you that you didn't see what you think you did. You claim to have seen a large glowing ball of blue light, but in reality, it was a fluorescent weather balloon."

She just stared at him. "You've got to be kidding. That's the best you could come up with, a glowing weather balloon? Why don't you just tell me it was swamp gas, or the planet Venus?"

"It doesn't matter what it was," his voice turned cold. "You tell anyone else this story, and your family and friends will be in serious danger."

"Give me a break. Why don't you just get out?"

Quickly reaching over, he grabbed Christina's throat with both hands and began to squeeze. "I am not joking, Ms. Anderson. You will comply, or you will die."

Christina was struggling wildly trying to break free of his hold. Pushing with all her breath, she tried to cry out for help, but only whispers welled up from her throat. Tears began to roll down from her eyes. Her face was beginning to turn a dull shade of blue due to the lack of oxygen.

Releasing her from his grip, he took a step from the bed. "Remember what happened here, Christina. If you repeat the story of what happened to you, or what took place here today, you and your family will be in grave danger. You have been warned." Turning around, he adjusted his suit and pulled off his leather gloves. Placing them back in his pocket, he walked out the door.

Sitting in awe of what just happened, Christina started taking deep breaths to try and calm down. Reaching over to her nightstand, she grabbed her asthma inhaler and immediately took two quick puffs off it. Setting the inhaler back on the nightstand, she noticed the business card Jake had left there. Snatching it up, she reached for the phone.

***

Jonathan Anderson snapped a pair of bloody latex gloves off and tossed them in a nearby trashcan. Sitting down in a chair near the wall, he adjusted his white lab coat. He was standing in a large operating room with polished silver walls and black tiled floors. In the center of the room, two banks of monitors and computers flanked a tall operating table. He was alone. Two assistants had just wheeled out a male subject on a stretcher. The procedure had apparently been a success...to his dismay.

Running his hand through his hair, Jonathan let out a long, exhausted sigh. Standing, he grabbed a vial off a nearby table. It was long, cylindrical and filled with a clear green fluid. Walking out the operating room, he made his way down the hall to his office. Grabbing the ID badge off his lab coat, he slid it through the control panel next to his door. Twisting the handle, he pushed the door open and strode in. Sitting down in the chair behind his desk, he stared around his office. There were still boxes in the corners he hadn't unpacked yet. His desk was empty, except for a few pens and a yellow notebook with varied scribbles on it.

Laying the vial of green liquid on the table, Jonathan began to stare at it. He felt a wave of nausea flow through him. Wrapping his arms around his midsection, he doubled over in pain. Beads of sweat began to well up on his forehead.

Suddenly, a knock at his door pulled him out of his stupor. Sitting up, he tried to clear his mind. Wiping the sweat off his brow with his sleeve, he stood and walked to his door. Twisting the handle, he slowly opened it.

"Hey, Jon. Congratulations are in order. We've been working on this project for years now and you've finally cracked it." Jim Yokama grabbed Jonathan's hand and began to shake it vigorously. Yokama was a short man of Asian heritage who wore thick, dark-rimmed glasses. He was considered by many in their field to be one of the top minds. Jim had been working with Jonathan ever since he had arrived and had even suggested him for the position. "All of us are going to meet in the lounge in about an hour to celebrate. Are you coming?"

Jonathan smiled. "Yeah, I'll be there." Another wave of nausea ran through him. "Are you okay, Jon? You don't look so good." Jim placed his arm on Jonathan's shoulder.

"Yeah, I just need to sit down." Jim guided him over to his desk and into his chair. Relaxing in his chair, he looked up at Jim. "Do you mind if I ask you a serious question?"

Jim sat down on the edge of the desk. "Sure, Jon. Go ahead."

Jonathan cleared his throat. "Do you ever feel what we're doing here is morally wrong?"

Jim's eyes widened. He had expected a different question altogether. "In what way?"

"You know what I'm talking about. We abduct people right out of their homes, bring them here and perform all sorts of experiments on them. What kind of people are we?"

Jim had gone down this road before. "We're the good guys, Jon. We do here what other researchers only wish they could do. We are finding cures for every disease known to man. Sometimes, we need to bypass the federal laws in order to speed up the process. But to do that, we need to test them on subjects..."

"In the process, possibly scarring the psyches of our subjects permanently. At what cost, Jim?"

Jim stood and moved to the opposite side of the desk. "Let me ask you a question, Jon." He adjusted his glasses. "If you had to sacrifice one life to save millions, wouldn't you do it? This is something we all have to come to grips with." He began to walk out the door, but stopped to face Jonathan. "I just keep telling myself this if for the good of the human race." He slipped his hands into his lab coat and walked out the office.

Jonathan leaned back in his chair. Jim was a good man. Jonathan knew he had no intention of hurting innocent people. He actually believed his quest was good and just. Jonathan knew the truth. While working on a test patient several weeks ago, he had inadvertently stumbled across the test results for some of the subjects. *This wasn't for the good of the human race. This was the end of it.*

*   *   *

Jake checked his watch. He knew he still had about half an hour before he had to meet Anne back at his room at seven thirty. His mind wandered to her identity. She claimed to know so much about this case and apparently, a lot about him. He was sitting in the same booth where he had spoken to

Anne earlier that day. Lifting his white coffee mug off the table, he took a long sip of the dark black steaming substance.

Laying the stolen file on the table, he flipped it open. The front page was the standard incident report, but it had several Polaroid pictures clipped to it. Removing the paper clip, he elevated the pictures to look at them. They were all shots of Christina standing in front of a white brick wall documenting her injuries. There were several pictures of her face. Just above her right eyebrow, there was a dark red bruise. Her right eye also looked like it was blackened, and a trail of dried blood ran down her face from her nose. Flipping to the next photo, he saw the long laceration on her left foot.

He put the photos down and began to flip through the report. According to the reports, they agreed with Jake in their conclusion that she had been raped. So far, they had no suspects and no leads. It seemed like they had come to a dead end. Closing the folder, he pushed it to the side of the table. Pulling the photocopied medical charts out, he spread them neatly on the table. Starting at the top, he scanned over her medical history. She apparently had never been a very healthy girl. Suffering from chronic asthma, she had been to the doctor at least once a month for the past sixteen years. He skipped ahead in the chart to her current medical status. She had a mild concussion and several bruised muscles, otherwise, she was as healthy as could be expected. In this last fall, she had exacerbated her concussion causing her to pass out and to get lightheaded very quickly. The doctors had predicted a full recovery. Stacking together the sheets of paper, Jake slid them into the folder containing the police report.

Reaching into his well-worn leather jacket pocket, he found one of his cigars. Pulling it out, he slipped into his mouth. Retrieving his lighter from his other pocket, he snapped open the top and lit it. He allowed the tall yellow flame to lick the end of his cigar. Taking several puffs, smoke began to flow. Glancing down at his watch, Jake noticed it was now seven twenty. Deciding he should be on his way, he pulled a couple folded dollar bills out of his pocket and tossed them on the table. Standing, he grabbed the folder and began to make his way toward the elevator. Pressing the 'up' button, he waited for the silver doors to slide open. Stepping inside, he took a long puff off his cigar. He watched as the lights slowly counted up to the second floor. A small ding sounded as it reached its destination. The doors slid open and he stepped out. Reaching around behind, he checked that his weapon was firmly in place in its back holster. *Never can be too cautious.*

Rounding the corner to the hall that led to his room, he spotted Anne standing in front of his door. Checking his watch again, he saw it was only seven twenty-two. Walking up to her, he gave her the once-over. She was wearing a formfitting black dress that hung down to her ankles. It seemed to be made of silk, flowing as she moved. She had her long brown hair up, except for a few loose strands that fell on both sides of her face and her long, graceful neck. She had on a pair of black high heels that made her about the same height as Jake. She smiled as he walked up.

"You're early, Anne."

"I know. I just couldn't wait."

Jake was slightly taken aback. The perfume she was wearing had a sweet scent to it, but wasn't overpowering. Fumbling with the room key in his pocket, he pulled it out and began to put it in the lock, when it slipped from his hand. Reaching down to grab it, he quickly plucked it off the floor and stood back up. He gave Anne a little embarrassed smile. She reached over and took his hand.

"Here, let me help you, Jake." The two made eye contact and just gazed at each other for a long moment. Still holding his hand, she guided it and the key into the lock. They heard the door click as it unlocked.

Reaching for the handle, Jake opened the door and stood to the side so Anne could walk in. "Ladies first."

She gave him a sensual smile and strode into the room. Stepping inside, Jake closed the door and locked it. Pulling off his jacket, he opened the door to the closet and reached for a hanger. Sliding the hangar through the sleeves, he put it on the long metal bar. Lifting the folder up, he set it on the top shelf. Closing the door, he made his way over to Anne, who was seated on the edge of his bed. "Can I get you something to drink?"

"Sure, what do you have?"

Opening the mini-bar next to the television, he searched through the contents. "Looks like you're limited to either a can of soda or a can of soda."

Anne smiled again and laughed. "I think I'll take the soda."

Pulling the can out, he clicked open the tab and handed it to Anne. "Here you go." Closing the door, he walked past the bed and seated himself at the small table next to it. Lifting his feet up, he rested them on the table. "Now, let's get down to business. What do you know about the case I'm working on?"

Standing, she began to walk over to Jake. "There's time for that later, Jake. Right now, I have something else in mind."

"Like what?"

She leaned over and began to kiss his neck. "Like this."

Placing his hands on her shoulders, he pushed her away. "You don't have anything to tell me about the case I'm on, do you?" He stood and began to walk away from her.

Reaching for his arm, she grabbed it and spun him around to face her. "Yes, I do. Remember that e-mail you received this morning?"

Jake nodded.

"That was me," Anne said, pointing to herself. "But how did you know me e-mail address?"

She let go of his arm and sat down on the edge of the bed. She motioned for him to sit back down in his chair. "I know a lot about you, Jacob Dean Silver, Junior." She crossed her long legs. "I know you're a former FBI agent, and that you quit shortly after you were reprimanded for attacking a suspect in a molestation case."

Jake's eyes widened. "How do you know all this?"

"It's very easy when you have the right connections, Jacob." "Stop calling me that."

Smiling at Jake, she rolled on her side and reclined on the bed, propping her head up with her hand. "All right. Now, do you want to know what I

114

do about the case?"

Jake knew he was in over his head. This situation was becoming very uncomfortable for him. He cautiously nodded, "Let's hear what you've got."

"I knew you couldn't resist." Kicking off her shoes, she reached back and pulled the barrette out of her hair. Giving it a shake, her brown hair fell in waves around her shoulders. "Christina wasn't raped."

"What happened then?"

"She's part of an ongoing experiment by aliens. They're genetically manipulating humans to breed their own master race in order to conquer this planet."

Jake stood and pointed toward the door. "Okay, that's it. Get out. I don't want to sit here and be lied to."

Anne didn't move. "Most people have that reaction when they first find out." She sat up. "I can only assure you that what I'm telling you is true."

"How can you assure me?"

"Have you ever heard of Area 51, Jake?"

He nodded. He had heard about it, but assumed it was nothing more than an urban legend.

"It's a secret government installation designed to research and combat the threat of these aliens. Its doors opened in the late 1940's after a crashed UFO was recovered in Roswell, New Mexico. Along with the crashed ship, they found several bodies and began to study them. In the beginning, it was just a research and development facility, but after about 1950, reports of alien abductions began flooding in. The US Government knew they had to do something to protect its citizens, so they refocused the base into a research and defense facility."

"How do you know that?"

"Because I'm a former employee of the base." She reached out her open hand to Jake. "Let me formally introduce myself. My name is Doctor Anne Carroll. I was a researcher at the base. I mainly concentrated on chemical and biological weapons to oppose the aliens."

Jake was in awe of what he was hearing. "And you can prove this?"

Anne sighed. "No. When I left, it was not on the best of terms, so they officially erased my identity."

"Convenient for you."

Ignoring his sarcasm, she continued. "When I heard about Christina, I naturally began to look into it."

"Naturally," Jake mocked. "Will you shut up?"

"Sorry. Please, continue."

She waited for a moment, regaining her train of thought. "From her accounts, this sounded exactly like an alien abduction. The aliens are obviously continuing their experiments." She stopped and looked at Jake intensely. "You've stumbled onto something bigger than you know."

Jake had never believed the stories about Area 51. He had always assumed science fiction writers had concocted the story to sell books. "Okay. Let me see if I'm following here. You're a former employee of the base. The base is designed to study and stop these aliens who are snatching our population and doing tests on them. And you think Christina is one of these people who have been taken by the aliens."

Anne nodded, "Sounds pretty wild, doesn't it?"

"Yes it does." Jake stood and began to pace. "So what am I supposed to do about this? The Andersons are paying me a lot of money to find out what happened to their daughter, and you want me to go to them with a story about little green men and government conspiracies?"

"That's all you can do. There is no way to stop these aliens. Believe me, we've tried."

Jake sat down on the bed next to her. "Do you realize you're stark raving mad?" A wave of shock hit her. "How dare you!" Anne stood and began to walk toward the door. "I have graciously come here tonight and given you the answers, and you have the nerve to call me mad?"

"You have to understand, Anne, the story you just told me is very difficult to believe."

She began to walk back toward Jake. "I understand. I need a little faith from you." Jake stood and walked to the door. "I really appreciate the information, Anne, but I think it's time for you to go." Reaching over, he grabbed the handle and opened the door.

She moved over to Jake. "Maybe you're right." She stepped out the door. Turning back, she glanced at Jake. "Just think about what I've said." She began to walk away.

Closing the door, Jake moved over to the table and sat down. What Anne had told him was now running wild through his mind. His phone began to ring. Picking it up, he held it to his ear. "Hello?"

An emotionless voice spoke on the other end of the line. "Mr. Silver?" "This is Jake Silver. Who is this?"

"That's not important right now. What I have to tell you is."

Jake let out a long, audible sigh. "Look, I've had enough of this espionage bull- shit already."

The voice became impatient. "You need to hear this, Mr. Silver. The woman you just met has lied to you. She was intentionally sent there to mislead you."

"By whom?" Jake was curious. "It's not important right now." "What is important right now?"

"Only this. We need to meet. I have information very valuable to your case." "Okay. Where and when?"

"I'll find you when I'm ready to talk." The line went dead.

Jake leaned back in his chair and put his feet up on the table. Turning his head, he looked out the window. He watched the millions of lights in Vegas flicker on and off. "I am definitely in the right city. This just keeps on getting stranger and stranger."

***

The group of men had moved into the conference area adjoining the control room. It was a long rectangular room with shimmering steel walls and no windows. The one door at the rear sat directly behind the chair occupied by General Perry. He sat at the end of a long wooden conference table flanked on his right side by his advisors, and on the left, by the staff of Area 51. "What do we have, gentlemen?"

General Davis stood and adjusted his uniform. "We have apparently tracked and are ready to

118

recover a 'fallen angel'."

The advisors began to whisper among themselves. General Perry looked straight at Colonel Hunter. "Colonel?"

Hunter quickly stood up next to Davis. "Yes, sir." "What is your take on the situation?"

Glancing over at Davis, Hunter began. "We did track something on radar last night. It had violated our airspace, so we sent a patrol craft out to meet it and turn it around. Upon intercepting the intruder, Red Bird was immediately destroyed. We theorize that Red Bird fired her missiles on the craft hitting it, but the intruder returned fire and destroyed Red Bird."

Davis continued. "Colonel Hunter led a recon team out to the wreckage of Red Bird and discovered an immense crater near it. This was probably due to the intruder hitting the ground and somehow bouncing off."

"It bounced?" One of the Navy's advisors stood and addressed General Davis. "How could a craft struck by a missile and falling to Earth at terminal velocity 'bounce' off the ground?"

Davis turned to face the advisor. "As you well know, sir, the aircraft we are studying here are not all that normal. You saw several extra-terrestrial vehicles in the hangar. We have tested several different types of projectiles on them, usually causing minimal damage to the exterior of the vehicle. These things can stand up to whatever we throw at them and are still smiling afterward." The advisor slowly sat down.

General Perry stared at Davis. "General Davis, I've called this debriefing to allow the advisors a chance to ask questions about your methods and procedures, not for you to criticize them." His tone was stern.

Davis sat down. "I am terribly sorry, sir." Swiveling his chair toward the advisors, he leaned forward on the table. "As you all well know, rational thinking does not apply here at Area 51. We have to be willing to examine the extraordinary and accept it." The advisors began to nod in agreement.

Perry folded his hands and placed them on the table. "What are your plans to recover the craft, General Davis?"

"We will send out another recon team led by Colonel Hunter to determine the condition of the craft. After we know that, a full salvage team will be sent out."

"What about the Moscow Convention's stipulation about recovered extra-terrestrial technology? It states that all technology and biological entities must be destroyed upon discovery or capture." The President's advisor adjusted his glasses.

Hunter stepped in. "That law was put into effect after the world leaders deemed the UFO phenomenon was a threat. I don't think it applies over forty years later."

"Why not? The law is still on the books."

Hunter had always enjoyed a good debate. "Yes, but now every major nation of the world has their own facility for retrieval and study of extra-terrestrial technology."

The President's advisor leaned back in his chair while removing his glasses. "I was not aware of that. I was given to understand that this facility was the only one of its kind."

"Unfortunately, no. Up until a few years ago, the Russians had the most advanced facility in the world until they went bankrupt. Now the most complete base in the world is located in southern France. It's maintained jointly by the French and English governments."

"Do we work with these other facilities?"

"No. Most governments still deny the existence of this kind of base, even though we all know these places exist."

General Perry cut in. "Back to the task at hand, gentlemen. When does the salvage operation begin?"

Davis thought for a moment. "We'll need time to brief our salvage team and get a recon team out there." He estimated the time in his head. "The quickest would be tomorrow evening. We'll have to reallocate personnel to the teams, possibly call staff back from leave."

Perry stood and glanced around. "Let's make this happen. I want a full report in my hands by this time tomorrow so I can advise the President of the situation. Now if that's all, excuse me, gentlemen." The military personnel in the room stood and saluted as Perry exited the room followed by the advisors.

Davis sat down at the table along with Hunter and Griggs. Griggs looked over at Davis. "General, permission to speak frankly?"

Davis rolled it over for a moment. "Granted, Major. What is it?"

"Sir, I think having General Perry and his advisors calling the shots could be very dangerous."

"How is that, Major?"

"Sir, they don't know procedures here. They could put one of us or one of my men in a potentially deadly situation."

Hunter jumped in. "I'm going to have to agree with Major Griggs, sir. It's obvious from the conversation we just had that they don't know what they're doing."

Davis stood and paced around the table. "That much is obvious, Colonel." Seating himself at the end of the table, he stared at the two men. "And there is nothing we can do about it." Waving his hand, he dismissed the two men. Sitting alone, his mind began to swim with possibilities. If General Perry and his advisors were really as ignorant of Area 51 as they seemed, Davis knew his plans would succeed.

CHAPTER SEVEN

Jonathan Anderson was riddled with guilt. Sitting in his home office, he held his arms crossed and his head down on his desk. He felt a huge knot in his stomach begin to well up and his head was pounding. Finding a moment of clarity, he opened the top drawer and removed an item wrapped in crumpled yellow notebook paper. Laying it on his desk, he began to unfold the sheets of paper, exposing a vial of clear green liquid. Lifting it in his hand, he studied the fluid. "This will be the end." Placing it in his pocket, he stood and walked out of his office.

Stopping near the front door, he grabbed his trench coat off the rack and began to pull it on. He was reaching for the door handle when Susan came around the corner. "Jonathan? What are you doing?"

He finished putting on his coat. "I'm going out for a little while."

She looked concerned. He hadn't told her what was bothering him, but she knew something was wrong. "Where are you going?" She walked up to him and put her hand on his left shoulder.

He looked away. "There is something very important I need to do." "Why?"

He reached down and opened the front door. "It's for Christina," he turned to stare right at her. "And for my own salvation." He stepped outside and closed the door.

***

Two lone figures stepped off the plane. It was an all-white 737 jet with a thick red stripe extending from the tip to the tail. Walking down the stairs to the tarmac, they began to make their way to the hangar in the pale moonlight. Looking up into the starry sky, the two figures watched as several helicopters cruised overhead. The large hangar had old white wooden walls with panes of dirty glass looking out onto the empty airfield.

Stepping up to a small wooden door, the two figures each took turns placing their right hands on a small touch screen adorning the wall next to it. They listened as the lock on the door clicked open. Grabbing the handle, the two made their way into a small room. It was heaped with trash and scrap wood. The walls were bare wood, except for a few spots where the drywall still clung to them. Moving to the back, one of the figures lifted a large plank of wood away from the wall revealing a small door and another touch screen. After placing their hands on the screen, the door slid open to an elevator. Stepping inside, one of the figures removed a key from his pocket and slid it into the lock on the elevator's panel. Giving it a click to the right, all the lights flickered to life. Pressing one of the buttons, the elevator whirred to life. The two figures felt the lift begin to fall.

The door opened to a sterile white hospital like environment. The two figures stepped off into the hallway. Anne turned to address her companion. "Did General Davis say why he wanted us back at the base?"

The man in the black suit with the scar on his face shook his head. "No, but to call both of us back

124

in the middle of our assignments would indicate this could be a very serious situation."

Anne laughed.

The man in the black suit looked confused. "What?"

"You've been doing this for too long. A simple yes or no would've sufficed." The man smiled. "I have indeed."

Patting the man on the shoulder, they began to walk down the hall. Reaching the end, they came to a door marked 'General T. Davis' in tall black lettering. Anne stepped forward and knocked on it. From inside the room, they heard a voice telling them to enter. Grabbing the handle, Anne carefully opened the door and walked in.

A somber Davis greeted them. Looking up from his seat at his desk, he commanded them to sit down. Anne and the man both took seats opposite Davis'. Anne looked around his office. She had only been here once before, when she was promoted to her current position. The walls were a dull white and adorned with plaques and trophies in various shapes and sizes. Photographs of him and important people he had met littered his desk and shelves. Anne had always liked the one of Davis and Nixon taken in the oval office.

"Let's get down to business." Davis' emotionless face stared at the two. "We are currently under evaluation by the White House and the Pentagon. General Perry has personally come to oversee this operation. It seems the powers that be aren't exactly satisfied with our performance here, especially mine."

The man leaned forward. "What does this mean

to us, sir?"

"If the evaluation goes well, nothing. But if something goes wrong, we could all be replaced." Davis set down the pen he was holding. "I've briefed all the major staff members of the situation, and you two are the last to know."

Anne looked mystified. "Sir, why is Washington unhappy with us?"

"Apparently, we aren't moving the program along fast enough. As you both know, ever since the Air Force gained control of the facility from the Army, we have been operating under a microscope. This could very well be the end of Area 51."

All three leaned back in their chairs trying to process the information at hand. The man straightened up. "So am I to assume, sir, that it's business as usual until we're notified otherwise?"

Davis nodded. "We have a rather strange event unfolding here at the base, so I'm going to need you two to continue your work in the field and get this 'Anderson Incident' taken care of." Standing up, he walked around to his door and opened it.

"Dismissed."

***

Jake sorted through the several files he had accumulated that day. He was sitting at the small circular table in the corner of his room. Shuffling the files together, he placed them all neatly in a yellow folder and set them aside. He rubbed his hands over his eyes. It had been a long day. Staring across the room, he glanced at the alarm clock on his nightstand. It was almost two in the morning. He stood and flipped off his boots while pulling off his t-shirt. Walking into the small bathroom, he stared at himself in the mirror. He twisted on the faucets and held his hands under the water waiting for it to warm up. Cupping his hands, he lifted the warm water to his face. He leaned over and rested his hands on the counter, just staring at the man in the mirror. Straightening up, he began to unbutton his jeans when he heard a knock at the door. *What now?*

Walking toward the door, he grabbed his shirt and began to pull it on. Stepping up to the door, he peeked through the peephole. Quickly grabbing the handle, he opened it. "Jonathan," Jake was surprised to see him here this late at night. Jonathan Anderson stood in the doorway, soaking wet. "Please, come in."

Jonathan walked past Jake and began to strip off his jacket. Setting it on the edge of the bed, he moved around to the small table where Jake had just been seated. "I need to speak with you."

Jake closed the door and turned around. "Sure, go ahead."

"Earlier this evening, you received an anonymous phone call claiming to know the real facts behind the case you're working on."

"Yes. How did you know?"

Jonathan shifted in his seat. "Because I made that call." Jake's eyes widened. "You? Why?"

"Because I am tired, Mister Silver. Tired of lying to my family." "I don't understand. What are you talking about?"

Jonathan pulled out the vial of green liquid and placed it on the table. "I'm sure you know by now I'm a government employee."

"Yeah, I know. I just don't know what kind of

employee."

"I am a genetic researcher. I've been called one of the top minds in the field. I've had a long and distinguished career in the science community." Jake felt Jonathan was reminding himself, not telling Jake. Jonathan began to mumble to himself.

"Jonathan? Are you okay?"

"Yeah, I'm okay." He looked away from Jake. "I just don't feel well, that's all." "Can I get you a drink?"

Jonathan shook his head. "No, thanks. I'm fine."

Jake began to reach across the table to grab the vial of green liquid. "What's this?"

It was almost in his grasp, when Jonathan's hand shot out and grabbed it. "No!" Pulling his hand quickly back, Jake felt like a child playing with his father's prize possession. "I'm sorry. I was just curious."

"We'll get to that. But let's start at the beginning." Jake nodded for him to begin. Jonathan raised his glance to Jake's. "I'm damned."

"I'm afraid you're going to have to be more specific." Jake smiled, trying to lighten the mood.

Jonathan stared right through him. "I have been involved with illegal experiments on the citizens of the United States. We take people right out of their homes against their will and then conduct medical experiments on them." "I'm afraid I'm not following."

"I'm an employee of Area 51."

Jake stood and began to run his hands through his hair. "I really don't want to go down this road again tonight."

"Look, Mr. Silver, I'm not crazy. The woman you met with tonight was lying to you. She is what's known as a 'plant'. She was enlisted by the powers at Area 51 to spread disinformation and to pull people off the right track—"

"What track? I'm here to investigate what happened to your daughter, not some secret base in the middle of the Nevada desert!"

"That is the right track, Jake. You have no idea what you've gotten yourself into here. Please, sit down." Jake moved back to the table and sat down across from Jonathan. "I'm a scientist. I hold doctorates in genetic engineering and chemistry. Before I moved my family here, I worked for a small research facility in Colorado. We did mostly smaller projects on bacteria and germs, testing them for immunities to several different strands of diseases and flu strains. I had worked there for several years, until I received an interesting job opportunity to do some real research here at Area 51. It was an offer no self-respecting scientist could turn down."

"Why?"

"Basically because we could do the work we wanted without the watchful eye of the government. We didn't have to report our findings to the FDA, or wait years until we could do actual human trials." He stopped. Reaching his hands up to his temples, he began to slowly massage them. "I'm sorry, I have a terrible headache."

"Can I get you some aspirin?"

"No. I'm fine. Thank you, though." He stopped rubbing. "I was recommended for the position by Doctor Jim Yokama. He was a prominent researcher until he faded out of view several years ago. It wasn't until I worked with him at the facility that I knew it was when he was recruited to Area 51. He was considered by many in his field to be one of the world's top minds. I feel as though I was recruited under false pretenses."

Jake struggled to take the information in. This story seemed very similar to the one Anne had told him only a few hours ago. Standing, he began to move toward the mini-bar. "I need something to drink. Please continue." He opened the door and removed a can of soda. Popping open the top, he took a long sip from it.

"As I was saying, I was recruited under false pretenses." Jake had returned to his seat. "In what way?"

"I had been told we would be doing good work there, but in all actuality, we were doing horrible things to people."

"What kind of 'horrible' things?"

"I was recruited for my expertise in genetic engineering. You know," he motioned with his hands, "identifying, splicing and studying DNA. I was part of a team that abducted subjects from their homes, then experimented on them."

"How did you 'abduct' them?"

"We used a top secret government aircraft known as the 'Aurora'. As I understand it, this craft was back-engineered from alien technology. It has a very ominous look, but is very hard to describe. Basically, it's just a big black triangle that flies. I'm not up on the logistics of the craft, I just know it takes us where we want to go all over the world in a manner of minutes."

130

"So you're in the craft, what next?"

"The subjects we go after are subjected to a long screening process. Once they are picked to be in the project, a crack team of commandos dispatched from Area 51 scrutinizes their lives. Most of these people never even know they're being watched. If the subject passes the surveillance, we abduct them. We do this by first flooding their room or house or car with a highly hallucinogenic gas. This gas serves two purposes. First, it makes the subject very susceptible to suggestion, and secondly, it makes them very manageable, except in certain extreme cases. Once the subjects are sufficiently gassed, soldiers dressed as aliens come in and take them."

"All right. Let me see if I'm tracking here. You take this strange craft out and gas people? What next?"

"Next we take the subjects aboard the craft and return to base. Sometimes, our ship gets spotted. This is where the majority of the UFO sightings come from." He rolled the vial of green liquid in his fingers. "Once back at base, we do tests on these people."

"What kinds of tests?"

"Basically these tests are to determine a subject's susceptibility to certain nerve toxins. It's all about biological warfare. We've found that certain types of people have a natural immunity to some of the chemicals we test on them. We then extract the DNA from these people and store it. Usually, the people are returned home safely with little or no memory of what happened."

"And the others?"

"Sometimes they don't survive the tests." Jake was horrified. "For what purpose?"

"Mr. Silver, we're creating a genetically perfect army. This 'super army' could be sent into battle with no effects from the toxins we would be hurling at the enemy. They could infiltrate and kill while the enemy was incapacitated. We are building an army of clones."

"For warfare? These people are being taken, gassed and cut open so you can build the perfect soldier!" Jake leaned back. He knew the story he was being told was true. He had been a P.I. long enough to know when someone was lying to him. "What does this mean to your daughter?"

Jonathan's body slumped. "She was one of the test subjects." He laid the vial on the table and rolled it to Jake. "As were you."

CHAPTER EIGHT

General Perry stood staring out the window in his makeshift office. Before he had arrived, this had been a storage room. It was small with bare white walls, but large enough to suit his needs. In the back behind his desk, a large observation window looked out onto the longest runway in the world. He watched as a bright blue light rocketed toward the end of the runway. No matter how many times he had seen the Aurora in flight, he never got used to it.

The Aurora was a top secret government ship back-engineered from alien technology. It was large, black and triangular in shape with incredibly bright running lights. The Aurora was the pinnacle of military technology.

He watched as the bright blue light touched down on the runway and taxied to a stop in front of the main hangar. The running lights faded away revealing the hull of the large black craft. Five men in black Army fatigues approached it. Upon reaching the ship, a large rectangular cargo door on its side slid open and several men dressed in white jump suits exited the door, along with a person strapped to a stretcher. Perry couldn't tell whether it was male or female. The Army personnel swiftly escorted the men in the white jump suits and the stretcher. He watched as the craft began to roll toward the now open hangar door. A knock sounded at his door. Not moving from his place at the window, he commanded the person to enter.

"General Perry?" Colonel Hunter opened the door and strode into the room. He snapped to attention in front of Perry's desk.

"What is it?" Perry asked sternly.

"Sir, I am saddened to inform you that we have a traitor in our midst."

Perry turned around to face Hunter. "You do understand that treason is a very serious offense, Colonel."

"Yes, sir." "Who is it?"

"It's one of our research team." Hunter clasped his hands behind his back. Perry sat down in his chair. "What has this person done, Colonel?"

"We just got word from one of our operatives in Las Vegas he's imparting top secret data to a civilian." "Which data?"

"About the 'Uber-Soldier Project'."

"This man must be eliminated," Perry advised. "Who else knows about this?" "Just you, sir. I thought it would be best to take this problem to the highest authority."

"Very good, Colonel." Perry stood and adjusted his uniform. "Dispatch a team to handle the problem."

"What about the man who's receiving the information?"

"I want everyone involved with this man to disappear. I want this to send a message to the rest of the employees here at the facility that treachery will not be handled lightly."

Hunter saluted. "Yes, sir." He made his way out the office.

***

Jake's eyes went wide at what he had just

heard. "What do you mean?" Jonathan lowered his voice and leaned closer to Jake. "This project is very far-reaching. We have records on every man, woman and child born since 1950." Jake gasped for air. "I was born in 1967."

"This is the biggest project the US government has ever undertaken. We have screened millions of subjects looking for the perfect genome."

Anger began to well up in Jake. He leaped up and grabbed Jonathan by his shirt collar, lifting him out of his chair. "You sons a bitches violated my rights, came into my house and took me? To do 'genetic testing' for your perfect soldier?"

Jonathan broke free of the hold. "Yes." His tone was still dead serious. He adjusted his now messed shirt. "They even have my sample on record." Jake tried to calm his temper. "This can't continue. This project has to be stopped!"

"That's exactly what I'm here to talk to you about. Did you ever wonder why we picked you for this case? Why we drove all the way from Las Vegas to Lake Tahoe?"

Jake nodded.

"I knew you were a former subject. That's why."

"You came to me because you knew exactly how I'd react when you told me. That I'd want some kind of retribution."

"Right."

Jake thought for a moment and then nodded in approval. "All right, I'm in. How do we do it?"

He pointed to the vial of green liquid on the table. "Take that. It's undeniable proof of what we're doing at Area 51. That's what you'll need when you take this story to the media." Jonathan extracted his key card from his pocket. "It's going to be very difficult, but you'll need this to access most of the base. Getting there will be the hardest part."

Jake picked up the card and began to examine it. Placing it in his jacket pocket, he continued to listen.

"As you may or may not know, Area 51 has some of the most state-of-the-art defenses in the world."

"What kind are we talking about?"

"Motion detectors every fifty feet and infrared sensors which can detect an insect flying past them at a hundred yards. Pressure sensors so sensitive, blowing dust sometimes sets them off. They'll know you're coming even before you do."

Jake rubbed his chin. "How do we get in then?"

"I've set up a contact for you in the base. He's a very high-ranking official with the clout to help us."

"Sounds good. When do we meet him?"

"Tomorrow night at eight at a bar downtown called 'The Factory'."

"How will we know him?" Jake began to get an uneasy feeling. Something was wrong.

"He'll be wearing a 'Yankees' baseball hat."

The door to Jake's room burst open in an explosion of wood shards. Jake's instincts went into high gear. Leaping over the table, he grabbed Jonathan and threw him to the ground. Quickly reaching behind him, he retrieved his weapon from its resting place on the nightstand. Cradling it in

136

both hands, he lifted it into a ready position. Moving swiftly, he knocked over the table in front of them to use it as a barricade.

Two men in black fatigues ran into the room carrying automatic machine guns with black ski masks concealing their faces. The room erupted as bullets sprayed from the attackers' weapons.

Jake plastered his back to the table, knowing it wouldn't last long under this kind of abuse. Jonathan was shouting in hysteria as the bullets pierced the wall directly behind them. Jake knew the men were advancing, and this wouldn't be a safe hiding place for very long. Searching for options, he spotted the bathroom. Moving his gun around the table, he fired several shots wildly toward the assailants. He turned to Jonathan. "When I say go, you run for the bathroom!"

Jonathan nodded frantically.

Hearing the tell-tale click of an empty magazine, both men jumped up from their cover. Time seemed to freeze as Jake immediately fired two shots, hitting the nearest attacker squarely in the chest. The man let out a groan as he clutched his wound and crumpled to the floor. Jonathan was less than a step from the bathroom when the second man reloaded his gun and began to fire. Jonathan let out a shriek of pain as he fell to the floor. Diving in front of Jonathan, Jake initiated a roll that carried him into direct sight of the second man. He quickly squeezed the trigger sending a bullet ricocheting off the second attacker's gun and knocking it to the floor. His next shot hit the man in the neck. The soldier grabbed his throat as blood began to spurt wildly from his severed arteries. Jake watched the soldier's eyes roll back as he crumpled to the floor in a bloody heap.

Staying in a ready position for a moment, Jake stared at the door for the next wave of assailants to enter. Nothing. Reaching over, he lifted Jonathan off the floor and carefully leaned him against the wall. A bullet had hit him near the heart piercing his right lung. Blood was dripping from his mouth.

With his last ounce of strength, Jonathan lifted his hand to Jake's shoulder. "Save my daughter," he made a gurgling sound as he spoke. "If they've come after me, she'll be next." His hand fell off Jake's shoulder.

Jake watched as his breathing stopped. Lifting his hand, he gently closed both Jonathan's eyes. "I will." Standing, he holstered his weapon. Grabbing his jacket and boots, he ran out the door.

***

Christina couldn't sleep. She rolled over in her hospital bed and glanced at the clock. It was almost three in the morning. Flipping over onto her back, she snatched the remote control off the nightstand and clicked on the TV. An infomercial was airing about a new kind of potato-slicer. Knowing that nothing good would be on at three in the morning, she watched it.

A cool breeze was blowing through her open window. It was rustling the curtain that separated her from the other patient in the room. She watched as the full moon cast strange shadows on the curtain and floor. She never knew why, but she'd always been a night person. Even when she had to get up early the next morning, she always stayed up late.

A noise caught her attention. The noise

138

sounded like very light footsteps on the hard floor. Knowing the nurse's rounds were finished for the night, her mind went on alert and her pulse began to race. Quickly flipping off the TV, she pushed herself back down in the bed and pulled the covers up to her chin. She heard the noise again. This time, it was closer. She watched as a long shadow began to creep into the room.

Rolling off her bed, she began to cower next to it. Peeking, she saw a tall man walk into the room. He was dressed entirely in black, including a mask covering his face. She recognized the night-vision goggles he was wearing from movies she had seen.

Christina watched as he moved closer to where she was hiding. Looking up, she saw the lamp over her bed. She took a long deep breath and quickly reached up for the switch. She knew she had been spotted. Finally finding the switch, she clicked it on. The light overloaded his goggles and he began to moan in pain as he tried to rip them off his face. Knowing this might be her only chance, she leapt to her feet and began to charge him. She slammed into his midsection as he was trying to pull off the goggles. The man toppled to the floor as she began to run past him. His hand shot out and grabbed her right ankle tripping her. She rolled over and began to kick wildly. Hitting her assailant in the nose, he loosened his grip long enough for her to wiggle free. Standing, she noticed his weapon lying on the floor next to him. Kicking it hard with her bare foot, she sent it flying under her bed. Turning, she sprinted out the room.

Christina frantically screamed for help as she tried to traverse the dark corridor. Reaching the nurses station, she searched for someone, anyone, to help her. Running around behind the desk, she found the three nurses on duty slumped over on their desks, each lying in a pool of their own blood. Thinking quickly, she lifted one of the dead nurses and crawled under her desk. Sitting as silently as she could, she heard the crisp click of booted feet walking toward her. She closed her eyes and hoped he wouldn't find her.

From under the desk, she could see he had rounded the corner and was coming around the nurses station toward her. She noticed he hadn't retrieved his weapon and that he'd abandoned the night-vision goggles. He stopped in front of her. She felt a momentary burst of adrenaline. Placing both her hands on the nurse's chair, she pushed as hard as she could. The body of the nurse went toppling over onto her attacker. Both hit the floor with a thud. Jumping up, she ran over to him and kicked him in the head as hard as she could. She heard a crack as the man began to scream.

Looking to her left, she spotted the elevator. She noticed the lights above it were still working and slowly counting up. Frantically, she dashed toward them. Hitting the down button, she spun around to see the man starting to push the body off him. She screamed and began to bang on the doors. She turned back around in time to see her attacker charging her. He jumped, hitting her squarely in the midsection, slamming her into the wall. The man slowly stood in front of her and flashed her a sinister grin. Reaching behind, he retrieved a small black pistol from his belt. Christina heard the elevator doors ding and begin to slide open.

Jake looked out into the dark hallway. It took his eyes a moment to adjust, but he immediately saw a man dressed all in black standing over Christina. Using all his strength, he leapt at the man sending both of them careening to the floor. The weapon in the man's hand went skidding off towards the nurses station. Swiftly pulling himself up, he sent a barrage of punches into the man's face. Recovering quickly, the man easily threw Jake off and leapt to his feet. Jake was still on his hands and knees when the soldier delivered several heavy kicks to his ribs. Grabbing the soldier's foot, he twisted it and sent him sprawling to the floor.

Jake reached for his gun. Aiming, he pulled the trigger. The gun clicked uselessly in his hands. "Damn, out of bullets."

The assailant quickly swatted the gun out of Jake's hands and began to deliver several hits to his ribs. Blocking the last one with his arm, Jake retaliated with an uppercut that caught the man in the jaw. The attacker stumbled back trying to regain his balance. Looking around, Jake spied a hallway that led to the staff's lounge. Realizing he had to take the battle away from Christina, he began to run full steam down the hall. Flipping around to see if he was being followed, he was caught in the face by a quick jab. Jake went reeling toward a window at the end of the hall. Catching himself on the window ledge, he watched as the man started another charge.

Jake suddenly had an idea. He readied himself as the attacker raced toward him with his face twisted with anger. Just when he was about to pounce, Jake quickly stepped to the side of the

141

window sending the attacker sailing through it in an eruption of glass and wood shards. Leaning back against the window frame, Jake let out a sigh of relief. He began to stand up when he was suddenly grabbed from behind. The two men toppled out the window, catching themselves on a nearby ledge.

The attacker lifted back up onto the ledge, where he stood mockingly over Jake. The ledge was at least six stories above the ground and no more than two feet wide.

"How do you like the view?" he sneered. "Better enjoy it, it'll be the last one you ever see." Lifting one of his booted feet, he began to smash Jake's fingers.

Jake fought off the pain while trying to keep his hold on the ledge. Gritting his teeth, he looked up at the attacker. "I think you'll appreciate this view more than I do."

Letting go with one hand, he snatched the soldier's foot and yanked. The attacker lost his balance and stumbled over the edge. Quickly grabbing the ledge, Jake listened as the man's screams faded, then stopped. He slowly pulled himself up on to the ledge, where he let out a long breath.

Christina startled Jake as she popped her head out the window. "Are you okay, Jake?"

Jake nodded since he was breathing heavily. "Yeah, I'm okay." He started to stand when he began to feel lightheaded. He hated heights. "Give me a hand here, will ya?"

Christina grabbed both his hands and helped him into the window. "Thanks for saving me."

Jake fell in a slump under the window. "It was

my pleasure." A smile appeared on his face.

She sat down next to him. "Why were you coming here so late?"

"To make sure you were all right." He patted her bruised knee. "Listen, Christina, we've got to get out of here. It's not safe for you anymore."

She nodded. "I know."

Jake stood. Extending a hand, he lifted Christina off the floor. "I also have some bad news."

She looked into his eyes. "What is it?"

He looked away. "I'm real sorry. Your dad," he felt the words get stuck in his throat. "He's gone."

"What?" Tears began to well up in her eyes.

"He was meeting with me when two of those goons dressed in black broke into my room and began to shoot up the place. I'm so sorry, Christina. I couldn't save him."

She began sob uncontrollably. "My dad's gone."

"He wanted you to know he loves you very much. That's why he hired me." She just cried. Jake opened his arms and pulled her to his chest. "I know you want to find who's responsible for this. He gave me names and places, but I'm going to need your help. Do you feel up to it?"

She stepped back and wiped the tears from her face. "Yes I do."

CHAPTER NINE

General Davis was awestruck. He had just learned General Perry had given the order to kill Jonathan Anderson. He was pacing around his office frantically. Sitting down, he pounded his fists on his desk. "This is not good policy, God dammit."

Colonel Hunter sat in a small wooden chair across from him. His arms were crossed in a very defensive position. "Sir, General Perry was just acting in the base's best interest."

Davis stared him right in the eye. "Bullshit. You know as well as he does sending troops into a heavily populated area is extremely dangerous."

"As I said before, sir, General Perry was just acting in the best interest of—"

"How the hell am I going to explain two dead soldiers in a hotel room and another one flattened on the ground after a six story fall?" He rubbed his hands through his gray hair.

"I don't know, sir."

Davis stood up. "How did he get the information before I did? This is my project!"

"Again, I don't know, sir."

Walking around the desk, he stood in front of Hunter. "I want you to talk to every man on this base who has access to this kind of information. I want to know if we have a plant, someone circumventing the chain of command. I want that person or persons in my office so I can rip their God damned heads off!" Davis kicked his desk full force.

"Yes, sir." "Dismissed, soldier."

Hunter stood up, saluted and exited the room.

Returning to the rear of his desk, Davis seated himself. He sat quietly for several minutes trying to curb his anger. Reaching down, he opened his top desk drawer. He removed a small gold-framed picture. Lifting it up, he set it facing him on his desk. It was a picture of a beautiful woman with long curly brown hair. What seemed to him like a lifetime ago, he had known this woman. Before he'd entered the military, he had loved this woman. He still did.

***

The room was buzzing with activity. Several men in lab coats checked and rechecked their computations. Some of the researchers were busy attaching several wires to the base of the object just below the glowing portion of the artifact. One of the men quickly stood and walked over to one of the computer banks. Tapping several keys, he was satisfied with the chart on his screen.

He turned to the others. "The device is ready when you are."

The main researcher nodded. "Very good. Let's proceed with the test immediately."

The soft white light filling the room switched to a harsh red warning light. The men quickly finished their final tasks and hurried out the door. The final man out of the room hit the door controls, slamming it shut with a thud.

Most of the researchers had joined the control team in the observation room directly above where the artifact was located. Looking down into the room through several sets of windows, they watched as the red light was again replaced with a soft white glow.

The main researcher stood over the control panel. He turned around to face a room filled with some of the top military and political brass in the country. He cleared his throat. "I'm glad you could make it to S-4, gentlemen." He hit a button on his control panel. A large TV screen lowered from the ceiling of the room. An image of the artifact appeared on the screen. "What you're seeing now is the device recently recovered in Egypt. We've tried to get an exact age on it, but that has proven to be an extremely difficult task. We do know, though, that it must be at least a thousand years old."

An older man in an Army uniform leaned forward. "What do you think it is?"

"We believe it's some kind of a power generator. What we're trying to accomplish here is to find out if we can tap this huge energy source inside it. From our estimates, the energy in this one artifact could power the Western United States indefinitely."

The old man though for a moment. "What are its military applications?"

The researcher thought for a moment. "If we could harness the energy in this device, we would have a weapon capable of wiping out the populations of entire continents."

The old man gasped, "My God."

He pointed to the large screen. "Now if you'll watch the monitor, we'll begin." He checked several items off on the clipboard he had been carrying under his left arm. Keying his control pad, he turned back to the room. "I'm starting the experiment," he hit the final key, "Now."

Everyone in the room watched the image on the screen intently. The artifact's pulsing orb became a steady glow. The main researcher turned to another man standing next to him. "Readings?"

He checked his many computer monitors. "It seems to be working. We are indeed siphoning off energy from the device." The orb began to glow a bright red. "Something's wrong."

The head researcher began to panic. "What's wrong?"

"We're taking in too much energy. The device is overloading our circuits!" "Shut it down!"

The man's console exploded in a shower of sparks. "I can't!"

The occupants of the control room watched in horror as the banks of computers located in with the device began to smoke and explode. The orb changed from a light red to a deep blood red. A huge wave of energy flowed through the device into the computer system. The lights in both rooms exploded. The TV screen blinked off and started to smoke. The windows separating the two rooms shattered allowing the high- pitched squealing of the device to permeate the observation room. Everyone scattered. Another wave of energy slammed through the wires sending shock waves through the two rooms.

The main researcher turned to look behind him at the chaos in the observation room. The researcher standing next to him grabbed his shoulder and spun him around. "If we don't stop this, we're looking at a total meltdown of the facility!"

The main researcher knew what he had to do.

Stepping up to the shattered windows, he leapt down into the room with the device. He heard cries of 'no' coming from above him. Pure energy was permeating the room. The hair on his body stood on end and he felt his heart begin to beat irregularly. He knew he only had one chance. Grabbing the wires with both hands, he pulled with all his strength to disconnect them. Electricity surged through his body, knocking him away and slamming him against the wall. He felt himself slipping away. Looking over at the object, he knew he had succeeded in unhooking the cords. The orb atop the device was returning to its normal white color. He closed his eyes and faded off.

***

Susan was sobbing uncontrollably. Christina was holding her in her arms trying to be strong for her mother's sake. Jake was sitting on a couch opposite theirs in the Andersons' large living room. The first time he had entered the house, it had seemed more vibrant than it did now.

Holding his hands in his lap, he tried to understand the pain they were feeling. He had never lost anyone close. "Mrs. Anderson, I will find the people who did this to your husband."

She looked up at him with tears in her eyes.

"I recently discovered your daughter was telling the truth about her experience. I've also learned I have had similar experiences." Both women looked up at him. "I have a personal stake in this now, and I'm devoted to bringing the men who did this to justice."

Susan wiped her eyes, smearing black lines of mascara down her cheeks. "Who did this to my

148

husband?" She looked at her daughter. "To my family?"

"The people he worked for." He stopped. "I don't want to tell you anymore because of the danger it could pose to your lives." He leaned forward and lowered his voice. "All I can tell you is that I will find the men responsible for this."

Susan stood and walked over to where Jake was sitting. Taking a seat next to him, she placed her hand on his leg. "I appreciate all you've done, Jake."

"It's what I do."

"I know, but this time, you'll have to go above and beyond the call of duty."

He nodded. Touching her hand, he slowly stood up. "I have to go, are you two going to be all right?"

Susan smiled her best smile at Jake. "Yeah, we'll be fine."

Walking toward the door, Jake stopped to look back at the two women. Tears were again rolling from their eyes. Stepping through the door, he pulled it closed behind him. Staring up at the gray overcast sky, he closed his eyes and felt the raindrops hitting his face. It felt refreshing. He had been up all night with the two, trying to console them as best he could. He needed to get some rest before his meeting later that night, but his hotel room had been blocked off as a crime scene. Hopping in his car, he slammed the keys into the ignition and started up the engine. Pulling out of the driveway, he headed downtown.

***

A long black sedan slowly pulled into the alley. It was littered with boxes and filthy trashcans filled

149

with puddles of rainwater. Steam rolled out of several grates in the cold, rainy air. Two ancient warehouses rose magnificently from either side. A man in a black trench coat got out of the sedan, accompanied by a tall man with short-cropped hair in a black leather jacket. The two shadowy figures walked toward the side of the alley. The man in the leather jacket stepped forward and opened an old wooden door.

Stepping inside, the two shadowy figures were immediately accosted by two well- built men in full Marine attire. "Sir, General Perry is waiting for you inside."

The man in the trench coat nodded and began to follow the two soldiers. The inside of the warehouse was strewn with boards and steel pipes of all shapes and sizes. Windows at the top of the walls created checkerboard shadows on the floor with the moonlight. Stepping through an archway that used to contain a door, the four men emerged into a large room. Inside, a lone lamp stood behind several wooden chairs and created long, eerie shadows across the floor. The two soldiers directed the men to be seated while they summoned General Perry.

The man in the black trench coat seated himself in the chair closest to the door. The light danced across his gray suit and shone brightly off his blue eyes. His gray hair was neatly combed and his long slender face was freshly shaved. The deep lines in his face showed the long history of a man in his seventies. By comparison, his companion was a young man. His face untattered by time and his brown eyes still sharp with youth and vigor. His black leather jacket hung loosely off his broad shoulders and around his slim torso. He was young, but by no means naive.

General Perry strode into the room followed by the two marines. Seating himself in a chair opposite the two figures, he reached into his breast pocket and removed a pack of cigarettes. Pulling one out of the pack, he lit it with a short, square lighter he had removed from his other pocket. Taking a long drag off the cigarette, he exhaled the smoke toward the two men, allowing it to linger in the light.

The man in the trench coat spoke first. "Why have you summoned me here, General?" He spoke with a gruff tone in his voice.

"I've found information I think you will find very interesting." Perry took another drag off the cigarette.

The man in the trench coat stared intently at Perry. "You presume to know something we don't?" The younger man studied Perry's two guards.

Perry shifted in his seat. "One of our main researchers has, of late, decided to take his work at the facility public."

"How?"

"His daughter had been placed in the project. Afterwards, he feigned ignorance of what happened to her, trying to play it off as a rape." Taking another long drag off his cigarette, he continued, "He hired a private investigator, who had also been involved in the tests, to look into what had happened."

"He told this man about the project?" "Yes."

"How has this situation been resolved?"

"We dispatched a team to deal with the

problem. We eliminated the scientist, but missed his daughter and the PI."

The man in the trench coat stood up and approached Perry. His voice was low and filled with rage. "We were already aware of your ignorance in this matter. You have three dead soldiers scattered around Las Vegas." He was in Perry's face. "You have overstepped your boundaries on this one, General. You will be reprimanded by the Assemblage when you return to Washington." He took a step back. "In the meantime, what do you plan to do about the private investigator?"

Perry crushed his cigarette out on the arm of his chair. "He has connections in the bureau. If he vanishes, someone will miss him. We've decided to make it look like an accident."

The man in the trench coat began to walk toward the door. "Perhaps you're not as ignorant as I first assumed. Make it happen." Turning to his companion, he motioned toward the door. "David, please ready the car." He nodded and walked away. "General, one more thing." Perry stood. The light cast a strange shadow across his face. "Deal with this correctly and immediately, or we will handle you." Turning around, he walked out the building. Perry again sat down. Lighting another cigarette, he watched as the smoke flowed around his head. Reaching over, he grabbed the small string hanging from the lamp and gave it a slight tug. The lamp clicked off, filling the room with darkness.

***

Jake found himself sitting on a bench at the city park. A large tree behind him was sheltering him from most of the rain. His eyelids were heavy from lack of sleep, and his body felt heavy and lifeless. He desperately needed to get some rest.

His mind began to wander. He kept flashing back to the dream he had the night he took the case. The inhuman figure he saw in his dream was haunting him. Was Jonathan Anderson telling the truth? Were there actually no aliens abducting people? Could it be that the government was actually behind the whole project? He tried not to trust his thoughts when he was this tired. Lack of sleep caused a person to think incoherently.

Pulling a cigar out of his jacket pocket, he licked the tip and put it in his mouth. Lighting it, he inhaled deeply from and slowly exhaled. Leaning back against the bench, he looked up into the overcast sky. The clouds rolled together with swatches of black, gray and white. Commenting to himself, he really found it quite beautiful. Taking another drag off his cigar, he stood and began to walk toward his car.

Opening the car door, he slowly got in. Closing it, he rolled down the window so the crisp air could flow inside. Resting his hand on the door, he watched the cigar smoke mingle with the raindrops. Leaning back in his seat, he felt his eyes slowly close. He began to drift off to sleep.

He awoke lying on a hard metal table in the middle of a rectangular room with no visible doors. The table was cool to his touch. This place reminded him of pictures he had seen of the inside of a human's body. Dark strips of material ran in asymmetrical patterns across the walls with flesh-like webbing in the middle, allowing light to flow into the room. He swore he could see veins running through the walls. He was still fully dressed, but somehow immobilized. Looking up, he saw a fine mist rolling out of a circular hole in the ceiling above him. Trying to lift his head, he found he was still unable to move.

Resting his head back on the table, he noticed something emerging from the hole in the ceiling. Its chrome skin was glistening in the dim light as it lowered toward him.

He could see several moving arms attached to a central cylinder. An arm on the right side of the device began to creep toward his face. He watched as a needle slid out of a tube at the center of the claw like object. The claws slid back as the arm inched closer.

From out of the corner of his eye, he could see several shapes moving toward him out of the mist. The two in the front immediately took flanking positions on each side of him, while the third stood silently at the foot of the table observing. Jake caught a quick glance of the two figures standing next to him. His heart began to pound. Their huge black lidless eyes reminded him of an insect's. He began to panic as both of them grabbed his head and held it firmly to the table. Their skin felt cold and moist, but smooth to the touch.

Jake strained with all his might to catch a glimpse of the figure standing at the foot of the bed. He could tell he was different from the others. He was tall and appeared to be proportioned like a human. He wasn't sure, but it looked like he was wearing a military uniform of some kind...

The beings tightened their grip on Jake's head, pulling his attention back to the lowering arm. It

154

was almost on top of him now. He was using all his strength to try and break free, but an invisible force was keeping him firmly atop the table. The being to his right reached up and grabbed the gyrating arm, slowly moving it into position above Jake's right eye. Terror welled up inside him as the needle edged closer and closer to his eye. He tried to shut them, but couldn't. The being on the left leaned in close enough so that Jake could feel its terrible breath on his face.

Sitting straight up, he found himself still in his car. A cold sweat had broken out all over his body. Leaning forward on the steering wheel, he wiped the sweat off his face. Peering out the windshield, he noticed a group of people had gathered around his car. They were all staring intently at him. He knew he was just having a dream, but it somehow felt very familiar and very real to him.

CHAPTER TEN

Hours later, Jake found himself wandering through a nightclub dubbed 'The Factory' by its inhabitants. Blaring industrial music began to assault his senses as soon as he walked in. It was packed with people of every shape and size dressed mainly in black and other drab colors. The main room was decorated to look like the inside of a steel mill. Everything from the tables to the bar was built using steel pipes and huge iron plates. Multi-colored lights flooded the hall, while powerful white spotlights careened off the walls and the band playing on the front stage.

Cutting his way through the mob on the dance floor, he found himself standing in front of the bar. Stretching to both ends of the room, the top seemed to be constructed of steel girders, complete with rust colored paint and rivets. Standing next to him was a tall black man with dreadlocks that hung to the middle of his back. He was sipping on a beer while smoking a cigarette. He dwarfed Jake in height by at least a foot.

Turning toward Jake, the man gave Jake the once over. Taking a drag off the cigarette, he crushed it out on the bar. "It's not polite to stare, mon," he warned in a thick Jamaican accent.

"Sorry. I didn't realize I was staring."

Stepping back from the bar, the Jamaican turned around and began to walk away. Jake shook his head. *Great. All I need now is to get into a bar fight.* Lifting his hand, he signaled for the bartender.

She was of medium height and had a very athletic build. She was wrapped in a tight black leather vest and a pair of black denim jeans. She seemed to have several piercings through every part of her body. Her hair was brown with blonde highlights. It hung messily down to the center of her back.

"What can I get for you, stranger?"

"Just a beer." He watched as she gracefully moved behind the bar and lifted a brown bottle out of a cooler. Twisting off the top, she placed it in front of him. She quickly collected the three dollars he had laid on the bar. "Can I ask you a question?"

She looked at him amusedly. "I'm married."

Jake smiled. There had been many times he had tried to pick up a good-looking waitress or female bartender. This wasn't one of them. "No, but thank you. I was wondering if you've seen a man wearing a dark blue 'Yankees' baseball cap in here tonight."

She thought for a moment. "It's hard to say. I see so many people come and go." Jake nodded. "I understand. Thanks a lot." He slipped her another dollar and moved toward an empty table in the corner. Placing his beer on the table, he seated himself and began to scan the crowd. He knew he stuck out like a sore thumb, but he hoped the person he was supposed to meet here would too.

The band finished the song they were performing with a flourish of lights and sound. The crowd erupted into wild applause and screams of joy. Announcing they were taking a brief break, the band marched offstage and tried to wade through the crowd toward the bar. As they went by, Jake caught sight of an older man sitting in a booth on the opposite side of the bar. He was wearing a tan

157

jacket and a 'Yankees' baseball cap. He seemed to be checking his watch like he was expecting someone.

Standing, Jake made his way through the crowd toward the man. Stopping short of the booth, Jake waited for the man to look up and make eye contact. He knew the man would be expecting him, but probably not without Jonathan.

The man glanced up at Jake. A look of confusion crossed his face, then recognition. Waiving a hand, he motioned for Jake to sit down across from him in the booth. "I appreciate you coming, Mr. Silver." He quickly cut to the chase. "I'm completely aware of Mr. Anderson's untimely death. I was hoping he had a chance to tell you of this meeting before it was too late."

Jake sipped his beer. "It's obvious you know me, but who are you?"

The man twisted the coffee mug he was holding between both hands. "I work at Area 51. My name is Tom Davis. General Tom Davis."

"And that means what to me?" Jake asked blatantly.

"It means that I am Chief of Operations at Area 51. I'm the man that makes the decisions." He gave Jake a scowl.

"Sorry. I wasn't aware. Please continue."

Davis cleared his throat. "Anderson has informed me that you were also one of our test subjects." Jake nodded. "I'm sure he also told you about the purpose of our experiments, so I'll jump to the point. I'm an old man and I'm ready to get out."

"What does that have to do with me, General?"

"Please don't call me that in public," Davis snapped. "They have ears everywhere."

"Who's 'they'?"

"The government. We need to proceed very cautiously." Davis glanced around to see if anyone was trying to eavesdrop on them. "First, I need to know if you're in."

"'In'? What do you mean?"

"In my line of work, you don't just exactly retire. I want out, and I want to take them down with me."

"Why?" Jake pulled out a cigar and lit it.

"I've become very tired of lying to the public I have sworn to protect. I want them to know the truth." He took another sip of his coffee. "I need your help to infiltrate the base and bring them down."

Jake's eyes went wide. "You want me to help you break into the base and stop the experiments? Is that what you're saying?"

"Yes."

"That's a little more than I bargained for on this case." He took a long puff off his cigar. "I'm all for bringing the bastards who did this to me to justice, but the whole operation?"

"It can be done."

Jake fidgeted in his seat. "How?"

"My plan is very simple." Davis began to explain. "You will be entered into the database at Area 51 as a newly transferred soldier. That will give you all the necessary keys and pass codes to traverse the base."

"What am I supposed to do once inside?"

"I have set up contacts for you throughout the

base, but your first priority is to find Major Griggs. He is one of many patriots to our cause. He will guide you through the base and be your acting commanding officer. Your second priority is to locate and free a researcher by the name of Doctor Alex Robinson."

"What's he got to do with this?"

"Actually, Doctor Robinson is a she." Davis smiled. "She was captured by our foreign intelligence division after she came too close to finding out the truth." "The truth about what?"

"Agree to help me, and you'll know everything."

Jake leaned back in the booth. Rolling the cigar between his fingers, he took another puff and slowly exhaled it. He stared at Davis for a long moment, trying to figure out what he wanted to do. "Okay. I'm in. When do we start?"

***

Alex's mind painfully came back to consciousness. Her eyes slowly opened, but saw nothing except blackness. Her lungs ached as she drew in a deep breath. Trying to sit up, she found she was completely naked and encased in a long glass tube. Looking toward her feet, she saw the end of the tube was constructed of metal with pipes extending into it. Glancing up, she distinguished the top was constructed of the same material with pipes also extending inside. Placing her hands on the glass, she peered out into the surrounding area. It was a sterile white room with banks of computers situated all around. Gazing across the room, she saw a man inside a similar tube suspended in a thick green fluid.

160

A long shadow crept across the tube. Staring up, Alex was confronted by a man in a white lab coat. He had strong Asian features with short dark hair and thick black-rimmed glasses. He was holding a clipboard as he checked various dials and readings on his computers. Alex began to pound on the glass to get his attention. "Let me out!"

The thick glass of the tube muffled the words. Yokama tried to understand. "What did you say?"

"Let me out!" she yelled again.

Yokama leaned closer. "I'm afraid I can't do that, Doctor Robinson."

Alex slammed her fists on the glass trying to crack it. "What are you doing to me?"

Yokama smiled and spread his arms wide open. "You are going to be involved in one of the most cutting-edge projects ever undertaken by the United States Government." He checked off another dial. "You should feel honored," he added with a tone of reverence.

"Honored? I've been taken against my will and now you're going to use me in some kind of experiment?"

"It's for your country." He marked off a final item on his checklist. "Try to be still while I inject the liquid."

"Liquid?"

Hitting a key on a nearby computer keyboard, the pipes leading into the tubes shuddered to life spewing a viscous green fluid into the tube. Alex struggled wildly as the warm liquid splashed against her skin. The tube was flooding quickly. She took a deep breath as it filled past her chest to her chin. Her body began to feel numb as the liquid engulfed it. Her eyes stung as the fluid encased her head and completely filled the tube. Her body convulsed as she finally succumbed to the pressure and exhaled the breath she had been holding. The liquid began to seep into her nose and mouth. A gagging sensation set in as she struggled against the fluid. She was barely able to turn her head in the thick fluid. She watched as Yokama hit another key at his console. A wave of electricity surged through Alex's tube. Her body tingled and twitched as the electricity permeated it. Almost instantly, the liquid began to solidify into a thick gelatinous substance suspending her body.

Yokama pressed the record button on a small black tape recorder sitting next to his computer terminal. "Subject Alex Robinson contained and ready for testing." Turning off the tape recorder, he set his clipboard down and moved across the room to the other tube. He stood staring into the tube remembering the conversation they had less than a day before. The fluid the man was immersed in was slowly healing bullet holes that riddled his torso.

"Dammit, Jonathan. Why did you have to go and get yourself shot?"

Jonathan Anderson's body hung motionlessly in the tube. They had pulled him out of the room he was shot in only moments after it had happened. After being airlifted back to the base, he was pronounced dead on arrival. It was deemed necessary to keep his body for research purposes, but Doctor Jim Yokama wasn't sure why. Yet.

CHAPTER ELEVEN

Christina found herself lying naked on the desert floor. She was curled into the fetal position with her knees up to her chest and her arms wrapped around her legs. Lifting up into a sitting position, she wiped her hand across her forehead. She felt as if a thick fog was swallowing her mind, making it difficult for her to think clearly. She struggled to comprehend what was happening to her.

Scanning the horizon, she watched the sun starting to rise creating a soupy mixture of reds, oranges and whites in the eastern sky. Standing, she felt a cool breeze blow past her naked body giving her the chills. Looking to her left, she saw a patch of sagebrush with a small jackrabbit huddled near its base. Taking a step toward it, the rabbit quickly dashed away.

The western sky was still dark with stars. For a moment, Christina lost herself in staring at it, but was immediately brought back by the sight of a familiar blue light. Her mind instantly cleared when she recognized the object. "Not again," she moaned.

The ball of blue light swooped out of the morning sky toward her. Instinct took over as she began to sprint away from it. The cool morning air was stinging her lungs as she ran. She abruptly froze as the object settled directly over her. A beam of blinding white light from the craft slammed against her chest, knocking her off her feet. She found herself unable to move. It was difficult to see, but she could make out the rough outlines of humanoid forms moving about.

Her eyes went wide and her heart began to pound with fear. She tried to scream as a hand pierced the light. A large bulbous head with large black almond-shaped eyes followed it. Her mind began to panic as the being started to run its long spindly fingers over her body. Its head bobbed back and forth like a bird's, but its body moved very fluidly.

Another being entered the light behind her. She tried to turn her head to look away, but found herself unable to even close her eyes. Her skin began to crawl as she felt the second being run its hand down to the small of her back. The first being was still examining her chest, running its fingers over her breasts. Christina was screaming at them to stop, but no sounds were coming out of her mouth. She watched in relief as the two beings slowly backed out of the light.

A strange feeling washed over her body as the light transformed from a harsh white to a softer red. She found she could now move her body, but she was slowly rising off the ground. Looking down, she saw not only the two beings standing below her, but several others. Out of anger and fear, she threw a kick that hit the nearest one in the head sending him sprawling on the desert floor. The others rushed toward him as a burst of compressed atmosphere began to spray from the top of his head. Looking up, she found herself nearing the bottom of the craft. A small round door just above her opened up just as she was about to hit it.

Christina crossed her arms in front of her face

as the red light became so intense, she could no longer see. Finally, she felt her upward momentum cease. Opening her eyes, she found herself lying in a rectangular metal box illuminated by an awful blue light. The polished silver surfaces inside acted like fun house mirrors, distorting her reflection into horribly misshapen images. It was barely large enough for her. A terrible wave of claustrophobia rippled through her body. She tried to lift her arms to bang on the top of the box, but discovered she couldn't.

She felt the box begin to shake. She knew she was being moved. Outside the box, she heard talking, but not in a language she had ever heard. It vaguely reminded her of hands being rubbed over a rubber balloon making various squeaks and pops. She listened intently trying to pick out what they were saying, but it was useless. Tears began to roll down from her eyes as a sense of hopelessness engulfed her.

Christina's head slammed against the box as it thudded to the floor. She heard what sounded like several latches being opened. Closing her eyes, she prepared for the worst. The lid of the box was flung open and several of the beings reached inside and began to pull her out. The touch of the creature's hands sent shivers down her spine. Opening her eyes, she saw several of the beings carrying her. Two had her arms, while two more had her legs. Trying to look away from them, she stared at the ceiling of the craft. The rows of lights on the ceiling reminded her of a hospital. The inside of the craft had a very sterilized feel to it with polished metal walls and ceilings. She watched as they passed through a large archway into a dimly lit room. The creatures slammed her down on a cold metal table. Chills ran through her body as they once again began to examine her. They seemed to be mainly interested in her reproductive organs. Trying to shut the terror out, she stared away from the beings toward the ceiling. Above her was a circular hole emanating a harsh white light. She could see some kind of device resting within it, but its outline was too vague to see exactly what it was. She felt something cold and hard being inserted into her vagina. Her body arched upward with discomfort.

One of the beings moved toward the right side of her head. She tried to turn away from it, but couldn't. It lifted something from a nearby table while running its left hand down her neck. It brought the instrument into her line of sight. It looked to her like a long needle. The being turned her head to the left and quickly jabbed it into her neck.

A shooting pain ran through her body as the needle pierced the muscles in her throat. A warm feeling began to wash through her head. The injected fluid coursed through her bloodstream. Her body began to feel very heavy and relaxed. The being to her right lifted a hand to her head and opened her eyelids. It watched as her eyes began to roll back. Christina slowly began to lose consciousness.

**

The morning sun was shining brightly overhead as Jake approached the Las Vegas Airport. Davis had instructed him to use a rear entrance near the parking garage that led to a private airstrip the military used. Walking up to the gate, he found himself confronted by an armed soldier who quickly stepped out of the guard shack. Lifting a flap on the bag he was carrying over his shoulder, he removed a small ID badge Davis had given him. Flashing it at the soldier, he waved Jake past. Stopping a few steps inside the airport, he turned back to the guard. "Can you tell me where I need to go? I've just transferred in."

The guard stepped toward Jake studying him. He looked suspiciously at Jake. "Yeah, you're gonna want to stay left and enter the terminal over there." He pointed at the nearest tan building. "Show the baggage clerk your ID and she'll point you to the correct flight."

"Thanks. I appreciate it." Spinning around, Jake headed off toward the terminal. It was a tall building with long observation windows built into the sides. The parking lot was filled with cars of every make and model gleaming in the bright Nevada sunlight. Passing the last row of cars, he made his way toward the terminal entrance. Two glass doors slid apart as he approached.

The terminal was eerily empty. The majority of space on the lower level was unused. The floor was tiled with green and white squares. Across the large room was a lone operational booth. Walking toward it, he made eye contact with a tall blonde woman in an Air Force uniform. Her hair was neatly done and the pair of wire-rimmed glasses she wore suited her. She smiled at Jake.

"ID please, soldier." Her voice was very gentle.

Pulling his ID badge out of his pocket, he presented it to the woman. "Here you go."

Checking it over, she slid it through a card reader next to her keyboard. Laying the badge back in front of Jake, the computer began to make several high-pitched beeping noises. Jake began to worry. It seemed like an eternity before the woman looked up from her terminal. "So," she said with a bit of amusement. "You're a new recruit, huh?"

"Yeah." Jake smiled, quickly snatching his ID and returning it to his pocket. "Okay," she examined her computer screen, "it says here you're fresh out of Austin, Texas."

Jake paused. He hadn't known what kind of background story Davis had created for him. "That's right."

"I've never been there. Is it nice?" She was trying to make small talk while she processed him through the system.

"About the same as here. Hot and dry." Jake had never been there either. Hitting several keys on her computer, the printer next to it whirred to life. "Your travel plans will be up in a second." Reaching over, she ripped the sheet off the printer and handed it to Jake. "You have about an hour before your plane departs. Make yourself comfortable."

Jake grabbed the sheet. "Thanks." He scanned the terminal. "What should I do for an hour?"

"Well, there's coffee in the lounge."

"Sounds good." Jake turned around and began to walk away. Stopping in his tracks, he spun back around to face the woman, "Where's the lounge?" She pointed to a door behind her. "Thanks," Jake laughed as he walked through the door.

The lobby was a small room with several chairs

168

scattered about and two long couches on either side. A long aluminum coffee table with a coffee pot and a stack of paper cups on it was in the center. The lobby was empty except for Jake. Walking over to the coffee maker, he lifted a paper cup and poured himself some coffee. Seating himself on one of the couches, he took a sip and began to relax. Glancing down at his watch, he saw that it was now eight thirty in the morning.

Jake looked up to see the tall blonde baggage clerk walk into the room. He watched as she moved over to the couch opposite his, and slowly sat down, crossing her slender legs. "So how'd you get posted to 'Dreamland'?"

"Just lucky I guess." He took another sip of his coffee. "Have you ever been there?"

She sighed. "Unfortunately, yes." "Why is that unfortunate?"

She adjusted her blue skirt. "Strange things happen there." Jake feigned ignorance. "Really? Like what?"

She leaned forward and began to speak in a hushed tone. "I've heard about the testing that goes on there. They steal people right out of their homes at night and experiment on them." She leaned back. "I was the general's assistant when I first arrived here. But after the things I saw, I wanted out. So, when this job opening came up, even though it was a step down for me, I took it."

"It was that bad there?"

She looked him straight in the eye. "Yes." Clearing her throat, she readjusted herself on the couch. "So, what are you, some kind of war hero?"

"No. Why?"

"The powers that be at Area 51 only recruit the 'best of the best'. They want this operation to remain Top Secret so they recruit only the most loyal soldiers."

"How can they be so sure?"

"This base has been operating secretly for over fifty years. They must be doing something right."

"Yeah, I guess you're right." He glanced around at the bare white walls of the room. "Where is everyone else?"

"Most of the other workers and soldiers take an earlier flight or the bus." "The bus?"

"Yeah. It runs in and out of the base four times a day." "Why do they run a bus when they have flights?" "Some people don't like to fly, that's all."

Jake nodded. "Have to be an equal opportunity employer, right?" She laughed out loud. "Equal opportunity employer. That's a joke." "Why?"

"You didn't hear about the law suit filed last year against the base?" "No. What happened?"

The woman stood up, walked over and poured herself another cup of coffee. "Last year, a widow filed a lawsuit on behalf of her late husband. Up until his death, he was an employee of the base. She claimed the base was illegally disposing of chemicals on-site. She also alleged they were burning most of the chemicals, releasing harmful toxins into the air and poisoning a lot of workers. Some of those chemicals were blamed for eventually killing several other employees."

"What happened to the lawsuit?"

"It was thrown out. The President signed into law a motion that allowed Area 51 to do whatever it wanted under the auspice of national defense."

Jake sipped his coffee. "So the President actually acknowledged that the base exists."

"Yeah, but then the base quickly faded back into myth."

Jake smiled. "That's the way the government wants to keep it, right?"

"That's right." Standing up, she placed her cup of coffee on the table. "I've got to get back to work. You've still got a while before your plane leaves. Why don't you try and relax?" Jake took another sip of his coffee as she walked toward the door. Stopping just inside the door, she turned around and smiled. "By the way, Jake, I'm also a patriot to the cause." She winked at him and walked out the door.

***

Christina awoke back inside the box. Her head felt very groggy, and it took a lot of effort to even wiggle her toes. She was no longer naked, now wrapped in what looked like a black body suit. It felt very restrictive when she tried to breathe. Her body ached as it moved.

She heard the familiar sounds of the latches opening on the box. Feeling too exhausted, she didn't even try to fight what was about to happen. The top of the box slowly opened, but this time, a human face peered in. A wave of relief flowed over her.

The man was of Asian heritage with thick black-rimmed glasses and short dark hair. She recognized the face, but couldn't place it. He was speaking to her, but she didn't comprehend what he was saying. He stood, turned his head and pointed down at Christina. Two large men dressed in gray jump suits moved over to her and carefully lifted

171

her out of the box. Her body went limp in their arms. The room she was in was busy in comparison to the craft. It was filled with men in white lab coats working on computers and checking long tubes filled with a thick green substance. She turned her head to the right and saw a woman suspended in one of the tubes. She realized then she had not been rescued. Panic ensued as her mind shifted into high gear trying to find a way to escape. She tried to struggle, but couldn't. The two men rested her on a nearby table and began to undress her. Unzipping the black body suit, they quickly pulled it off her. Staring off to the right, Christina saw an empty tube being checked by the same man that had opened her box. She knew it was intended for her.

One of the men lifted her up and slung her over his shoulder like a sack of bricks. She was still too weak to move, and she had gone past the point of caring what happened next. He slipped her into the glass tube on her back. Her head fell loosely to the left. She watched carefully as several men in lab coats examined another tube with a man inside. The man seemed familiar somehow...

Yokama moved over in front of Christina's tube. His mouth was moving, but all she could hear were muffled sounds. Tapping a button on the top of her enclosure, the glass lid slowly slid shut locking her inside. She didn't even try to struggle. Letting her head fall to the left again, she stared at the man in the next tube. One of the men had opened the tube and was reaching into the green fluid. She watched as they turned the man's head to the right to examine his neck.

Christina began to sob as the green liquid

flowed into the tube. Turning over to her right, she placed her hands on the tube and tried to shout, but all that came out was a whisper. "Daddy." Christina stared at the lifeless body of her father in the next tube. The green fluid in her own was already up past her head. She mustered all her strength to ball up her fists and pound on the glass. She mouthed the words 'I love you, Daddy'. She looked up in time to see Yokama hit another button on his console. A shock of electricity shot through her tube solidifying the fluid inside. Still conscious, but immobilized, she stared with wide eyes at her father's tube. She desperately wanted to close her eyes, but couldn't.

***

Davis made his way back into his office. Several messages lay strewn about on his desk. Picking them up, he quickly looked over them and placed them in his pocket. Sitting down in his chair, he heard a knock at his door. "Come."

General Perry opened the door and strode in. Davis immediately jumped up and stood at attention. Perry nodded for Davis to sit back down. Seating himself across from Davis, he pulled off his hat and laid it on the desk. "I want to know where you were last night."

Davis was taken aback. "Pardon?"

"You left the base last night." His tone was firm. "I want to know where you went." Davis' heart began to pound as he struggled to find an excuse. "I needed a night off, and I was sure the base was in your capable hands, General." He spat the words at Perry.

"Bullshit." Perry stood up. "I don't care what you think of me, but you have a base to run. I don't think you should be off in Vegas fucking around."

"I agree."

"Then why did you do it?"

Perry stood up and placed both of his hands flat on his desk. "I don't care if I'm guarding a crashed UFO or a God damned merry-go-round, sometimes my men and I need a little rest."

"Then why wasn't I informed?"

"Last time I checked, I was still the CO of this facility." "I am your superior officer!"

"By one star."

"It wouldn't matter if you were a private, you still have to report to your senior officer!"

Davis knew he had picked a fight he couldn't win. "I apologize, sir." "That's not good enough for me, or the President."

Davis' eyes went wide. "I'm not sure I understand."

Perry returned to his seat and motioned for Davis to sit as well. "This morning, I posted my report on this facility to the President. Understandably, he was very disappointed."

"In what?"

"The way you run this ship. This is the most Top Secret base in the United States and it needs a commander that understands this. So as of eight hundred hours, I was appointed Temporary Commanding Officer of Area 51." Davis felt his stomach twist. "When I leave in a week, Colonel Hunter will be promoted to general and will take over from me." Pulling a folded packet of papers out of his pocket, he laid it on the desk in front of Davis. "These are your walking papers, Tom."

"How can you do this to me?" Davis slumped

174

down in his seat. "I've been a damn fine officer for a long time and now you do this?"

"I'm sorry, Tom. I really am, but this is for the good of the nation."

"The hell it is." Davis chewed over what had just happened. "What are you planning to do with me?"

"We can't just put you back in the population because of what you know, so we've decided to transfer you."

"To where?"

"Better pack your parka, because you're off to Alaska." "What?"

"You'll like it there. I hear the wilderness is beautiful and the fishing is incredible." Davis was too shocked to speak. "This transfer is effective immediately." Perry stood and tucked his hat under his right arm. "Nothing personal, Tom." Opening the door, he stepped outside and slammed it behind him.

"The hell it's not." Davis knew the timetable for his plan had to be moved up substantially. *This won't give Jake long to finish his tasks.*

***

Jake stepped aboard the plane. The 737 had been modified for the line of work it was in. There were no windows in the passenger compartment and several rows of seats had been removed in the middle to accommodate a table and two couches. From the computer banks built into the walls, it looked as if this plane could operate as a mobile base if necessary. Loading his bag into the overhead compartment, he took a seat near the back of the plane.

175

A female stewardess emerged from the cockpit. She scanned the passenger compartment until she spotted Jake. Walking up to him, she leaned over. "Are you the only passenger on this flight?"

Jake nodded. "As far as I can tell." Jake quickly noted that she looked very good in her blue uniform.

She stood up. "I hate the nine o'clock flight. It's such a waste of time." "Why?"

"Because there's never anyone on it."

Jake smiled. "I could've sworn I was someone."

She gave him a mystified look. "You know what I mean." Sitting in the seat next to him, she leaned back. "All right, I'll give you the usual drill." She took a deep breath, "The plane will be taking off in about five minutes and we'll arrive at the base in about forty-five. Soldiers usually take this time to get into their uniform or take a nap."

"If you don't mind me saying so, you sound very cynical."

"I know." She shook her head. "It's this job. I got into the Air Force because I wanted to fly, not be a stewardess. I could've done this without going to boot camp." "I'm sorry."

She smiled at him. "That's okay, I'll live." She stood. "Get buckled in, we're about to take off." She returned to the front of the plane.

Jake grabbed the two sides of the seat belt and snapped it around his waist. He then realized there was one major flaw to Davis' plan. He was to impersonate an Air Force officer, when he hated to fly. Closing his eyes, he gripped the armrests as the plane began to shudder to life. He had been on

176

many flights in his life, mostly when he was in the FBI, but the part he hated most was the take-off. He felt the plane taxiing around the tarmac until it was stopped again on the runway. Gritting his teeth, he felt the plane begin to accelerate as it cruised down the runway. His stomach lurched as the pilot eased it into the air. Leaning back in his seat, he felt the aircraft climb at a forty-five degree angle. Slowly, it began to level off. Keeping his gaze forward for what seemed like an eternity, he watched the seat belt sign turn off.

Removing his seat belt, he stood up and stretched. The stewardess emerged again. "Are you all right?"

"Yeah, why?"

"Your face is very pale."

He smiled. "I'm just not very good at flying."

"You joined the Air Force and you don't like to fly?"

"I've seen stranger things. A buddy of mine joined the Navy right out of high school and he couldn't swim. Didn't even really like the water."

She laughed. "Sounds like he made a bad career choice."

"That's what we kept telling him." Jake glanced around. "Where are the bathrooms?" She pointed with her thumb behind her. "Thanks." Grabbing his bag, he scooted past her and made his way to it. Stepping inside the cramped room, he laid the bag on the sink and unzipped it. Inside were several Air Force uniforms Davis had provided him. Lifting out the one on top, he began to pull it on. The jacket was a little tight in the shoulders, but he could live with it.

Buttoning the last button, he stared at himself in the mirror. Jake flashed back to an image of his father putting on his green Marine uniform in their bathroom. He was seven years old. His father was a tall, well-built man with dark hair. His deep blue eyes burned with intensity and a sense of purpose. He stood in the doorway watching his father straightening his necktie. "Dad? Why do you have to go?"

Turning around, his father knelt down and placed his hands on Jake's shoulders. "My country needs me, Jacob."

Jake began to sob. "But it's my birthday! Can't you stay?"

"I'm sorry, little man, but I've got to go." As far back as he could remember, his father had always called him 'little man'. His mother had told him it was because he was so much like his father. "When you're older, you'll understand." Standing, he grabbed his hat and his duffel bag and left the bathroom. He watched as his father gave his mother a kiss. Turning back to Jake, he smiled. "Save a piece of cake for me, okay?" Jake nodded. "I love you, son, and I'll be home very soon."

"I love you too, Dad." His father waved good-bye and was gone.

He ran to his mother and wrapped his arms around her. She rubbed his back and held him tightly. His mother had always seemed to be the most beautiful woman he had ever seen. She always knew how to comfort him in a way only a mother could. Her dark wavy hair hung to the top of her blue blouse. She had large brown eyes always filled with love and warmth. "He'll be back soon, Jake.

Let's go open those presents." Jake wiped a tear away and nodded. He had no idea it would be the last time he would ever see his father.

The letter came three weeks later. He remembered it vividly. His mother was cooking dinner and he was watching a western on TV. There was a knock at the door. Wiping her hands on her apron, she walked to the front door and answered it. "Yes?"

Two men dressed in Marine uniforms stepped inside and removed their hats. "Mrs. Silver?"

"Yes, I'm Rachel Silver."

The two men glanced at each other. "I'm afraid we have bad news." Jake watched as his mother began to cry as the two men handed her a folded American flag. "We're saddened to inform you that your husband, Captain Jacob Silver, has been shot down over Vietnam during combat." Jake's mother dropped to her knees, crying uncontrollably. The man pulled a square black box out of his pocket and opened it. "He was awarded the Congressional Medal of Honor." He handed the box to Jake's mother.

"Why?"

The two men replaced their hats and turned to leave. As they took a step out the door, the man at the rear paused. "We're very sorry for your loss, ma'am, and if it's any consolation, he died bravely." He closed the door behind him.

Rachel lay on the floor in a heap with her head buried in the folded flag. Jake rushed over to her and sat down beside her. "What does that mean, Mom? Is Daddy coming home?"

The words seem to cut her to the bone. She sat

up and pulled Jake into her arms. "No, sweetie, Daddy's not coming home." The two sat wrapped in each other's arms for what seemed like an eternity sobbing uncontrollably. From that day on, Jake hated the military for taking his father away from him.

Adjusting his tie, Jake leaned over and splashed some cold water on his face. Shaking the thoughts from his mind, he unlocked the bathroom door and stepped out. After putting his bag back in the overhead compartment, he sat down. Closing his eyes, he tried to catch a quick nap before arriving at the base.

CHAPTER TWELVE

The plane finally rolled to a halt, much to Jake's relief. The stewardess walked up to Jake's seat and informed him that he could now exit the plane. Standing, he grabbed his bag out of the overhead compartment and slung it over his shoulder. Putting on his hat, he walked down the center aisle of the plane toward the door. One of the pilots was already standing there opening it. He looked up and smiled at Jake. "Welcome to Are a 51, soldier." He opened the thick door.

Stepping onto the stairs, Jake was assaulted by the scorching heat of the Nevada desert. At the bottom of the stairs stood several men dressed in black fatigues. Reaching the bottom, Jake snapped to attention and saluted. "Lieutenant Jacob Silver reporting for duty, sir." Davis had given him a crash course in military etiquette and chain of command. Scanning the symbols on the man's collar he knew he was a major.

The major saluted and stepped forward, extending his hand. Jake grabbed it and shook it. "Glad to have you here, Lieutenant. I'm Major Jason Griggs, I'll be your CO." Letting go of Jake's hand, he turned and pointed to his men. "This is Lieutenant Steve Harris, my second-in-command."

Jake stepped around and shook his hand. Harris was a tall man, though not as broad as Jake. His cleanly shaven face and red hair shone in the sunlight. "Pleasure to meet you, sir." Jake knew, even though they were the same rank, Harris was

181

still his superior officer.

Griggs pointed past Harris to the next man in line. "This is Private First Class Jack Lansinger." Lansinger saluted Jake. Jake returned the salute, then shook his hand. Lansinger was a tall, wiry man. He had shortly cropped blonde hair and a dark goatee. "Next in line is PFC Dan Altone." Altone saluted. He was larger than Lansinger, but not by much. He was well built with dark skin, dark curly hair and steely blue eyes. "And finally, PFC Wendy Black." Black saluted, then shook Jake's hand. She was a thin woman with wire-framed glasses and short blonde hair. "Now that you know the team, Lieutenant Silver, let's get to work. First things first, we've gotta get you out of that uniform."

"Why is that, sir?"

"Because the top brass doesn't really like anyone on the base walking around in their dress blues. We have Russian birds fly over this place at least once every few hours that can easily spot a man in uniform."

Jake knew he was talking about spy satellites. "Yes, sir."

The group of men started to walk off the tarmac toward the main hangar. Lansinger jumped out in front and opened the door. Griggs nodded and walked inside. Jake was the last one through. Taking a step inside the hangar, Jake found himself in awe of the sheer size of it. It looked to him to be carved straight out of the mountain itself.

Griggs stepped back and grabbed Jake by the arm. "Come on, soldier. We'll get to the tour later."

"Yes, sir. Sorry, sir." Jake snapped back into line. Following the men through the giant hangar, they stopped at a door at the far left. Griggs pulled out his ID card and slid it through the control box next to the door. Jake watched carefully as he did so, trying to memorize the process. After his card was through, a green light flashed on and the door slid swiftly open. The group moved went through the door into a long hallway. Moving past several doors, they stopped in front of an elevator.

Griggs spun around. "Harris, stay put, Silver and I need to check in with General Davis." Pressing the button next to the elevator, the door slid open. Jake and Griggs stepped inside just as the doors slid shut behind them. Griggs reached over and hit the bottom button on the panel. Turning to Jake, he whispered. "I'm a patriot."

Jake nodded. "Davis told me you would be, but not why."

"Let me simply say this. I am a sworn protector of the United States of America. What they're doing here at Area 51 makes me sick. They say they do it under the rubric of National Security, defending our citizens from an alien invasion, but we're abducting those very same citizens out of their homes and conducting ghoulish experiments on them."

"I understand."

"I am a patriot, Mr. Silver. In every sense of the word." "Then it's a pleasure to be working with you, Major Griggs."

The elevator came to a halt. The door slid open revealing a room bustling with activity. Griggs snapped back into military mode. "Lieutenant Silver, welcome to the brain center of Area 51." The two stepped inside the room. "We are now deep within the mountain. This operation center could survive a direct nuclear assault and continue to function." They waded their way through the sea of people, heading toward the center console. Griggs stopped short when he saw Perry sitting in the chair. Stepping forward, he saluted. Jake followed suit. "General Perry, what an unexpected surprise."

Perry returned the salute. "What can I do for you, gentleman?"

Griggs stood at attention. "We were looking for General Davis, sir. I wanted to introduce our latest recruit."

"I'm sorry you haven't been informed, Major. General Davis has been relieved of duty. He has been transferred to another base."

Jake and Griggs were shocked to hear what Perry was saying. "Sir?"

Perry slowly stood and adjusted his uniform. "All you need to know, soldier, is that I'm in command now."

"Yes, sir."

Perry waited for a moment. "Well? Aren't you going to introduce me to our new recruit?"

"Yes, sir. This is Lieutenant Jacob Silver. He's just in from the Gulf." Jake saluted.

"Welcome to the base, Lieutenant. Did you see action in the Gulf War?" Perry extended his hand to Jake.

"Some, sir." He grabbed Perry's hand, giving it a firm shake.

Griggs stepped in. "He was a fighter pilot stationed aboard the aircraft carrier *Enterprise* during the first engagement."

"Very good. You'll be a welcome addition to the base." "Yes, sir. Thank you, sir."

Perry returned to his chair. "You have your orders, Lieutenant?" "Yes, sir."

"Then that's all. Dismissed."

Jake and Griggs saluted, then made their way out. The elevator doors slid open as Griggs punched the button. Stepping inside the elevator, they watched silently as the doors closed. Griggs quickly turned to Jake. "This is a serious setback to our plans." Jake nodded. "They must've found out that Davis talked to me."

"Then there's a good bet he knows about you, too."

"I'll take that bet." Jake snapped his fingers. "We need to talk to Davis. Do you think he's still on base?"

"I'm not sure. Let's find out."

***

Davis was sitting in his office with a stack of boxes next to his desk. He was holding a picture frame. He carefully ran his fingers around the woman's image, caressing her face and running his hands down her long brown hair. Long forgotten remnants of loss slowly welled up in him as he stared at the photo. A loud knock at his door quickly brought him back to the present. Placing the picture face down on his desk, he cleared his throat. "Come."

Colonel Hunter stepped in. "General?" "Yes, Colonel?" What can I do for you?"

Hunter seated himself across from Davis. "Sir, I've just come to say it's been a pleasure serving under you."

Davis stood and leaned toward Hunter. "You son of a bitch. Why did you do it?" "Sir?"

185

"Don't 'sir' me, Colonel. I know you gave General Perry the information to send out the squad after Jonathan Anderson. You also alerted him to the fact I went off base last night." Davis walked around his desk to stand right in front of Hunter. "You greedy little bastard."

"I'm afraid I don't know what you're talking about, General." Hunter was smug.

"I may not be your CO anymore, but I am still your superior officer, and I will see you brought down for this."

"For what, sir?"

Davis stayed calm. "Mutiny." He spat the words at Hunter. "Now get out of my office."

Hunter stood and began to walk toward the door. "Don't you mean *my* office, sir?" He smiled as he walked out the door.

Davis sat back down. Leaning forward, he lifted the picture off his desk. Anger welled up in him. Rearing back, he threw the picture at the wall as hard as he could. The frame shattered on impact falling to the floor in pieces.

***

The two men stepped inside the soldiers' quarters. The room was a dull shade of tan with bunk beds placed along one wall and lockers along the other. Jake and Griggs walked to a nearby locker and cracked it open. Black fatigues hung inside. Griggs pulled out the black jump suit and handed it to Jake. "Put it on."

Jake began to unbutton his coat and pull it off. "We need to speak with Davis. He's the key."

"I know." He pulled a pair of boots out of the locker. "If he's on his way out, our timetable

186

must've been moved up."

Jake nodded as he pulled off his pants and boots. Quickly pulling on the jumpsuit, he grabbed the boots and slipped them on. "What do we need to do first?"

"I think it's best if we speak with Davis," he thought for a moment. "Then we need to carry out the rest of our mission."

Jake slipped on his vest and belt. Griggs reached over and began straightening his pins and insignias. Jake reached up to the top of the locker and pulled out a pistol and holstered it. "Agreed. We have to see Davis first."

***

"Sir," Hunter spun around in his chair to look at General Perry. "Alpha team has reported that the second crash site has been scouted."

Perry leaned forward in his chair. "What were their findings, Colonel?"

"They report the object must be some sort of extra-terrestrial craft. It's remarkably different from those we have in the hangar."

"Any signs of life?" "Minimal, sir."

Perry leaned back in his chair and thought about his options. "We need a team inside the craft. Suggestions on personnel, Colonel?"

"Sir, Major Griggs' team is one of the best Recon teams we have."

"Very well. Assign Major Griggs to the job. I want this done immediately, Colonel.

I want them in that craft by dawn."

"Yes, sir." Hunter turned back to his console.

***

Jake followed Griggs down the long hallway

187

toward Davis' office. The boots Jake had been assigned were a size too big, making it harder for him to keep up with Griggs' brisk pace. He glanced around as he clunked along. Jake was astounded at the halls and rooms that seemed to be carved out of solid rock. Rounding a final corner, Jake saw a door with Davis' name on it. Stopping in front of it, Griggs rapped loudly on the door. From inside, they heard Davis' voice telling them to enter.

Griggs opened the door and stepped inside, followed by Jake. "Sir, Lieutenant Silver has arrived at the base."

Davis was stooped in the corner picking up shards of glass. He quickly stood and shook Jake's hand. "Good to see that you made it, Jake."

"Thanks, General." Jake cut to the point. "Is what we heard from General Perry correct? You've been relieved of duty?"

Davis leaned back against his desk. "Yes it is. I'm on my way out. It seems they're shipping me off to Alaska immediately."

Griggs stepped forward. "How can they do this, sir?" "They're on to me. That means you two may be next."

Jake was still straightening his uniform. "How did they find out?"

"You're forgetting where we are, Jake. Here, the walls have ears." He stood and walked around his desk, then seated himself in his chair. "Gentlemen, Colonel Hunter is a traitor. He has aligned himself with General Perry. I was counting on him being on our side. Then we would have control of all the major systems of the base, but now, you two will have to be extra careful."

"But we are still planning to go through with the mission?" Griggs had seated himself across from Davis.

"We are, Major." Davis folded his hands on his desk. "Your first priority is still to locate and free Doctor Alex Robinson. She is the key to unlocking most of this base's secrets."

"Why is that, sir?"

"Alex is a renowned UFOlogist that has studied phenomenon worldwide. She was detained recently on a dig in Egypt, where she discovered an ancient extra-terrestrial artifact."

"I'm not sure I understand, General." Jake had also sat down across from Davis. "You will when you get her." Davis reached inside his pocket and pulled out his ID card. "Here, take this. It will give you access to everything on the base, except the secondary hangar."

Griggs took the card. "Why not the secondary hangar, sir?"

"It requires the ID card and a handprint. I didn't have enough time to set it up for either of you."

"Understood."

Davis took a long breath before continuing. "I'll be leaving the base soon, so you two will be on your own." He stood up and saluted. "Good luck and God speed, gentlemen."

CHAPTER THIRTEEN

The five members of Major Griggs' team sat quietly in the belly of the helicopter. The word had come down from Colonel Hunter about an hour before sunset they had been assigned to the detail. Jake and Griggs knew Hunter was aware of their mission and was doing everything in his power to stop them. The major was keeping an outwardly strong appearance for the benefit of his men.

The men were bathed in a dark red light. The constant thrum of the rotors drowned out most of the sounds, making it extremely difficult for the men to talk. Jake and Griggs sat opposite Lansinger, Altone and Black in the rear of the helicopter. Lieutenant Harris had opted to sit next to the pilot in the cockpit.

The red light began to flash, telling the men they were near the target area. Hunter reached around and tapped Griggs on the shoulder. Twisting around, Griggs watched as Hunter slammed his fist into his open palm. Griggs nodded and turned back to his team. Twirling his finger in the air, his team moved into action. Altone reached up and flipped a switch killing the red flashing light. Lansinger removed several harnesses from a bag he had next to his seat and began handing them out. Black began to uncoil several repelling cords she had in front of her and locking them onto a long steel bar that crossed above the door on the left side of the chopper.

Griggs grabbed Jake and pulled him close. "Do

everything I do! Never hesitate!" Griggs was practically screaming in his ear. Nodding emphatically, Jake glued his eyes on Griggs.

Altone was the first one in his harness. Reaching over, he started to help Black pull hers on. Jake watched intently. Quickly, he began to pull his on in a similar fashion. Lansinger snapped the last buckle into place and moved toward the helicopter door. Threading the rope through the harness, he pulled a pair of leather gloves out of his back pocket and slipped them on. Altone was next, followed by Black and Griggs. Jake was the last one on the line. He carefully threaded the rope through the harness and pulled on his leather gloves.

The team members slowly leaned out the helicopter. Thrusting their free hands forward, they laid them on top of each other.

"Recon!" They all shouted with one voice. All at once, they pushed away from the helicopter and quickly lowered themselves to the crash site.

Jake's hand slipped off the guide rope. He swiftly began to free-fall toward the ground. Trying to stop himself, he inadvertently began to twist around until he was facing the desert floor. The ground was shooting up at him.

Thinking quickly, Altone shot a hand out and grabbed Jake's guide rope slowing his fall. Griggs quickly dropped down to where Jake was hanging and righted him in the harness. Grabbing his guide rope, Jake slowly lowered himself to the ground.

Griggs and Altone hit the ground immediately after him. Altone stepped up to Jake. "What the hell were you doing?"

Griggs stepped in front of Altone. "At ease,

191

Private. It was an accident." Jake took a step back from the two and wiped the sweat off his face. He addressed Griggs. "Sorry, sir. Won't happen again."

Griggs nodded. Turning to his men, he shouted, "Pull off those harnesses and form up. We have a job to do. Move it!"

Jake pulled Griggs aside. "Sir, why are Lieutenant Harris and the helicopter leaving?"

"We're on our own, Lieutenant."

"What if we need to evac in a hurry, sir?" Jake was trying to sound as professional as he could in front of the team.

"Then we'll have to call in support."

Griggs stepped away from Jake. The team was standing on a small rise above the crash site. Scanning over it, Griggs found himself in awe. The craft was partially buried in rubble and debris. The scar from the crash stretched for miles along the desert floor Jake stepped up behind Griggs. Instantly, his mouth dropped open at the sight of the craft. The silver metal skin glistened in the moonlight. In the darkness, Jake found it hard to estimate its exact size, but he could tell it was immense. It was the shape of a saucer with what looked like a dome in the center.

Griggs spun around and held up two fingers. "I want two teams. Altone and Lansinger, you're Team One. Black, you come with me and Silver. Team One," he pointed at them, "I want you to stand guard outside. Team two is heading inside. I want full safeties on. The possibility exists that we could encounter a live E.B.E. and my orders are to take them alive." The teams nodded. Griggs looked over his team for a moment. "All right, let's do this!"

The two teams split up and hurried toward their individual tasks. Lansinger and Altone took up flanking positions next to the craft. Team Two began to search for an entrance. Jake stood in front of the craft staring up at it. The sheer size of it intimidated him. "Jesus, this thing is huge."

Black agreed as she walked along the side of the ship. "Sir?" Griggs peeked his head around the corner. "What is it, Private?"

"There are no seams. It looks like it's one fluid piece of metal." She was running her hand along the side of the ship.

"Noted, Private."

Jake walked past Black toward the partially buried front of the ship. "Private, come take a look at this."

Black jogged up to the front of the ship. "Sir?"

Jake pointed to what looked like a rupture in the ship's skin. "Seems like when this thing hit, it buckled. We'll have to dig it out, but I think we can get in that way."

Black leaned in closer to the opening. "I think you're right, sir. I'll start digging." She dropped to her knees and started clawing at the dirt. Pulling his knife from his belt, Jake dropped down next to her and began to help.

***

Colonel Hunter sat at his desk in his office. It was a small room, only large enough to fit his desk, a chair, and one potted fern in the corner. His walls were plastered with awards and decorations he had received throughout his distinguished military career. Sitting in front of him on his gray steel metal

193

desk was a small black laptop computer. Reaching down, he flipped the latch on the front and lifted the top. Pressing several keys, the laptop whirred to life. His fingers flew over the keys with accuracy. A window opened up in the center of the screen. Lifting a headset off the desk, he slipped it over his head and hit a final key.

The screen fluttered to life with an image of the crash site. "Hunter here. Go ahead."

A voice crackled to life over his speaker. "I'm at the site, sir. Are you receiving my video feed?"

"I've got you clearly. Report."

"Sir, Major Griggs has split us up into two teams. Team one has been posted on guard, and Team Two is going inside."

Hunter tapped several keys to widen the angle of the camera. "What is the condition of the craft?"

The voice paused for a second. "From my vantage point, it seems to be in very good condition. The outer hull looks to be in one piece except for a small area at the front where it appears to have buckled upon impact."

Hunter smiled. "Any signs of life?"

"Not as yet, sir. Team Two is about to enter and then we'll know for sure." "Very good." Hunter adjusted his mic. "You are still aware of the plan?" "Yes, sir. I am to eliminate Major Griggs and the impostor, Silver."

"I never want to see the bodies again. Do you have a plan?"

"Yes, sir. There's a lot of soft soil around here, it will be very easy to bury the bodies."

"And if the others interfere?" "Then they will be eliminated, sir."

194

"Impressive. Don't forget, you are my lone man on the inside. Don't fail me or you will suffer the same fate as your targets."

"I won't, sir. You can count on me."

"I sincerely hope so, Private. Hunter out." He tapped several keys on his computer killing his mic. Leaning back in his chair, he studied the shot of the craft. He watched as Jake slowly passed through the frame. He reached over and tapped a button pausing the video feed. Anger burned in him as he stared at Jake. "No one makes a fool out of Colonel Rick Hunter."

"Major Griggs!"

***

Griggs ran around the side of the craft toward Jake and PFC Black. "What is it, Private?"

Black stood out of the pile of dirt she had accumulated at her feet. "Sir," she pointed at the hole in the side of the craft triumphantly, "we're in."

"Good work, Private. Inform Lansinger and Altone of our progress and let's get inside." He watched as Black took several steps away from the craft and keyed her mic. Stepping up to Jake, he patted him on the back. "You're looking a little pale, Silver."

Jake cleared his throat. "I'm fine, sir. I've just never done anything like this before."

Griggs consoled him. "None of us have, Lieutenant. None of us have."

Black returned to the group. "Major, Altone and Lansinger report ready. There's something strange, though."

"What is it, Private?"

"My signal is very poor. I could barely get a signal to the others, and I was having a lot of problems with disruption."

Jake fielded the question. "Could be that the ship is somehow interfering with communications."

Griggs turned to look at the craft looming over them. "Could be, Lieutenant. We have to remember what we're dealing with. We could encounter anything inside this craft." Griggs kicked at the dirt. He was nervous, but he didn't want anyone to know. "Private, why don't you go set up an antenna on that ridge? It should boost our signal."

"I'm on it."

Jake leaned in close to Griggs. "Do you have any idea what's inside?"

Griggs shook his head. "A day ago, Hunter had a Recon team here investigating, but they were pulled out early and we were assigned."

"Hunter knows something he's not telling." Griggs nodded in agreement. "But what?"

They turned and watched as Black ran down from the ridge. "We're ready, sir. The signal is already better."

"Well, let's get inside." The three figures stood in front of the hole in the craft. Black pulled her weapon off her shoulder and cocked it as she stepped toward the hole. She was followed inside by Jake with his pistol drawn, then Griggs.

The inside of the craft was dimly lit, except for random shafts of light which shot out the walls at random angles. The hallways were huge. They were tall and wide. Probably built for a large being, Jake assumed. The wall seemed to be made of some kind of organic material. Running her hand across them,

Black found they were oozing with some kind of slime.

Wiping her hand off on her trousers, she retrieved a small black flashlight from her vest. Flicking it on, she was startled. "What the hell is that?"

Griggs turned his attention from the walls to the thing up ahead in the hallway. Jake let out an audible gasp as he caught sight of it. The three slowly moved toward it with weapons raised. It wasn't moving, whatever it was. Griggs knelt down next to it. Reaching up, he grabbed the flashlight from Black and began to inspect it.

"It's an alien, boys and girls."

The small being lay sprawled out on the floor with its head turned away from them. Shining the light across its chest, Griggs saw it had massive damage to the left side of its body. Reaching over, he touched the head and gently rolled it over to face the three. Gasping, they all jumped back away from the dead creature. Its head was massive compared to the rest of its thin body. The huge black lidless eyes stared at them from the soulless corpse. It had a large laceration through its skull, allowing part of its brain to spill out onto the floor. A blue substance they all assumed was blood caked the wounds and the floor around it.

"What happened here, Major? Why did this ship crash?" Jake couldn't take his eyes off the dead being in front of him.

"It was attacked by one of ours. The patrol helicopter thought it was a civilian craft and tried to warn it out of our airspace, but when it didn't deviate from its course, they shot it down taking themselves out at the same time."

Jake was horrified. "We did this?"

"I'm afraid so." Griggs shined the light up ahead in the hallway. "Let's get moving. We've got a lot of ship left to explore." Griggs handed the flashlight back to Back and pulled out one of his own. Jake followed suit pulling out his own and clicking it on. "Let's split up, we can cover more ground that way. Remember to keep in constant contact with each other. I don't want anything happening to one of my people in here. Black, you keep heading down the hall, Silver, you go in the opposite direction, and I'll see what's behind this hole in the wall." Everyone nodded, then turned to go his or her separate ways.

"Dan! Get over here, man!"

***

PFC Dan Altone stood on the rise near the small antenna Black had set up. Turning his head, he saw PFC Jack Lansinger waving at him from near the base of the craft. He began to slowly jog down the hill toward Altone. "What's up, Jack?"

Lansinger lifted a small piece of metal up out of the dirt. "I was just walking past here and I spotted this." Turning it, he noticed something seemed to be written on one of side of it. "This is alien writing! Damn cool." He handed it to Altone and stood next to him.

Flipping it over in his hands, Altone stared at it as it glimmered in the moonlight. It was shaped like a triangle and was about two inches in diameter. "You better hang on to this. It could be very valuable." He began to hand it back to Lansinger, when he dropped it in front of him. "Sorry, man."

198

Lansinger shrugged. "It happens." He began to reach down to get it, when he heard Altone cock his gun. Feeling the cold barrel of the gun in the back of his head, he raised his hands to show he had no weapons. "What the hell are you doing?"

Altone pulled the trigger sending Lansinger to the ground in a heap. "Just following orders, man." Returning the gun to its holster, he made his way back up to the antenna. Lifting his booted foot, he crushed it with one swift blow. Turning his attention back to the craft, he began to make his way down the hill.

***

Jake was legitimately scared as he made his way down the corridor. He was holding his pistol in his right hand while he had the flashlight in his left. The speaker in his ear crackled to life with Griggs' voice. "Report."

Jake listened as Black reported in. He keyed his mic. "Silver here."

The walls seemed to have patches of very thin areas scattered through them. The thin areas were emitting a strange orange glow. Walking up to one of the patches, he ran his hand across it. It was pliable to the touch, but unbreakable, no matter how hard he pushed. Leaning close, he tried to see through the semitranslucent surface. He jumped back as he saw a figure cross behind the patch. Jake's heart was racing. He hit his mic. "Major, there's something alive in here besides us."

"What was it?"

Jake tried to catch his breath. "I'm not sure, but it looked like one of those things!" "Stay on it, Silver! We want one of them alive!"

That was not what he wanted to hear. "Yes, sir. Silver out." Shining the light up ahead of him, he saw a Y in the corridor. Moving ahead, he shined the light down both halls. *Door number one, or door number two.*

***

PFC Wendy Black was moving quickly down the long corridor. Beads of sweat rolled down her forehead. As she moved away from the door, she had noticed the temperature steadily rising. Coming around a corner, she encountered an immense room. It was easily a hundred feet across and thirty feet high. It was different from the rest of the ship in that it had smooth black walls instead of the patchwork ones she had previously encountered. Stepping into the center of the room, she found herself standing in a large circle carved into the floor.

Looking around the circle, she saw a carved relief that vaguely reminded her of Egyptian hieroglyphs. Kneeling down, she ran her hand over the smooth lines in the floor. She heard a clicking sound as she passed her hand over a second one. Stepping back, she watched as the hieroglyphs quickly began to light up.

The room around her began to flicker to life. What looked to be large viewing screens began to power up around the sides and rear of the room. Individual screens showed the outside view of the ship and system statistics. "Wow, this is great."

She tapped a button on her belt turning on her mic. "Major, this is Black. Do you copy?" She waited for Griggs to reply, but heard only static. "Major Griggs, this is Private Black. Do you copy?"

Nothing. "Damn. Something in this room must be interfering with my signal."

She started to make her way out of the room to get a clearer signal, when a loud crackling sound caught her attention. Spinning around, she caught sight of a huge view screen behind her twinkle to life. "What the hell?"

A giant image of Earth appeared on the screen. She watched as it spun peacefully in the void of space. A low rumble began to fill her ears as she stared at the screen. Suddenly, the Earth was ripped apart at the center in a fiery explosion. Fragments flew in all directions, leaving the view screen empty. The image was replaced by what looked to her like film footage of World War II. The film was black and white and scratched as it showed soldiers being shot and blown up, as well as planes bombing entire cities into submission. The image flashed again, this time, showing canisters of toxic waste being dumped into one of the oceans and the polluting of the environment.

She was in shock at the images flashing before her. "What does this all mean?" A single word in white lettering flashed across the black screen. She gasped as she took several steps back. "Extinction? I don't understand!"

A voice startled her. "You don't need to."

She flipped around to see who it was. "Altone? What are you doing here?" She relaxed. "Why did you abandon your post?"

"It's very important that we talk."

He was acting strangely. She cautiously took a step back. "About what?" "Wendy, I've always liked you and I don't want to see you come to any harm.

That's why I'm here."

"That's very nice of you to want to protect me, Dan, I just—"

"No, that's not it," he cut her off. "I'm here to make you an offer." She slowly put her hand on her weapon. "What kind of offer?"

He looked around to make sure no one else was listening. "We have an infiltrator in our midst. The powers that be back at the base have instructed me to seek out and destroy this infiltrator and his partner. I want you to help me."

"What are you talking about, Dan?"

"Our new lieutenant, you know, Silver, he's not who he says he is." She leaned a little closer. "Who is he?"

"He's a private eye sent in to infiltrate the base and bring it down." "What? How could one man bring down a whole base?"

"That doesn't matter now. All I need to know is that you'll help me stop him."

"Or what?"

"Or you'll have to be killed too."

Her eyes widened. "I don't know about this. It all seems awfully strange." Altone nodded. "I understand. I'll give you a little while to think it over."

She turned her back to him as she thought over the information just presented to her. Slowly, Altone reached up to his belt and uncoiled a thin piece of nylon rope. Wrapping it around his hands, he raised it up and slowly moved toward her. With one fell swoop, he had the rope around her neck and was choking her. She gasped for breath as she struggled to break free. Balling her fist, she threw several elbow jabs into his ribs. His hands were like steel as he pulled. She felt the lack of oxygen begin to hit her brain. Trying to think quickly, she squirmed to the right and sent her left hand backward into his groin. The rope went slack as he doubled over in pain. Seizing her chance, she flipped around and sent a kick into his midsection sending him toppling to the floor. She kicked again, this time, hitting him in the head. He rolled over on his back moaning in pain.

Taking a step back, she watched him for a moment. Lifting her foot, she readied herself to kick again. Quickly, he rolled over and grabbed her foot knocking her off balance and sending her to the floor. Jumping to his feet, Altone swiftly removed his pistol from its holster and aimed it at her.

"Sorry, Wendy." He pulled the trigger.

***

Jake stopped dead in his tracks. Up ahead in the hallway he could feel something staring at him. Quickly lifting his light, he caught a glimpse of a small gray creature as it darted around the corner away from him. His adrenaline took over as he rushed headlong after it. He was running full bore, but was falling behind.

Rounding the corner, he caught the creature leaping into a small hole in the wall. Jogging up to the hole, Jake cautiously peered inside. It was a long tunnel. His light flashed across the creature as it moved deeper into the passageway. Dropping down on his hands and knees, he made his way after the creature.

The tunnel was oozing with some sort of slime

pooling at the bottom. Jake tried not to be disgusted by the feel of it as he waded through. It was making the bottom of the crawl space very slick and difficult for him to traverse too quickly. Shining his light ahead of him, he saw the creature moving quickly and easily.

He took a deep breath, but quickly exhaled it. He'd noticed when he first entered the ship, but its rank smell had steadily grown worse as he had traversed deeper inside. The smell was starting to turn his stomach. It vaguely reminded him of a moldy piece of fruit. He stopped to catch his breath. The smell was making it increasingly harder for him to breathe.

He shined his light around the tunnel. It was scarcely big enough for him. He quickly began to move again, not wanting to lose sight of the creature. Pointing his light in front of him, he caught sight of the creature's foot as it swiftly rounded a corner. He moved as quickly as he could toward it. Rounding the corner, he brought his light to bear, but saw nothing.

"Dammit, I lost him." His flashlight began to flicker, then died. He pounded it against the wall trying to make it work. It remained dark. Replacing the light on his belt, he cautiously turned to look behind him. Darkness. Turning ahead, he caught a small light. His heart began to race. "I hope that's the light at the end of the tunnel."

Cautiously, he began to inch his way toward the light. He moved his right hand slowly forward in the slime. He rested it on what felt like some kind of tube. He slowly moved his hand along the length of it. He unexpectedly felt it move.

Jumping back, he accidentally slammed his head against the ceiling of the tunnel. He tried to stifle the pain as it thundered in his head. He held his body perfectly still. Beads of sweat began to roll down his forehead. He carefully started to back out when the flashlight on his belt slipped off and splashed into the slime.

The flashlight sparked to life. Jake's eyes went wide as he stared at the creature directly in front of him. The creatures almond-shaped black eyes studied him as his pear-shaped head bobbed back and forth like a bird's. One of his spindly arms reached out for Jake. Trying hard not to gasp, Jake slowly backed away from the creature. The creature cocked its head to the right. Shifting around, it quickly moved toward Jake.

Jake panicked. "Get back!" It reared back and emitted a shrill scream from its tiny mouth. "Jesus Christ!" Jake jumped back and fell face first into the slime. Lifting himself out of the sludge, he gasped for air and quickly wiped the slime out of his eyes. By the time he opened his eyes, it was gone.

CHAPTER FOURTEEN

He stared at his empty desk drawers. He had been in the same office throughout his entire career at the base. It had grown to feel like his second home. Emptying the last of his possessions into a small brown cardboard box, he carried it over to where several other boxes sat stacked in the corner. Seating himself at his desk, he stared at his now barren office. He had once been told one could judge one's life by how long it takes to pack. It had taken fifteen minutes. He wasn't sure what that meant.

Davis stood and walked over to his door. Twisting the knob, he slowly opened it. Stepping out into the hallway, he moved toward the exit at the end. Lifting his spare ID card out of his pocket, he slipped it through the control box next to the door. Two red LED lights blinked on instead of the usual green light.

"What the hell?" He slid it through again with the same response. He stared at the two red lights. Reaching up, he tapped his personal access code into the keypad. The red lights appeared again. "Damn."

He strode briskly back to his office and slammed his door. Picking up the receiver on his desk, he dialed the number for the control room. The phone rang several times before someone picked it up. "Control room."

"This is General Davis. Let me speak to General Perry." "Hold on a minute, sir."

The phone went silent as he was put on hold. Davis waited patiently for Perry to pick up. "Hello?"

"Perry?"

"Yeah, Tom. Go ahead."

"What the hell is going on? Why have my pass codes been removed from the system already? I still have a whole day here at the base!"

The phone was silent for a moment. "Tom, I'm going to level with you. I've assumed full operational control of this facility. That means you're no longer needed, so your access has been limited to your office until you're shipped out."

"Jesus Christ! I've been working here for fifteen years! I already know what goes on here! You're not keeping me out of anything I don't already know about!" Davis' anger was building.

"Calm down, Tom. I did this in the facility's best interest. You are to be transferred off-base in one day. That means I need to be able to do my job without your interference."

"You can't do this to me!"

"Sorry, Tom. I just did." The phone went dead.

"You son of a bitch!" Davis slammed the receiver on the desk breaking it. Knocking the phone to the floor, he kicked his desk as hard as he could. Grabbing his chair, he pulled it over and slumped down into it. Laying his hands on the armrests, he leaned his head back and stared at the ceiling. "It's up to you now, Jake."

***

Jake lifted his head out of the slime. He tried to wipe it off his face the best he could as he reached for his now operational flashlight. He looked ahead

207

in the tunnel, and then looked back. Twisting around, he started back the way he came. Finally making it back to the entrance, he slowly pulled himself out and stood. He flattened himself up against the wall as a long shadow appeared from around the corner. He reached for his pistol, but found only an empty holster. *I must've dropped it in the slime.* He readied himself.

"Silver?" It was Griggs. "Right here!"

Griggs jogged around the corner. "We've lost contact with PFC Black. Have you seen her?"

"No I haven't."

Griggs stared at Jake. "What happened to you?"

He glanced over his slime-covered uniform. "I fell in."

Griggs smiled as he walked past. "Welcome to the Air Force, Silver."

The two men made their way back to where they started. Jake leaned his head out into the cool night air and took a deep breath. Griggs checked his watch. "I lost contact with Private Black almost forty minutes ago. I heard what sounded like a message from her on the comm., but it was very fuzzy and I couldn't make it out."

"What are our options?" Jake was still trying to get the slime off.

"The way I see it, we only have one." "Find her."

Griggs nodded. "She went down this way," he pointed down the hall with his hand. Griggs looked at Jake. "Let's go."

***

Black slowly came back to consciousness. Pain shot through her body as she tried to sit up.

208

Reaching up to her chest, she felt the bullet hole in her right side. It had ripped through her body just above her right breast. Opening her eyes, she carefully looked around. She was still in the center of the circle she had discovered. *I should be dead by now.* She was confused.

Looking around, she saw all the hieroglyphs were brightly lit and emanating some kind of blue light forming a bubble around her. Slowly lifting herself to a standing position, she glanced up at the top of the bubble just above her head. Reaching up, she passed her hands easily through the top. *It's not a containment field...*

She mustered her courage and took a step out of the bubble. She dropped to the floor like a sack of bricks. Blood started flowing out of her wound onto the floor. Her mind screamed with pain and she could taste the blood welling up in her throat. She could feel herself dying. Struggling with all her strength, she pulled herself back into the bubble.

Rolling onto her back, she felt a warm sensation flow over her body as the pain receded. Reaching over, she felt the bullet hole stop bleeding and begin to close. Her mind cleared. *This field is keeping me alive.*

***

Jake and Griggs came to a dead end. The corridor they had followed the entire way was blocked with a large black wall with no markings. "What the hell is going on here? This is the only way she could've come. There were no doors or forks in the road leading here."

Griggs twisted around and began to recount his footsteps. "It just doesn't make any sense."

Crossing his arms, Jake shifted his weight to lean on the wall, but instead, fell through. Jumping up, he tried to put his hands on the wall. "Griggs?"

"Where the hell are you, Silver?"

"I'm behind the wall." Jake pushed his hand through for Griggs to see. "It's not real. Just step though."

Griggs hesitated. "This place is really getting strange." Lifting a hand, he easily passed it through the wall. Pulling it back, he lifted one of his booted feet and stepped into it.

"Fun, huh?" Griggs was not amused. Jake turned around and scanned the room. It was immense. In the center of it was a tall blue bubble. "What the hell is that?"

Griggs nodded. "Better check it out." The two men walked briskly toward the bubble. Griggs' eyes widened as they neared it. "That's Black inside!"

The two men rushed toward her. Jake stopped short of the bubble. "Private, are you all right?"

She slowly turned her head toward them. "I'm okay." She sounded as if she was talking through glass.

Griggs looked down at the large pool of blood on the floor. "What the hell happened here and why are you in that bubble?"

She sat up and looked at them. "This bubble is the only thing keeping me alive." Jake ran his hand through the light, then pulled it out again. "I don't understand.

How is it keeping you alive?"

"I don't know." She pointed to her wound. "I was shot. I thought I was going to die, but I woke up in this bubble. As long as I'm inside it, I'm fine, but if I come out, I won't make it to the door."

Griggs knelt down next to her. "Shot? By whom?"

"By me." A voice boomed out of the darkness. "And you two are next." Griggs and Jake turned around toward the voice. "Who's there?"

Altone slowly stepped out of the shadows with his weapon raised. "It's me, Major. Private Altone."

Griggs quickly raised his weapon. "What do you think you're doing, soldier?"

He smiled a devilish grin. "Not that it's going to matter in a few seconds, but I'm here to kill the three of you."

Griggs stepped forward. "You son of a bitch."

Altone fired off a round hitting Griggs in the shoulder. Griggs moaned in pain as he fell to the floor clutching his wound. "I don't want to hear anything else out of you, Major." Jake slowly tried to pull his pistol out of its holster. "Keep your hands where I can see them, Lieutenant. Or should I say, *Mr*. Silver?"

Jake reluctantly raised his hands. He knew his secret was out. "You'll never get away with this, Altone."

"Oh yes I will. You have no idea how high up this order came from."

"No, but I bet I can guess." Jake's eyes wandered down to Griggs, who was slowly aiming his weapon. He needed to keep Altone talking. "These men you're taking orders from respect no one. As soon as you return to base, you'll be disposed of just like us."

"That's not true."

"It is, Private. They want someone to do their

dirty work *and* take the fall for them." Griggs was almost ready.

"I've had just about all I can take of—" Griggs jumped up and fired at Altone. He doubled over in pain as the bullet tore through his left upper thigh. He screamed as he jolted up and began to fire wildly.

Jake bolted toward Griggs, knocking him out of the way. Turning, Jake squeezed off several rounds toward Altone. His bullets ricocheted off the wall next to Altone. Rolling to his left, Altone pulled the trigger again. One final bullet whizzed past Jake's head. In frustration, Altone slammed down his weapon and began to charge.

Before Jake could return fire, Altone was on him. A vicious right jab caught Jake in the jaw stunning him momentarily. Jake returned the favor by sending several quick jabs into Altone's midsection knocking him off. The two men scrambled to their feet. Standing opposite each other, the two combatants stared intently at the other. Reaching behind him, Altone brandished a large knife. The jagged silver blade reflected the blue light of the bubble toward Jake. Glancing down in front of him, Jake caught sight of the weapon knocked out of his hand during the initial struggle. Next to him, Griggs was trying to pull himself up to help in the battle.

Altone leapt at him again. The blade whipped past Jake's chest, then his face. Dodging the blade once again, Jake threw a punch that connected with Altone's jaw.

Altone stumbled backward, giving Jake enough space to tackle him. The two men went sailing to the floor once again. Jake grabbed Altone's wrist and slammed it on the ground repeatedly until the knife tumbled loosely from his hand. Quickly reaching over, he sent the blade skidding away from them. Altone shot his hands up grabbing Jake's head, then delivering a nasty head-butt. Jake reeled back, blood gushing from his nose. Lifting his boot, Altone kicked Jake squarely in the chest.

Jake hit the ground hard. Quickly rolling to his left, he narrowly avoided another kick from Altone. The two warriors jumped to their feet glancing over at Jake's gun. They jumped. Altone threw a backhand into Jake's face knocking him back. Altone skittered to the floor grabbing for the gun. Turning around, Altone pointed the gun toward Jake. Lashing out, Jake knocked the gun from Altone's hands, then kicked him in the head dropping him.

Slowly, Jake moved over to the gun and picked it up. Turning around, he aimed it at Altone. "Who told you to kill us?"

Altone sat up and stared at Jake. "Go fuck yourself," he spit at him.

Cocking back the hammer, he pressed the barrel into Altone's head. "Who gave the order?" Altone said nothing. "You have ten seconds to live, my friend. Either you tell me who gave the order, or you will die. Ten…nine…eight…seven…six…" Silence. "Five…four…three…two—"

Altone broke. "Hunter!" he screamed the name. "Colonel Hunter gave the order." "Now that wasn't that hard, was it?" Altone glared at him.

A moan from Griggs caught Jake's attention. Taking the opportunity, Altone rammed his shoulder into Jake's gut knocking the wind out of him. His gun fell to the floor next to the bubble protecting Black. Altone quickly dipped down and scooped up the discarded weapon. Quickly jumping to his feet, he drew a bead on Jake's head. "It's your turn, PI." He started to squeeze the trigger.

Jake watched as Black slowly rose to her feet pulling a knife out of her belt. Jake wanted to stop her, but before he could, she jumped out of the bubble tackling Altone and burying the blade deep in his back. Altone let out a blood-curdling scream as Black twisted the blade. Altone shook violently, then stopped as he crumpled to the ground. A pool of blood slowly formed beneath him. Black lifted up her head to look at Jake as she ripped the knife from Altone's back.

"What are you doing? Get back in the bubble!"

She looked up at him. "It's too late for that now." Blood was dripping from her mouth. "I couldn't just watch you die."

He knelt down next to her and placed a hand on her back. "Thank you."

She smiled. "You're welcome." She made a gurgling noise. "Get them for me, okay?" Her eyelids slowly closed as she stopped breathing.

"I will." Standing, he walked over to where Griggs was lying. "Come on, Major. Break time's over." He slipped his hand around his arm and began to lift.

"Good job, Silver." Griggs slowly made it to his feet. He slowly pressed his hand against his wounded shoulder. "Damn, that hurts. What's your plan?"

Jake thought for a moment, "It's obvious

214

Hunter is on to us. We need to complete our mission."

Griggs nodded. "First, I need to get this wound bandaged up."

215

CHAPTER FIFTEEN

The lights were off in General Perry's office when the two figures entered. His chair was turned slightly toward his large picture window. The light from the moon was creating eerie shadows across his face and the floor. His chair creaked as he slowly twisted to face them. He motioned with his hand for them to sit down. Walking up to the desk, they pulled out chairs and seated themselves.

"I've called you into my office for a very important reason." Perry sat at his desk across from Anne and his man in black. "Our operative in the field has failed."

Anne crossed her long legs. She was wearing a white button up shirt with a pair of blue jeans. "What happened?"

Perry tapped the pen he was holding on the desk. "Private Altone has been eliminated. We didn't count on Private Black being a patriot, too."

The man in black leaned forward. "So they're headed back here?"

"As far as we know." Slowly, he twisted his chair around to face the window again. He watched the buzz of activity on the tarmac in front of the main hangar. They were rolling out two of the silver saucers, followed by one of their many stealth jets. "As you both know, tonight is a very important night here at the facility. We're testing both of our newly rebuilt saucers. This test needs to go off flawlessly."

Anne shifted in her seat. "We understand. What

216

do you want us to do?"

Perry stared at the two gleaming saucers. "You two will be my last line of defense against these two men. We've found out they will be trying to rescue Doctor Robinson and the Anderson girl. That must not happen."

"What's so important about Doctor Robinson?" The man in black adjusted his tie. Perry swiveled around in his chair and slammed his fist down on the desk. "I called you in here to listen, not to question!" He stared at his two wide-eyed employees. "I need your complete cooperation in this matter. Your main task is to stop and eliminate Silver and Griggs." He stood. "Dismissed."

Anne and the man in black quickly stood and exited the room. Turning around, he stared out his window at the project transpiring below. Men in white jump suits were scattered randomly around the craft. Bright spotlights illuminated the ships and the stealth jet. The advisors, wearing their cheap suits, stood near the hangar door watching the activity. Several of them were conferring and pointing toward the saucers. Perry knew he needed to get down there, but he was enjoying the calm before the storm.

***

The base was lit up like a shopping mall during Christmastime. From atop Freedom Ridge, Jake and Griggs flattened themselves to the ground as they watched the activity below. The mountain's terrain was covered with sand and sagebrush while large jagged rocks jutted skyward out of the soft soil. It was a very hostile environment.

Griggs stared down from the highest point near

Groom Lake with a pair of binoculars. "Look at that." He handed Jake the binoculars.

"What the hell are those?"

Griggs retrieved the binoculars and stared at the two saucer-shaped crafts being wheeled out onto the tarmac. "Those are two of our recovered extra-terrestrial crafts. Tonight's the test."

"What test?"

Griggs handed back the binoculars. "Several of the military's top advisors are currently at the base. This test is to prove to them that alien technology can be reverse engineered and used in our stuff."

Jake stared through the binoculars at the silvery ships. "They look very similar to the one we were just in."

"They are." Griggs moved a piece of sagebrush out of his face. "Tonight will be the first test in almost five years."

"Why so long?"

Griggs adjusted the binoculars. "Our scientists are good, but this technology is years ahead of ours. It took them almost ten years to figure out how to get inside one of the damn things."

Jake snickered. "Our tax dollars at work." He grabbed the binoculars. He slowly panned across the tarmac watching all the men in white jump suits scurry about. He stopped on a group of men standing near the hangar door apparently overseeing what was happening. "Who are they?" He handed Griggs the binoculars.

"Where?"

"The group of men standing in front of the hangar door."

Griggs paused as he found his target. "Those

are the advisors, but I'm not sure who the two men are at the end. I've never seen them before." He adjusted the binoculars. "One of them is an older guy wearing a long black trench coat, and the other looks younger," he squinted hard, "he's wearing a leather jacket."

"Friends of yours?"

Laying the binoculars down, he turned to Jake. "This will be our best opportunity to rescue the doctor. The base will be focused on this test."

"All right. What's the plan?"

"We have to assume by now the entire base has been alerted about us, so they'll be on the lookout. We're also still a good half hour from the base. We'll have to cross this barren terrain on foot and try not to be spotted."

"I thought this place had the most sophisticated security system in the world." "It does, but they're mostly on the outer perimeter."

"Why didn't they use it throughout the entire area?"

"They felt if they kept the border heavily guarded, the need for security in the interior would be pointless. And for the most part, it is. We've never had anyone make it all the way to the base without being stopped." Griggs looked around the mountaintop. "In fact, this whole ridge used to be public property. That changed when every camera crew in the country used to come up here and photograph the base."

Jake smiled. "For a secret base, it's not very secret."

"That's part of the disinformation campaign they're running. They've promoted the base in such a way as to give it a mythical quality. Sure everyone knows about Are a 51, but they all think the stories about it were made up in some writer's overactive imagination."

"But they do have regular patrols?"

"Yes they do. Officers dressed like we are and driving white Jeep Cherokees."

"They have vehicles," he muttered to himself. Jake snapped his fingers. "That gives me an idea." He stood up.

"What the hell are you doing? Get down! You'll be spotted!"

He smiled. "That's what I want."

Griggs reached up to pull him down, then stopped. "I get it." He stood beside Jake.

Slowly, Jake scanned the area around them. "There's one." He pointed to the west of them. A white Jeep was parked on an opposite peak. "I wonder how long they've been watching us?"

"Hard to say. One thing's for sure, though, they have backup on the way."

No sooner had Griggs said the words, than a white Cherokee pulled up behind them. Gunfire erupted. The two men hit the ground and rolled near the front of the vehicle. Jake glanced to Griggs. "You don't think they'll try and run us over?"

They listened as the Jeep kicked into gear and started to roll forward. Jumping up, Griggs ducked out of the way. Jake rolled to his left away from the vehicle, accidentally hitting the edge of the mountain.

"Shit!" Jake grabbed wildly at nearby plants as he teetered on the edge. His hand snatched the base of one of the sagebrush. Slowly, he tried to pull himself up. Griggs and the vehicle were just out of his line of sight. He heard the Jeep's doors open and footsteps approaching him. The sound of machine gun fire broke the silence, then it stopped. A soft moan filled his ears. Fearing the worst, he screamed. "Griggs!"

Looking up, he saw the form of a soldier stagger over to him, then fall hard on a large rock near the edge. The crack of his skull against the rock made a sickening sound. He watched as the soldier slowly slipped off the rock and over the edge. His body dropped several hundred feet to the rocky floor below.

Pulling with all his strength, Jake slowly lifted himself back up. Peering over the edge, he saw Griggs kneeling with his hands behind his back in front of the second soldier. A shiny pistol was reflecting the lights from the Jeep's headlights as the soldier held it firmly to the back of Griggs' head. Carefully, Jake removed one hand from the bush and reached for his weapon. Pulling it out of his holster, he drew a bead and fired.

The soldier dropped to the ground behind Griggs as the bullet slammed into the back of his head. Dropping his gun in the sand, Jake pulled himself up. Quickly standing, he moved over to Griggs. "Are you okay?"

"Yeah."

"What happened?"

"I had this one pinned down," he pointed to the one lying behind him. "Then I saw the other one approaching you. I had to take him out, and that gave the second one a chance to get me." Griggs stood. Turning around, he delivered a swift kick to the dead soldier's ribs. "Come on, let's go."

The two men climbed into the still running vehicle. Griggs pressed down the clutch and threw it into reverse. Looking behind him, he slowly drove it off the mountain.

***

Perry stepped out of the doorway and adjusted his blue uniform. A soldier spotted him and quickly ran over. He saluted, then leaned close to whisper in his ear. Perry nodded and eagerly dismissed him. The floodlights positioned around the tarmac were hurting his eyes after spending so much time in his dark office. He turned to his left and spotted the advisors still standing near the hangar door. He moved toward them.

"Good evening, gentlemen." He rubbed his hands together as he approached them. "I trust you're all ready for the test."

One of the advisors glanced at his watch and sighed. "Can we hurry this up, General? We all have to be back at the Pentagon in the morning."

"It'll just be a few more moments." He looked over at the figure in the trench coat, "Excuse me for a moment." Perry made his way over to the man. "I wasn't made aware you were here, sir. I'm glad to see you could make it."

"This isn't a social call, General. We're here to see if your little pet project is a success." His black trench coat rustled slightly in the breeze.

"I understand. I think you'll be pleasantly surprised when it begins."

He tapped his finger on Perry's chest. "I better be, your job's on the line."

***

222

Griggs stomped on the accelerator sending the Jeep flying over a large bush and slamming into the desert floor. Cranking the wheel hard, he righted the vehicle, sending it screaming toward the base.

Jake was gripping the dashboard for dear life. "What happened to inconspicuous?"

Griggs swiftly guided the Jeep through a maze of sagebrush and rocks. "Look behind us." Jake twisted around to see another white Jeep following them. "That's the vehicle we saw on the ridge opposite ours."

"Damn. What do you plan to do?"

"There's nowhere to lose them, so I'm trying to outrun them."

"Do you think of these things beforehand, or do you just act impulsively?" Jake turned around in the seat to see another white Jeep rushing headlong toward them. "Turn!"

Griggs stayed cool. "I see it."

Jake's eyes widened as Griggs held his course. "Turn!"

He didn't. "Shut up!" Jake stared as the Jeep came closer and closer. Reaching over, he grabbed the wheel and tried to turn it. "Get off!" Griggs threw Jake back into his seat. "I know what I'm doing!" Griggs gripped the wheel with all his strength. He kept his eyes firmly locked on the approaching vehicle. He felt the wound in his shoulder begin to bleed again due to the pressure of his flexed muscles.

"They're going to hit us!" Jake locked his arms around his head.

"It's just a simple game of chicken." Griggs began a countdown in his head as the other vehicle's headlights glared in his eyes. He could now clearly make out the writing on the license plate. Beads of sweat began to roll down his forehead. Checking his rear view mirror, he made sure the other Jeep was still right behind him. He knew it was now or never. Suddenly, he cranked hard on the wheel sending the Jeep skidding by the oncoming vehicle.

The two white Jeeps crashed headfirst into each other. The divers of both vehicles slammed into the windshields shattering them. The passenger in the vehicle following them slammed his head on the dashboard, knocking himself unconscious. The passenger in the second vehicle wasn't as lucky. Wearing only his lap belt upon impact, he was tossed forward like a rag doll snapping his spine instantly.

Griggs slammed on the breaks, throwing his Jeep into a three hundred and sixty degree spin. Jake stared at the mayhem Griggs had just caused. "Remind me never to doubt you again."

Griggs turned to him and wiped the sweat off his forehead. "Just like I said. It was a simple game of chicken. I just had to know when to flinch."

Jake stared at him for a long moment, then started to laugh. "You are one twisted son of a bitch." Both men laughed for a moment, then stopped. "What next?"

Griggs removed his binoculars from his belt. Holding them up, he scanned the horizon. "Looks like General Perry's little party is about to begin." He turned to Jake and smiled. "What do you say we crash it?"

"I just want you to know that I am expecting to

survive this whole ordeal." "I am, too." Griggs kicked the Jeep into gear and floored it.

***

Colonel Hunter seated himself in the Command Room and pulled on his headset. Running his hand over the keyboard, he typed in his password. Hitting the enter key, his screens flickered on with views of the tarmac. He watched as several men in white jump suits readied the two saucers and the black stealth jet for the impending test.

He wheeled around in his chair. "Monitors up. I want this to go off without a flaw." The other soldiers moved through the control room with ease and purpose carrying out Hunter's command. Twisting back around to his console, he tapped in the code to switch all monitors to the main hangar and tarmac. He was sure his crack security force would be able to handle any intrusions they might have during the test.

***

Perry stood in front of one of the immense saucers staring at it. He watched as the support crew removed several hoses connected to it. Reaching up, he ran his hand across the rough surface of the shiny craft. He watched intently as his slightly warped reflection moved along the side of the saucer. Pulling his hand away, he walked around to the front. Several members of the crew were moving in and out of the craft through an open hatch.

He stared at the steel steps leading up to the hatch as he walked up them. He had only been inside these things once before. He stopped at the hatch. Grabbing the sides of the door, he slowly leaned inside and inhaled a deep breath of air. He hated the smell of these things. Stepping inside, he took a quick look around. The first time he had come aboard, the halls had been dimly lit and dank. The engineers at the base had installed track lighting along the base of the halls and lights along the ceiling. The black patchwork walls had been replaced by thin sheets of glistening aluminum giving the ship more of a human feel.

The walls were stenciled with arrows and area designations. He glanced at the arrow pointing down the hall to the cockpit. Turning to his left, he followed the arrows through the twisting passages until he reached it. Stopping at the door, he watched as members of the support crew checked the readouts on the newly installed computer banks. Three chairs arranged in a triangle stood in the center of the room with control panels flanking each. Two more chairs stood at the front of the room directly under a huge electronic view screen. The screen was flashing images of the tarmac and computer diagnostics.

Stepping into the cockpit, he made his way to the center chair and seated himself. It had a steel frame with vinyl cushions that wasn't entirely uncomfortable. Reaching over, he ran his hand across the smooth control board. He longed to be at the helm of the craft when it lifted off, but his presence was needed on the ground.

Standing, he gave the bridge one final look before turning around. He was approaching the door when a young soldier stopped him and saluted.

"What is it, Private?"

He was panting. "Sorry to bother you, sir," he tried to catch his breath. "But we've got an intruder

226

heading our way."

"Damn. Do we know who it is?"

"It's Major Griggs and Lieutenant Silver, sir."

"Son of a bitch." He placed his hand on the young man's shoulder and pulled him out of earshot of the other crewmembers. "What the hell happened?"

"They disposed of Private Altone, then commandeered a Jeep. So far on their way here, they've killed four more of our men and wrecked two vehicles."

"Jesus Christ." He pulled his hand off the young man's shoulder and quickly turned around to make sure no one else was listening. Turning back, he quickly began to think. "I want all our available men on this right now. Inform Colonel Hunter he is to assign several of his men to be on watch for Griggs and Silver."

"Yes, sir." The young man saluted, then went about following his orders.

Perry slowly spun around and glanced over the bridge one last time. Turning, he slowly made his way back toward the hatch. He passed five men wearing green flight suits. They saluted as they walked by. He envied them.

Stepping through the hatch, he slowly walked down the stairs. Glancing over at the advisors, he saw they had now separated into small groups and were discussing something. *Things aren't going well.*

Suddenly, shouting filled the night sky followed by the sound of gunfire. "Shit." Whirling around, he saw a white Jeep roar onto the runway with guns blazing out the windows. Perry shouted at the top of his lungs. "Get those bastards!"

Waves of soldiers took up firing positions around the tarmac unleashing a torrent of bullets toward the Jeep. The bullets slammed into the hood and doors of the vehicle sending it careening out of control toward the main hangar door. Soldiers jumped out of the way as the Jeep skidded past them on its collision course.

Perry watched the advisors scatter as the jeep slammed full throttle into the hangar door shredding it. Fragments flew in all directions. Running toward the first soldier he saw, Perry began to bark orders. "Private!"

The soldier was surprised to see the general. He quickly snapped to attention. "Yes, sir?"

"Gather a team and get in there! I want those men dead!"

The soldier quickly saluted, then took off. From where he was standing, he could see a gaping hole in the hangar door. Grabbing another soldier, he reached for his weapon. "Give me your sidearm, Private!" The private quickly relinquished his weapon.

Holding the sleek black pistol in his hand, he cocked back the hammer and swiftly jogged toward the hole in the hangar door. Glancing around the edge, he saw the Jeep rolled onto its side in front of another black stealth jet. The rear of the vehicle was slowly burning due to the leaking fuel. With several soldiers behind him, Perry slowly crept toward the injured vehicle with weapon raised. Motioning with his hands, his soldiers spread out.

The Jeep was lying on the driver's side with the roof facing the hangar door. Perry slowly crept around to the front. The windshield was shattered and the hood flung open. Engine oil was leaking out in huge pools in front of the vehicle. One of the soldiers slowly made his way to the passenger side window. Quickly aiming his weapon inside, he fired several rounds. Perry walked to the window and peered inside. Nothing. "Where are they?" Perry demanded.

The soldier shrugged.

Stepping back, Perry swiveled around and began to scan the hangar. Fear gripped him. "Do you see them?"

Machine gun fire erupted around the hangar. The sound of bullets ricocheting off the concrete floor echoed loudly. "Get down! Get down now!"

Two soldiers who were hit square in the chest crumbled to the floor. Perry and the other soldiers scrambled for cover next to the battered Jeep. "Get those bastards!" Perry's men jumped up and started firing wildly in all directions. One by one, his men fell to the floor dead.

***

Jake and Griggs had taken up position behind the stealth jet, which had been knocked over in the wreck. When the Jeep tipped, they had scrambled out of the passenger window with only minor scrapes.

Sliding down, they sat with their backs to the jet while bullets whizzed overhead. "How are we going to get out of this?" Silver sat holding his rifle in the ready position.

"Give me a second. I need to think of something." Griggs jumped up and fired several rounds over the top of the plane.

229

Jake twisted his head around and stared at Griggs. "What about one of those?" He pointed at a small round object attached to Griggs' belt.

Griggs yanked the grenade off his belt and assessed it. "That's not a good idea." Jake jumped up and fired off several more rounds before he slid back down next to Griggs. "Why not?"

"We're surrounded by very highly explosive objects. If I throw this," he twirled his finger in the air, "the whole hanger goes up in flames."

A gunshot slammed into the plane's hull right behind their heads. "Do we have any other choice?" Jake asked.

Griggs leapt up and fired off several rounds just as a wave of bullets skimmed over his head. "I see your point." Both men moved into a crouching position. "When I pull the pin and throw the grenade, run for that door to your left."

Jake nodded and readied himself.

"Okay, here we go." Griggs quickly pulled the pin. Standing, he tossed the small green ball over the plane toward the group of soldiers.

The two men leapt to their feet and hit a dead run toward the door. Machine gun bullets rained down around them. They hit the door just as the grenade exploded into a giant ball of flame. The sound of the soldiers' screams filled the room as the force of the blast slammed the Jeep into the nearby stealth jet engulfing both in a giant plume of flame.

"Open the door!"

Jake grabbed the handle and twisted it. "It's locked!" He shouted above the roar of the flames and explosions.

Griggs spotted the security box next to the

door. "Damn! We need a security card to get in!"

The flames were quickly nearing the two men. "Davis gave us his card!" Jake remembered. Digging into his vest, he removed the card and quickly slid it through the box. Two red lights immediately blinked on.

"Shit!" Griggs grabbed the card out of Jake's hand and quickly slid it though the reader again with the same result. "Davis' pass codes must've been locked out of the system. Stand back." Tossing the useless card to the ground, he lifted his weapon and fired directly into the machine. A cascade of sparks erupted from the small black box as it exploded.

With only moments to spare, he holstered his weapon and dug his fingers deep into the edge of the door. Pulling as hard as he could, he slowly managed to open it. Pushing Jake through first, Griggs dove to the ground just as a wave of fire burst through above them.

"Jesus!" Jake covered his head with his hands.

Griggs reached over and grabbed Jake. "Crawl! We need to get out of here!" The two men lifted themselves to their knees and quickly crawled out of the hallway. Jumping to their feet, they tried to catch their breath. Jake glanced around the bare room they found themselves in. It had two doors on the left and one on the right. Directly ahead of them was another hallway.

"Where are we?"

"This is kind of like Area 51's main lobby. From this room, you can get anywhere on the base." Griggs stared down the opposite hallway.

"We need to find out where they're holding

Doctor Robinson. How do we do that?"

Griggs thought for a moment. "It's not going to be that easy. There isn't any kind of base directory we can follow. On top of that, the base will now be alerted to our presence, making our job that much harder."

Jake snapped his fingers as he thought. "Might as well just start looking around. Lead on, Major Griggs."

Griggs assessed his options. He decided on the single door to the right.

***

Perry slowly came back to consciousness, his body racked with pain. Trying to lift himself, he found himself pinned down by an immense piece of scrap metal. Looking over, he saw two other wounded soldiers slowly lifting themselves off the charred floor. The two soldiers immediately spotted him and came to his aid. Kneeling down, they used all their strength to lift the piece of metal and slide it to the side. Reaching down, they grabbed Perry's outstretched hands and lifted him off the floor.

Perry tried to dust himself off and sustain his dignity, only to feel a trickle of blood run down his forehead. Pain rushed through his chest when he tried to take a deep breath. He knew some of his ribs were broken. Grabbing his side, he surveyed the damage. The hangar was wrecked. The grenade had triggered a chain of explosions that had annihilated everything in sight. Charred piles of metal that used to be jets littered the hangar's floor.

Anger welled up inside him. "I want those sons a bitches dead!" His two remaining soldiers staggered out of the hangar to find backup.

Removing a small white handkerchief from his pocket, he dabbed it at the cut on his forehead and tried to wipe off the blood. He felt a large painful bruise forming over the cut. Folding up the handkerchief, he replaced it in his pocket. Turning around, he made his way past several smoldering piles of rubble as flames burned unchecked on all sides.

Stepping out of the smoke-filled hangar, Perry coughed to try and clear his lungs. The tarmac was in shambles. Bodies were scattered about and equipment was on fire. Looking around, he spotted the advisors huddled near one of the saucers. He jogged toward them.

"Is everyone okay?"

The advisors turned to look at Perry. "General, consider your career over." "What?"

The President's advisor adjusted his glasses on his nose. "This is a Top Secret military installation and you've allowed two men to come in here and destroy what the government has worked so hard to attain!"

"You have no authority over me!"

The advisor folded his hands. "You are correct in that, General, but my employer does. When I get back to Washington in the morning, I will advise the President of your actions and recommend your immediate dismissal."

"You have no right to do this to me!"

"Yes I do, General. You gave me that right when you destroyed billions of dollars' worth of government property." The advisor briskly re-joined his group.

Perry turned away from the men. His eyes

focused on the man in the black trench coat. His long black coat was slightly rustling in the cool night breeze. He slowly shook his head as he turned away from Perry. At that moment, he felt the cold wind blow through his soul. He knew he was alone.

Walking back toward the hangar, he grabbed one of his soldiers by the arm and pulled him aside. "Get a team together and find those two men." The soldier nodded and began to leave. Perry grabbed his arm again. "Keep this quiet, Lieutenant. Report to no one except me."

"Yes, sir." He saluted and made his way toward a small group of soldiers gathered near one of the saucers.

Perry rubbed his hands together. "If I'm going down, I'm taking you two with me."

***

The two shadowy figures moved stealthily though a darkened corridor. Upon Griggs' suggestion, they had been following this same hallway for quite a ways now.

Both men had their weapons drawn as they crept along.

Jake tapped Griggs on the shoulder. "Where are we going?"

"To the main research lab." Griggs kept walking as he answered Jake. "Before you arrived, I had a meeting with General Davis. He informed me that Doctor Robinson was being held there."

Jake stopped. "Why is she being held in the main lab? Why wouldn't they have her in the stockade?"

Griggs quickly spun around. "Doctor Anderson told you about the 'Uber-Soldier Project', didn't he?" "Yeah, but—"

"That's why she's being held in the main lab. All prisoners of the base are subjected to DNA testing to see if they have the correct genomes. This facility never wastes an opportunity to have fresh test subjects."

"So what do they do with the prisoners if they don't have the correct genes?" "They are disposed of." His answer was cold and heartless.

"Do you hear what you're saying?" Jake was slowly raising his voice. "You sound just like one of *them*."

"Lower your voice," he scolded. "You're forgetting I was one of *them*. I don't know if you have any actual military training, but they teach you to keep calm in this kind of situation." He glared at Jake, "So if my answers sound harsh, I apologize, but you'll just have to live with it for the time being."

Jake was stunned. Griggs had never spoken to him that way before. "Now let's keep moving before we're spotted."

A door a few feet up the hall suddenly burst open and several soldiers emerged through it. "Too late."

Griggs quickly began to fire his weapon knocking down two of the soldiers as Jake charged the remainder with his gun blazing. Another soldier slammed to the ground with a bullet in his head.

Picking up one of the soldier's discarded rifles, Jake wielded it like a staff. Swinging it hard, he hit a fourth soldier squarely in the jaw with the butt of the weapon knocking him back against the wall. Quickly stepping up, he threw a right hook that caught the soldier in the side of the face and knocking him down. Aiming the gun down, he pulled the trigger sending a shell into the man's head. In the meantime, Griggs had finished off the remaining two men with his weapon.

The two men quickly backed up against the wall on opposite sides of the open door. Jake slowly peeked his head around the corner. He motioned with his hands for Griggs to follow as he charged into the empty room. It was brightly with a desk on the far wall with plants in all the corners. Unopened moving boxes littered the floor.

"Somebody's office?"

Griggs lifted the top on one of the boxes and removed a framed picture. "We're heading in the right direction."

"How can you be so sure?" He handed Jake the picture.

"This is the Anderson family." Jake lifted his head and looked around the bare office. "This was Jonathan Anderson's office?"

Griggs nodded. "Where to now?"

The tall man thought for a moment. "I think the main lab is just down the hall." Jake followed Griggs out of Anderson's office. Turning left, they made their way down a long corridor. Passing several doors, they found themselves standing in front of a large observation window. The two stared in horror at the contents of the room. Hundreds of long tubes with men and women suspended inside them loomed in the darkly lit room. Neither man could find the words to express the discomfort they were feeling at the sight of the tubes.

Griggs pointed into the room. "That's where

she is." "Doctor Robinson?"

Griggs nodded as he began to progress toward the door leading into the room. Jake slid to the side of it and reached for the handle. Griggs readied himself for any soldiers possibly lurking behind it. Jake slipped his hand around the handle and carefully twisted it. The two men made eye contact to signify they were ready. Jake flipped open the door as Griggs charged inside. He quickly scouted the room. He snapped his fingers once. Jake ran inside with his weapon at the ready. "There's no one here."

Jake slowly ran his hand along the nearest tube. A naked woman was floating in the green fluid. "What are they doing with these people?"

Griggs stared in horror at the tube. "I don't fully understand the tests myself, but I know the subjects have to be prepped for them. As far as I know, this is just a way to store them until they're ready to be tested on."

Jake struggled to understand. "Do you know what Doctor Robinson looks like?"

A blank expression washed over his face. "No, I've never seen any pictures of her."

"Great." Jake threw his hands up into the air. "Neither have I." He knelt down next to the tube.

"What are you doing?"

"For clerical reasons, you would think these tubes would have names on them, wouldn't you?" He scanned the tube. "Here it is." He pointed to a strip of white tape with the subject's name emblazoned on it in bold black letters.

"I don't want to check every tube in here." He looked around at the hundreds of tubes.

237

"Same here," his mind raced for a solution. "But that's all I can come up with." Griggs reluctantly began to go from tube to tube reading off the names. Jake did the same. They had each gone through about fifty when they heard a door on the far wall begin to open. Both men hit the floor as footsteps entered the room. Jake swiftly bobbed his head out for a second to see who it was.

"All right, Mr. Stratton, let's see how you're doing today." The man hit several keys on a nearby control pad. The patient's vital signs popped up on several small screens in front of him. "It looks like you're doing very well."

Jake stared across the room at the hidden Griggs. Motioning with his hands, he indicated he wanted to grab the researcher. Griggs shook his head furiously as he motioned for Jake to stay down. Drawing himself up to his knees, Jake quickly made his way across the room toward the unaware researcher. Griggs sighed and followed him.

Slowly, Jake stood behind the small Asian researcher. With a quickness Griggs had never seen, Jake snatched the researcher around the neck with his arm and quickly drew his gun and held it to the man's head. "Cooperate and I won't kill you."

The man nodded as best he could. "Who are you?"

He strained to get the words out. "I'm a researcher. My name is Doctor Yokama." "So you know what's going on around here, right?"

The small man nodded again.

"Good. I'm looking for Doctor Robinson. Can you take me to her tube?" Jake slowly released his grip on the small man.

Griggs stepped up next to Jake. "Are you sure this is a good idea?" "Do you have a better one?"

The two men followed the researcher through the rows of tubes until he reached a door on the far side of the room. Jake jabbed his gun into the man's side as he started to reach for the doorknob. "What are you doing?"

"Doctor Robinson is in a separate room."

"You mean there are more rooms like this one?" "Yes."

Jake let out a sigh of exasperation. "Step back from the door." He watched as the small researcher stepped back from the door. He turned around to Griggs. "Major, do you want to do the honors?"

Griggs nodded and stepped over to the door. Reaching down, he twisted the doorknob and slowly opened the door. Raising his weapon, he cautiously stepped into the smaller room and looked around. Turning his head back, he nodded at Jake.

Jake pushed his gun into Yokama's back. "All right, let's go."

The two men followed Griggs through the doorway into the small room. Three occupied tubes sat side by side. Jake glanced into the first tube. An unfamiliar naked woman was floating in the green fluid. Reading the tag on her tube he discovered it was Doctor Alex Robinson. "Major!"

Griggs walked over and stared into the tube. "Is she alive?"

They both turned to Yokama, who was already pulling up her vitals on his computer screen. "Yes she's alive, and in perfect hibernation."

Jake glanced across the room to the other two

239

tubes. "Shit!" Running around, he stood over the next tube.

Griggs turned around. "What is it?"

Jake pointed to the second tube. "It's Christina Anderson."

Jake moved over to the second tube. Christina's familiar face and blonde hair were still frozen in the tube. She had a look of grief on her face. Spinning around, he grabbed Yokama by the throat and slammed his face on Christina's tube. Shoving his gun hard into the back of Yokama's head, Jake leaned close to his ear. "Get her out of there right now," he growled Yokama's face was smashed against the tube. "I will, if you let me up." Griggs stepped over and placed his hand on Jake's shoulder. "Let him up."

Jake turned to look at Griggs. He nodded as he complied. Letting go of Yokama's neck, he slowly holstered his pistol.

Yokama slowly lifted himself up and straightened his lab jacket. "This will take several minutes to get both of them thawed out. You'll need to back off and let me do my work."

Jake agreed. "If you do anything sneaky, I swear I'll shoot you dead where you stand."

Yokama nodded and went hastily to work on his keypad.

Griggs put his arm around Jake and walked him to the far corner of the room. "I realize you know that girl, but you've got to keep a cool head. You could blow our whole mission."

"I lost my head. I'm sorry."

"It's all right. Just try and keep your personal feelings in check."

Jake understood. Looking past Griggs, he stared at the third and final tube in the room. Pushing past Griggs, he stopped in front of the tube and carefully laid his hands on it. "Major, could you come look at this?"

"What is it?" He walked up to the tube. "This is Jonathan Anderson."

Griggs stared at Anderson's lifeless body. "I thought he was dead." Yokama cut in. "He is."

Jake turned around to face the small Asian researcher. "Then why is he here?" "His genes are still salvageable. When new personnel come to the base, they are all checked for the correct genes for our test."

Griggs stepped forward. "You mean when I arrived you tested me?" "Yes. It's part of the basic physical. We always take a blood sample." "Son of a bitch," Griggs muttered.

Jake tapped his fingers on Christina's tube. "How long until the procedure is done? We need these two girls out of here."

Yokama checked his screen. "I'm almost ready to begin thawing them out."

***

Perry slammed his fist down on his desk. "How could they do this to me?"

Hunter was calmly sitting across from him. His legs were crossed with his hands laid leisurely on top of them. "I'm confident the President will overturn their decision. After all, you are his top military advisor."

Perry leaned back in his chair and steepled his fingers. "I wish I was as sure as you were about this whole situation," he rubbed his chin. "The

241

President's policies on the military aren't quite what they used to be. After that whole draft dodging bullshit surfaced in the media, he has been very quick to do whatever it takes to silence his military detractors. 'Commander in Chief' my ass," Perry muttered to himself.

"Sir, the President would be lost without you." Perry stood up. "The man's already lost."

Hunter folded his hands in his lap. Inside, he knew this would be very good for his career. "That may be, but you are a five star general. They just can't kick you out with all the things you know."

Perry turned to look out his window. Crews were now on the tarmac dragging the bodies off and cleaning up the wreckage so the tests could continue. "Let's put that all aside for now. I have a feeling as soon as the advisors see this successful test, they'll change their minds." He returned to his padded leather seat. "My main priority right now is to find Major Griggs and Jake Silver. I've already assigned a team to locate them, but these men have proven to be extremely resourceful. I want you to put the base on full alert until we find them."

Hunter nodded. "What are you going to do with them once you find them, sir?" An evil smirk slowly spread across Perry's face. "I will *personally* see to their deaths."

***

The ancient computers slowly struggled to life. When it had impacted, some of its systems had been damaged. Several workers had been moving briskly over the ship repairing it as quickly as possible. It had been sent here to complete a task. Its creators were trying to rectify a situation they had

242

inadvertently created over a millennium before. Lights and dials whirred with electricity as the computer slowly powered up. It would complete its task.

CHAPTER SIXTEEN

Jake watched as a surge of electricity flowed through Christina's tube. Before their eyes, the green fluid slowly began to liquefy. Christina's still body began to move and her hair flowed in the liquid. Her mouth opened and a bubble of air surfaced to the top of the tube. Griggs watched carefully as Yokama hit several keys on his computer.

"How much longer will this take?" Griggs was getting impatient.

Yokama calmly turned to the two men. "You must give me the necessary time to work. If I rush the process, they could go into shock and die from being pulled out of hibernation too quickly."

Jake wondered if he was telling the truth or just buying time. He had to make a decision. "Speed the process up, Doctor."

"Are you insane! Didn't you just hear me? It could kill them!"

Jake pulled out his gun and jammed it into Yokama's ribs. "Speed it up, or you'll die." He watched as a bead of sweat rolled down the man's forehead.

"Okay, okay. Just give me room to work."

Pulling his pistol away, he took several steps back. He carefully watched as the two tubes surged with life. Several pipes connected to the top and bottom of the tubes quickly filled with the green liquid as they pumped it out. He watched as the two girls inside began to shiver as the heated solution was removed.

"Are they okay?"

Yokama nodded. "This is a completely normal response. A person's body engulfed in the fluid for long periods of time shuts down its internal heater because of the constant heat of the fluid. In essence, it will take them a little while to relight their furnaces."

Jake didn't even pretend to understand. He turned around to see Griggs standing over Anderson's tube. He slowly walked over and stood beside him. "What's wrong?"

Griggs shook his head. "I just can't get over the fact we're treating people like this here at the facility."

"What did you think they did here?"

"I knew they tested Top Secret aircraft and alien technology," he rubbed his hand across his face, "but not abduct citizens right out of their homes and detain them indefinitely in these tubes."

"Were you assigned here, or did you ask for this tour?" Jake asked quietly.

"I wanted to be here. In the service, this is considered the best tour one can get. One sees action almost every day and the person is protecting our nation."

"But you're also violating the nation's rights by taking people and lying to them about the nature of this facility."

"I realize that now."

Jake patted him on the shoulder and turned around. He knew Griggs needed some time to sort things out in his mind. He stared at Yokama. "Are we almost done?"

245

Yokama was carefully keeping an eye on the two women's stats on his monitors. "They seem to be coming out of the hibernation very well. It's probably because neither of the women were in stasis for more than two weeks."

"Good. Is there anything I can do?"

Yokama pointed to a door on the opposite side of the room. "Get some robes out of that closet."

Jake complied. Opening the door, he found stacks of plain blue robes and several pairs of sandals on the bottom shelf. He quickly pulled out two robes and two pairs of sandals and laid them on Anderson's tube.

Yokama directed him toward Doctor Robinson's tube. "She'll be the first out. I need you to be prepared to open her tube."

Jake nodded and moved toward her tube. "How do I open this thing?"

Yokama pointed to a small red button on the tube's control panel. "When I say so, press the red button. That will open her tube. After that, you'll need to help her out."

Jake watched as Yokama returned to his instruments. He tapped in several commands on the keyboard. "Get ready."

A fine mist filled the tube but was immediately sucked out. "What was that?" "Merely a cleaning and disinfecting agent."

Jake quickly made his way over to Anderson's tube and grabbed one of the robes. Returning to Robinson's tube, he laid the robe over the end and knelt down by the control panel.

"Here we go." Yokama clicked a button. "Open her tube."

Jake hit the button and was met by a loud hissing sound. Standing, he watched the tube slowly open. Robinson's eyes shot open and she let forth a primal scream. Jake quickly pressed his hand over her mouth and tried to quiet her.

"Please stop," he said in a quiet, comforting voice. "My name is Jake Silver and I'm here to help you."

She stopped screaming. She wasn't sure why, but she believed him. She was violently shivering. "I'm so cold." Her teeth were chattering.

Jake grabbed her hand and slowly helped her out of the tube. Her legs were weak from inactivity, making it very difficult for her to stand. Jake reached over and grabbed the robe. Opening it, she quickly slid into it and wrapped it around herself. "Is that a little better?"

She nodded. "Yes." She looked around the room. "Where am I?"

Yokama stepped forward. "You mean you don't remember being brought here?" She shook her head trying to loosen the cobwebs. "Vaguely." She ran her hand through her wet hair. "The last thing I remember is being in Egypt and running from several soldiers..." she trailed off. "I feel terrible."

Jake helped her over to a row of chairs on the far wall and seated her. "Just sit here for a moment and relax. The effects of the hibernation will wear off in a few moments."

Yokama turned around to Jake. "Christina is ready."

Jake knelt down next to her and placed his hand on Alex's shoulder. "I'll be right back."

She nodded as he stood and walked toward

Christina's tube. He shot Yokama a look. "Same as before?"

Yokama nodded as he stared at his screens. "Hold on." He rechecked his screens. "Something's wrong!" He quickly moved to Christina's tube and hit the release button. Jake and Griggs watched as Christina began to shake violently. "She must be having a reaction to the fluid!"

"Why would she be having it now? You just drained it out of the tube!"

"When we inject the fluid, it slows down the patient's metabolism." He grabbed a syringe off a nearby table and filled it with adrenaline. "If a patient has a reaction to the fluid, it won't register it until we bring them out of hibernation."

Jake was panicking. "Has this happened before?"

"Only once. Hold her down." Jake and Griggs grabbed her arms and tried to steady her.

"What are you going to do?"

"I'm going to inject her with a shot of adrenaline. This should speed up the reaction, or..."

"Or what?"

"Or it will kill her."

Jake stared at the small Asian man. "Rest assured, Doctor, if she dies, so will you."

Yokama looked at Jake with fear in his eyes. Slowly, he stabbed the needle into Christina's chest just above her heart. Placing his thumb on the plunger, he quickly injected the adrenaline into her heart. Christina let out a blood-curdling scream. The three men stepped back. Yokama returned to his monitors to see what was happening.

Turning back to Jake, he smiled. "The injection

is working. It's moving the reaction faster through her body. She's going to be fine in a moment." He hit a key on his panel and another fine mist sprayed over Christina's body. Yokama watched as some of the spray flew out of the tube. It gave him an idea. Slowly reaching into the tube, he redirected the nozzle upwards and quickly hit the key again. Mist sprayed out toward Jake and Griggs.

Jake fell backward when the soapy mist hit him in the eyes. Griggs doubled over, trying to rub the mist out of his eyes. Seizing his opportunity, Yokama ran to the main door and jumped through it. On the other side, he quickly located a small red box with a glass plate over it. The box had a small white label on it that read 'Alarm'. Reaching back, he sent his fist crashing through the glass revealing a small red lever inside. Quickly pulling it, several klaxons immediately began to sound. Red security lights went on all over the research quarter of the facility. He leaned up against the wall. He knew the base security force would be here any moment.

Jake tried to rub the mist out of his eyes to no avail. Drawing his pistol, he muttered several curses under his breath. His eyes were welled up with tears making it extremely difficult to see where he was going. He bumped into Alex's empty tube as he made his way toward the door Yokama had run through.

Stepping through the door, he stumbled over Yokama's outstretched leg. Jake hit the ground hard. Quickly moving forward, Yokama kicked the gun out of Jake's hand and delivered a savage blow to his head. Jake moaned in agony. Yokama turned and started to run toward the dislodged gun.

Thinking quickly, Jake rolled over and shot his hand out wildly toward the researcher's legs. Luckily, he hit his mark and tripped him.

Standing, Jake blinked his eyes several times trying to clear the tears from them. Before he could reach the gun, Yokama was on his feet. The small researcher threw off his lab coat and sent a barrage of punches into Jake's face and stomach. Jake stumbled back toward one of the tubes. Yokama advanced, kicking Jake in the knee. Jake dropped to the ground in pain. All he could see through his blurry vision was a dark form moving toward him.

Yokama leapt off the ground and caught Jake squarely in the face with a high kick. Jake fell to the floor bleeding. He knew his nose was broken. He felt the researcher grab him by the collar and stand him up. Jake tried to cover up, but not before Yokama delivered another blow to his stomach. Jake doubled over. Grabbing the back of his head, Yokama slammed Jake's already broken nose into his knee dropping the bleeding man to the floor.

Yokama reached over and started to pick up the gun when he heard a voice behind him. "Don't move, Doctor."

Yokama quickly scooped up the gun and pointed it toward the voice. He was startled to see Alex standing in the door with her weapon trained on him. He smiled. "How are you feeling?"

Alex sneered. "You need to pay for all the people you've done this to. You are one sick son of a bitch."

"I think not. I—" The sound of the gunshot startled him. Slowly looking down, he saw blood gushing from a bullet hole in the middle of his chest. Wiping his hand across it, he stared at the blood on his fingers. Looking up at Alex with disbelief in his eyes, he quickly dropped to his knees, then to the floor.

"I couldn't stand to listen to another word." She dropped the gun on the floor and leaned up against the doorway. Griggs and Christina joined her.

Stepping past her, Griggs moved to his friend lying on the floor. Lifting him up, he leaned Jake against one of the tubes. "You okay?"

He wiped some of the blood running from his nose on his hand. He looked up at Griggs with a smile. "When did they start teaching martial arts at MIT?" Griggs laughed as he helped Jake off the floor.

***

Colonel Hunter stood on a small platform in front of ten men dressed totally in black in an empty gray room. The men stood at attention with their hands clasped behind their backs and their feet spread shoulder width apart.

Hunter addressed the men. "You are the base's finest, and I expect the best from you."

The men stood stone-faced as they looked at Hunter.

"I'm sure you're all wondering why I've assembled General Perry's crack team."

Hunter paced back and forth on a platform in front of the men. "Two renegade soldiers are loose on the base. I want you to apprehend them." He folded his hands behind his back. "These men have proven to be extremely dangerous and crafty. This will be a difficult task for you, but I'm assured by your past performances that you will succeed." He stepped down off the platform and approached the CO of the group. "Captain Dylan, can your men handle this?"

Dylan nodded. "Yes, Colonel," he replied in his loudest voice. "My team is the best there is. We will not fail."

He walked around Dylan and stood in front of his men. "Very good. You'll find your objectives and surveillance photos of the two men in a folder on the table in front of you. Good hunting, gentlemen." Hunter turned and briskly strode out of the room.

Dylan quickly snapped around and faced his men. "I want full gear and weapon checks in ten minutes. We are going to find these men and bring them in. We have a reputation to uphold."

His men answered in unison, "Yes, sir!"

"Very well. Dismissed." Dylan watched as his men swiftly exited the room.

Pivoting on his left heel, he spun around and began to walk toward the table. He flipped open the brown folder and browsed the first page.

APPREHEND MAJOR JASON GRIGGS AND LIEUTENANT JACOB SILVER. DEADLY FORCE IS AUTHORIZED, BUT ONLY IN A FINAL CAPACITY.

Flipping the page, he removed two black and white surveillance photographs of Griggs and Silver and placed them in the right breast pocket of his vest. Closing the folder, he tucked it under his arm and slowly made his way toward the door. His team had never failed a mission and he would be damned if this was the first. He wondered why Special Forces had been called in to capture two renegade soldiers. He felt his time was too valuable to be wasting on two loose cannons. Stepping out the door, he started the long walk down to the armory where he would find his men suiting up for the task at hand.

***

The four of them walked slowly along the corridor. The wide gray hall was dimly lit. It had base directories hung on the wall every few feet. Griggs was deep in thought leading the group, while Jake was humming to himself while he brought up the rear. Christina and Alex were still wet and shivering as they clasped the robes tightly around their bodies.

Jake quickened his pace to catch up with the girls. "Are you two okay?"

Both women nodded. Christina turned to look at Jake. "I knew it all the time." He was confused. "Knew what?"

"That you would come and get me."

He smiled. "That's what I'm here for, kid." He looked at the other girl. "I don't think I ever caught your name."

"My name is Alex. Alex Robinson." "What were you doing in Egypt, Alex?"

"I am a UFOlogist. My research led me to a major find in Egypt." "What kind of find?"

"That doesn't matter." Her voice was cold. It was obvious to Jake that she didn't want to talk.

He took on a sarcastic tone. "I apologize. I thought it might be nice to find out a little about the person we risked our lives to save."

She stopped and pointed a finger in his face. "Don't you dare pin that shit on me." She startled him. "I—"

"I watched one of my best friends die because of what I found there! Then I was taken by soldiers and stuck in a vat of that green shit!" She lowered her finger and stepped back. "Now if you don't mind, I'd rather not talk about it."

Jake's eyes were wide. "I'm sorry. I had no idea you lost your friend. I figured you were one of the run of the mill abductees."

"Well you 'figured' wrong."

"All I know is that General Davis sent us here to get you out. I'm standing up to my end of the deal." He turned around and took a couple steps away from the group.

"Did you say General Davis?" "Yeah, so what?"

"General Thomas Davis?"

Jake thought for a moment. "Yeah, I think that's his first name. Why?" She turned around and started walking. "It's nothing."

"Oh, no." He trotted up to her and grabbed her by the arm. "You don't arouse my curiosity then tell me it's nothing. How do you know General Davis?"

"He's..." She kicked her feet like a child not wanting to tell their parents they had lost their best pair of mittens on the schoolyard. "He's my father."

Griggs spun around. "What?"

"We haven't seen each other in almost fifteen years. When my mother died, he decided to pursue a full-time military career. I guess he thought that keeping himself busy was the best way to deal with mom's death." She got lost in the memories of her mother for a moment.

Jake shook her arm gently. "Then what, Alex?"

She snapped back to the present. "He ditched me with my grandparents. I never saw him again. Sure, he sent the occasional birthday or Christmas card, but that was it."

"Then why do you have different last names?"

"I was so angry at him for abandoning me, I changed my name to my mother's maiden name. I was only fifteen when he left."

Griggs stepped up to Alex and Jake. "That's a very touching story, but we've got to keep going." The two nodded and startled to move behind Griggs and Christina.

"Davis said you were they 'key'. Do you know what he was talking about?" Jake asked curiously.

"The key to what?"

"I was hoping you could tell me."

"I'm sorry. I don't know what you're talking about."

Jake cursed under his breath. "So we were probably sent here to rescue you because you're his daughter." He turned around and took a couple of steps away from the group. He started to mutter to himself.

Suddenly, machine gun fire erupted from behind them hitting the wall right next to Jake. Startled, he spun around and caught sight of a large group of fully armed men charging up from behind. "Shit! Run!"

Everyone in the small group broke into a dead sprint. Machine gun fire slammed into the walls all around them. Griggs spotted an open door up ahead. "In there!"

Griggs stood at the door, directing the two women in. Jake dove through it landing on the floor with a thud. Griggs followed him into the room just as a volley of bullets tore through the wood, right where he had been standing. Griggs quickly scanned the room. It was a small office with one desk on the far wall and several potted plants in the corners. The walls were bare except for a framed portrait of the President and a large picture window behind the desk. "Dammit." Griggs knew his options were limited. "Jake, get the girls behind the desk. You and I will hold them off at the door."

Jake nodded and quickly moved the two women behind the desk. "Stay there and keep your heads down."

Another wave of bullets slammed into the doorframe sending slivers of wood flying in all directions. Griggs quickly threw his arm over his face and jumped back. Both men quickly flattened themselves against the wall.

Griggs turned to Jake and smiled. "Just hope they don't have anything bigger than a machine gun."

"That's a comforting thought."

Griggs rolled around the edge of the door and snapped off three short bursts from his weapon, then quickly retreated. "We're outnumbered. There's no way we can beat these guys."

Just then, a small cylinder-shaped object slammed against the door and fell on the floor next to the two. Griggs, to his horror, immediately recognized the object. "It's a tear gas canister! Get back!" With one foot, he kicked the canister out of the door just as it began to spray the noxious chemicals into the air. "We need to get out of here right now!"

Jake quickly weighed their options. Raising his gun, he fired at the window shattering the glass. "We're going out the window!"

Griggs leaned out into the night air and looked down. "Are you insane? We're a full story up!"

Jake pointed down to a truck with a canvas top. "That should break our fall." "No way!"

One of the soldiers wearing a full-face gasmask broke through the fog rapidly filling the room. He spotted the two standing next to the window and started firing. Jake quickly spun around and unleashed a wave of bullets from his gun hitting the man squarely in the chest.

"We don't have a choice! Go!"

Griggs climbed up on the windowsill and stared down at the ground. Mustering his courage, he leapt out the window and sailed down toward the truck. Hitting the canvas top hard, he sat up and slowly slid off to the ground. He waved up to Jake.

Reaching down, Jake grabbed Christina's arm and lifted her to the window. "Jump, Christina!"

She screamed. "I can't! I'm afraid of heights!"

Jake squeezed the trigger and fired off several rounds through the door. "If you don't, you'll be dead!"

She closed her eyes and jumped. Jake watched as she landed on the top of the truck with a thud. She quickly slid off into Griggs' waiting arms. Jake returned his attention to the door as another soldier broke through the fog. He fired twice hitting the desk and the wall next to Jake. Returning fire, Jake hit the soldier in the head knocking him to the floor writhing in pain.

He grabbed Alex. "You're next!"

Alex was climbing up into the window just as two more soldiers emerged from the fog. Jake quickly snapped off several rounds hitting the first soldier, but the second one fired, hitting Alex. Letting out a scream, she slipped awkwardly out the window and fell.

"No!" Jake pulled the trigger. Nothing. "Out of ammo." Tossing the gun as hard as he could at the soldier, Jake jumped over the desk and delivered several swift punches to the soldier's midsection dropping him. Turning around, he sprinted for the window as three more soldiers jumped through the thick haze of chemicals. Bullets whizzed past his head as he leapt onto the desk, then dove headfirst out the window.

The world seemed to slow down as he watched the ground rushing up toward him. Inadvertently twisting his body in the air, he landed on the roof of the truck flat on his back. Pain shot through his body as the windows of the cab exploded with the force of his impact. A bullet slammed into the roof of the truck right next to his head. Looking up, he saw several soldiers leaning out the window and firing at him. Swiftly, he rolled off the top and onto the hood. Scooting to the edge, he jumped off and ran toward where the other three were waiting.

Looking around, they found themselves standing in front of the massive doors to the hangar. Jake smiled. "Well, we're back to where we started." He looked at Alex. "Are you okay? Where did the bullet hit you?"

She pulled up the robe to show where the bullet had grazed her leg. "It's not bad. Just startled the hell out of me."

"Good." He looked at the other two. "You guys all right?"

Christina nodded. "I think I landed wrong." She held up her hand. Two of her fingers were smashed in at the knuckles and quickly turning a deep purple. "The major says I broke my fingers, but I'll be okay."

Jake slapped Griggs on the shoulder. "Where to now, boss?" "We have the girls. We just need to get out of here."

"How do you propose we do that?"

Both men turned and looked behind them. The tarmac was empty except for the two silver saucers. Jake looked at Griggs. "Can you fly?"

"A helicopter." He stared at the saucer. "That's probably very different from a helicopter.

***

Captain Dylan stared at the cloud of gas at the end of the hallway. He tapped two of his men on the shoulder and pointed down the hall. "Go see what the hell happened in there." Both men quickly jogged down the hall and stepped in the door. Dylan waited patiently for their return.

One of the men came running back. "Sir, the targets have escaped." "How?"

"It seems they jumped out the window." "How many of our men are wounded?"

"One, sir. The other three you sent in are dead."

Anger rapidly welled up inside him, but he tried to remain calm. "Lieutenant, split the remaining men up into two groups. I'll take group one, and you'll command group two. Take your team back the way we came, just in case they decide to double back. I'll take my team downstairs."

259

The lieutenant nodded and started off toward the men. "Lieutenant?"

He stopped and turned around. "Yes, sir?"

"I am authorizing deadly force. Those bastards killed three of my men. I want them dead."

"Yes, sir." The lieutenant turned around and continued back toward the men. Dylan took several steps forward and stopped. Reaching up to his throat, he keyed his mic. "Colonel Hunter?"

The speaker in his ear crackled to life. "Yes, Captain. Go ahead." "We found the subjects."

"Good, do you have them in custody?"

"No, sir. They have eluded us and killed three of my men."

The speaker was quiet for a moment. "I thought I assigned the best, Captain Dylan."

"You did, sir."

"Then I want results!" Hunter yelled through the speaker.

"Yes, sir. I'm splitting my team up into two groups of three. This way, we have more of a chance of finding the subjects and apprehending them."

"Good. See to it that you don't fail me, Captain."

"Yes, sir." Dylan released the button on his mic shutting it off. He despised being threatened. He hated Hunter even more after that. Turning around, he made his way back to his men. They were standing in their respective groups waiting for the order to begin the search. "Team one, you're with me. Team two: you're with Lieutenant Lynn. I want safeties off. You are authorized to use deadly force to bring in the subjects." He stared at the two groups of steely-faced men. Lifting his weapon, he cocked it and hung it at his side. "Lock and load."

CHAPTER SEVENTEEN

The ancient ship slowly whirred to life. The humming sound of electricity filled the hallways of the darkened craft. Lights on the ceiling of the halls and rooms began to flicker on and the mighty engines slowly began to turn.

For eons, this craft had been one of the flagships in its fleet. It had been involved in battles, and was there when new civilizations had been discovered. Its computer banks recalled when it had first run across this small, backwater planet. It had been part of an armada of ships sent to Earth to study mankind. They were living in caves and had just discovered fire when the armada arrived.

It summoned its workers to the bridge. Several lanky beings immediately emerged from a door. Their large heads and huge almond-shaped black eyes were their most outstanding feature. The race of machines which had spawned the ship and its brethren had genetically engineered this race of beings to handle minute repairs during space travel the craft itself couldn't. They were also used a great deal in examining creatures brought aboard for study. The beings were also designed to have extremely long lives due to the lengthy travel times associated with space flights. The ship had the same core crew since it went online thousands of years ago.

Through a series of beeps, clicks and squeaks, the computer instructed the workers to remove the bodies of the two soldiers killed in the control room

what I've been looking for my whole life. Undeniable proof of the existence of extra-terrestrials."

"What are you talking about, Alex?" Christina was staring at the shiny silver walls. Alex turned to look at the young girl standing next to her. "I'm a UFOlogist. I've spent a good portion of my life in search of UFOs and the existence of extra-terrestrials, and this is it. *This* is what I've been looking for."

"Why have you been looking for them?"

"It really started out as a hobby after my father left, but after a while, it just became my passion. I attended college at UCLA where I received a Ph.D. in ancient history."

"Why did you get a degree in ancient history if you wanted to study UFOs?"

"I *was* studying them. I began to realize that if I went back and studied some of the ancient texts, including the bible, I'd find literally thousands of references to beings who came down from the sky and influenced our culture. I wanted to find out if these were in anyway relatable to our modern day depiction of extra-terrestrials and UFOs. That's why I got a degree in ancient history."

Griggs snapped around. "Be quiet. If there's any one in here, they'll be able to hear you. You're giving away our location."

The two women realized what they had been doing and quickly stopped talking. Griggs turned back around just in time to see a man rushing him. The man threw his weight against Griggs knocking him to the floor. Jake sprinted toward the two men pushing Christina and Alex out of the way. Quickly

265

reaching down, he ripped the man off Griggs and delivered a strong right jab to his jaw. The man crumpled to the floor at Jake's feet.

Griggs lifted a hand to Jake to be helped up. "I could've handled him by myself." "I know." Jake lifted him off the floor.

"He just got the jump on me."

Jake smiled and patted him on the back. Suddenly, Jake watched as Griggs' eyes widened. He reared back to throw a punch. Quickly dropping down, he saw Griggs throw a punch over his head.

Jake stood up. "What the hell are you doing?"

Griggs pointed over Jake's shoulder to a man slowly sliding down the wall. "Looks like we're even."

Jake nodded and walked back toward the two women. Checking to see if they were all right, the four continued on their way. Griggs rounded another corner and stopped when he realized he was standing on the bridge. The walls and floors had been done in the same way as the rest of the ship. Thin layers of aluminum had been laid down to cover the craft's interior. Three main chairs stood in a triangle formation in the center of the room. Each of them had a bank of controls on their left side. Two more chairs sat under a large view screen with a row of computers and controls running along the front of the ship.

Alex and Christina slowly crept into the room and stood with their backs against the back wall. "Jesus," Alex muttered.

Jake stepped into the room and stood next to Griggs. He looked around the bridge in awe. "Well, Major, do you think you can fly this?"

Griggs let out an uneasy laugh. "Maybe when hell freezes over. This is so far removed from a helicopter."

"We don't have a lot of options here, Major. We need to get the hell out of here." "God dammit! I don't know what I'm doing!"

Machine gun fire erupted throughout the bridge. Everyone immediately hit the ground and covered their heads. "What the hell is going on?" Christina screamed.

Griggs quickly popped his head up. Two armed soldiers were standing in the doorway with weapons drawn. He ducked his head back down as gunfire filled the room again. "Two guards blocking the door."

Jake drew his pistol and fired at the soldiers unsuccessfully. Griggs carefully leaned around the chair and fired hitting one of the guards in the chest. Jumping up, he and Jake each emptied an entire clip into the remaining soldier.

"It's probably a pretty good bet they know what we're trying to do."

Alex helped Christina off the floor and stared at the two dead bodies lying in the doorway. "We need to get out of here!"

Griggs agreed. "I'm not going to be able to fly this thing, Silver."

Jake nodded grudgingly. He knew heading back into the base would be very difficult and all four of them would most likely end up dead. He felt like he was between a rock and a hard place. His mind was rapidly searching for alternatives. They could hide in the large ship, but they would eventually be rooted out and killed. Their options were very, very limited. "We need options. Any suggestions?" The other three members of the group stood silently as they thought. In turn, they each looked at Jake and shook their heads.

Jake finally made a snap decision. "Come on. We're getting out of here." Walking out into the hallway, he checked for soldiers. "Coast is clear. Let's go."

The other three quickly followed Jake back through the winding passages that led to the main entrance. Cautiously, he peered around the edge of the portal and was met by a wave of machine gun rounds slamming against the silvery hull of the ship.

"We're surrounded." He slowly turned around to the others with a strange look on his face. "Do any of you feel that?"

CHAPTER EIGHTEEN

The workers had finally completed their task. No trace of the gaping tear in the hull was visible, where it once was, there was now only a smooth surface. Standing, the three stepped back and checked their work for flaws. Turning around, they made their way back to the control room. Stepping into the cavernous room, they stopped and stood at attention.

The huge view screen at the center of the room flickered to life. Images of the nearby base were replaced with several images of the recovered saucers inside. The computer clicked and whistled its instructions to the workers. Swiftly turning around, the workers strode out the room toward their next duty.

It thought about its workers. It knew it couldn't operate at full capacity without them. They had become part of the ship, yet somehow, still very detached. The machine inhabitants of the ship's home world had engineered the beings to be completely reliant on them. They were devoid of free will and personal thoughts. Upon reaching maturity, each individual worker was implanted with a specially designed chip which allowed the computer to link directly to the being's mind. In this fashion, the computer was aware of what every worker was doing at all times. In essence, becoming a living piece of the ship.

The ship shuddered to life. It was time. The ground began to shake as it slowly pulled itself out of the crater it had created upon impact. Lifting slowly into the sky, it turned south toward the base.

***

General Davis was sitting alone when a low frequency rumble began to rattle his office. Grabbing the side of his desk, he tried to keep it still as the tremors worsened. The desk clattered its way across his office, smashing his fingers between it and the wall. Pulling his hand out quickly, he yelled out in pain. Quickly standing, he cupped his hands over his ears to try and block out the noise pounding in his head. The boxes stacked in the corner crumbled to the floor spraying their precious cargo in all directions. Running toward his door, he watched as the translucent pane of glass shattered in front of him. A shard of glass rocketed away from the door slicing across his right cheek.

Blood spilled from the open wound onto the collar of his white shirt.

Grabbing for the doorknob, he flung open the door and stepped into the hallway. The florescent lights above him shattered one by one in a blaze of sparks, leaving him in the empty darkness of the hall. Red emergency lights quickly lit up, only to be shattered by the low rumble.

Feeling along the wall, he found his way to the door and tried to open it. "Damn, still locked," he moaned to himself. Rearing back, he sent his balled fist into the control panel smashing it. He pulled away his bleeding knuckles and smelled the smoke emanating from the panel. He hoped knocking out the control panel would kill the power to the door. Pushing on the sliding door, he felt it budge. A large smile crossed his face as he pushed it open.

270

Stepping into the next dark hallway, he felt his way along the wall until he reached the door that led into the main hangar. This was easy for him. He knew this base like the back of his hand. He could walk it blindfolded and never run into anything.

The rumble was steadily getting louder. He felt it pounding in his head. Pushing on the door, he slowly slid it open and stepped into the devastated hangar. "What the hell happened here?" He stared at the charred corpses of soldiers and the piles of smoking rubble that used to be jets. Flames still burned out of control on all sides of the cavernous room.

Running toward the tarmac, he caught sight of several armed soldiers firing on one of the saucers. One of the soldiers was dead on the ground, and several others were running away from the tarmac trying to get away from the rumble.

Drawing his weapon, he carefully walked around until he could see into the small hatch of the ship. A man quickly ducked his head out and fired several rounds wildly at the soldiers. The general's eyes went wide. "Silver!"

***

Colonel Hunter's monitors exploded sending shards of glass shooting in all directions. Covering his face with his arms, he fell out of the chair hitting the floor. Looking around, he watched the other screens in the room crack and explode. His men fell to the floor engulfed in flames from their short-circuiting terminals. Screams of horror and pain flooded the room as a low rumbling reverberated off the steel walls while smoke poured out of the damaged screens and terminals. Hunter stood and

271

ran for the door. Grabbing two of his men off the floor, he instructed them to force the door open.

One of his men stopped pushing and looked back at him with char marks on his face. "Sir, it won't budge!" Hunter could hear the fear in his voice.

"The hell it won't. Stand back!" he shouted over the roar of the flames. Drawing his pistol, he squeezed off several rounds into the control box. "Now try!"

The two men leaned into the door and pushed it open. Throwing the two men out of the way, Hunter quickly made his way down the hallway and to the next door. Repeating the process, he shot the control box and forced the door open. Stepping into the hangar bay, he was tripped by several soldiers running toward him blindly with their hands over their ears.

The rumble affected him too. His vision began to blur while he was trying to maintain his footing. The sides of his head began to pound as the rumble worsened. Suddenly, blood spurted from his ears as his eardrums exploded. Grabbing his ears, he completely lost his balance and tumbled to the floor. Struggling to lift himself, he crumpled back down to the floor.

Using all his determination, he quickly hit his mic and yelled into it. "General Perry! We've got a problem!" A wave of nausea swept over him as his vision grew dark. He fell a final time to the floor.

***

General Perry had problems of his own. Only moments before, he was watching the action on the tarmac below. Captain Dylan's soldiers had the

272

fugitives cornered inside one of the saucers. The room was abruptly filled with a low-pitched rumble that began to rattle his desk and knock over his plants. Taking several steps back away from the window, he turned to run out the door when he heard a cracking noise. Cautiously turning around, he saw a huge crack in the window behind him. Fear gripped his mind as it began to web out in all directions.

"Shit!" The giant picture window exploded into millions of tiny, razor-sharp fragments. One of the larger shards of glass sliced through his uniform and embedded itself into his chest. Stumbling toward the door, he tripped over one of his fallen plants and stumbled to the floor. He quickly rolled over just in time to see his desk topple over on top of him breaking his right leg. He screamed in pain as he tried to lift the heavy steel desk off himself.

***

The low frequency was still assaulting the base. Stepping forward, Davis easily picked off the three remaining soldiers with his pistol. Holstering it, he walked toward the open hatch of the saucer. "Silver!"

Jake slowly peeked his head out and caught sight of the four dead soldiers lying in front of the saucer. Redirecting his attention, he caught sight of Davis. "General!" He turned back to the three accompanying him. "Let's go."

The four people walked out of the ship and down to Davis. Davis grabbed Jake by the arm and led him into the hangar. Alex and Christina were covering their ears to try and stop the pounding. Then as suddenly as it began, it stopped. They all stood straight and looked around in confusion.

Jake glanced at Davis. "What the hell was that?"

"I don't know, but it sure wreaked havoc here at the base." He turned and caught sight of his daughter. He breathed a sigh of relief. "Alex." He walked toward her. "Are you all right?"

She shot him an icy gaze. "No thanks to you."

"What do you mean?"

"I mean, if you hadn't sent your goons out to get me, I never would've been here in the first place."

"I had no idea that was you in Egypt, Alex. As soon as I found out, I devised a way to get you out of here."

"I really appreciate that, *Dad*," she said with anger.

Griggs stepped between the two. "I really hate to break up this family reunion, but right now, we need to get out of here."

Christina nodded. "I want to go home."

Jake agreed. "This has been fun, but I really think we should all be going. How do we get out of here?"

Davis turned his attention away from his daughter and thought for a moment. "Major Griggs, you are qualified to fly a helicopter, aren't you?"

Griggs nodded. "But I haven't logged a lot of flight time under my belt." "We've gone down this road before, General. He can't fly the saucer." Davis shot Jake a bewildered look. "What the hell are you talking about?"

Jake smiled sheepishly at Davis. "We wanted Griggs to fly us out of here in the saucer."

"What in the hell possessed you to think of that?"

"It's the first thing that popped into my head. Isn't that what you were talking about?"

"No." He continued to stare in awe at Jake. "I was thinking of using that helicopter over there." He pointed at a chopper parked on the far side of the tarmac.

"Okay." Jake turned and started to walk toward the chopper followed by Griggs and Christina.

Davis took a step closer to Alex. "You're still angry at me for leaving after your mother died, aren't you?"

"Jesus Christ, Dad. Mom died and you left. How do you think that made me feel?"

"I realize you think I abandoned you, but—"

"You did abandon me. I grew up with Grandma and Grandpa."

He tried to hold her hand, but she pulled it away. "I needed a way to get through it. I chose to work." He grabbed her hand and stared into her eyes. This time, she let him hold it. "That was my decision and I regret it every day."

Tears welled up in her eyes. "I felt like you didn't love me."

"I'm so sorry, Alex. Your mother meant the world to me and when I lost her, I was devastated. I loved you so much, but I knew I would never be a good father to you."

The tears broke loose and streaked down her face. "You could've explained it to me. I was old enough to understand."

"I couldn't face you. I felt like a failure."

Just behind them, Hunter slowly began to

275

regain consciousness. Looking up, he saw Davis and Alex standing together in front of him. Lifting his weapon, he aimed the best he could and pulled the trigger. Davis screamed as the bullet tore through his upper back shattering his spine and puncturing one of his lungs. The force of the shot knocked him to the ground. Using all his strength, he rolled over and pulled his weapon out of its holster. Quickly aiming at Hunter, he pulled the trigger. The bullet slammed into Hunter's head.

Alex reached down and grabbed her father. "Dad! Are you okay?" He smiled. "No."

She placed her hands on both sides of his face, "Stay with me!" She quickly stood and screamed across the hangar for help.

Jake and Griggs came running across the room and stopped over Davis. Jake looked to Alex. "What happened?"

Alex was crying hysterically. She pointed to the dead body of Hunter lying behind them. "That man shot him!"

Griggs walked toward the body and kicked it over onto its back. "It's Colonel Hunter. He's dead."

Jake knelt down next to Davis. "General?"

Davis looked at Jake. "I don't think I'm going to be able to finish this journey." He looked over at his daughter and ran his hand across her face. "I love you, Alex."

She kissed his hand and held it tightly. "I love you too, Daddy." He grabbed Jake's shoulder. "Take care of my daughter, Silver." He nodded. "I will."

Davis' hand slipped off Jake's shoulder and fell

to the floor. Alex squeezed his hand tightly and quietly cried as he died. The two remained hunched over the fallen man for several minutes before standing. Jake scooped Alex into his arms and held her as she cried.

Jake muttered to himself. "Two dead fathers and two daughters under my care." Slowly, she pulled away from him and looked him in the eye. "Thank you for letting me see my father one more time, Jake." He nodded and smiled.

Griggs walked over and stood next to Jake and Alex. "We need to get going before reinforcements arrive."

The three began to walk briskly toward the awaiting helicopter when a bright flash of light filled the hangar. Holding his hand over his eyes, Jake struggled to see what was causing it. They slowly made their way toward the light. Walking out of the hangar, they caught sight of it. Alex let out an audible gasp.

A huge craft was hovering over the tarmac. Several apertures on the bottom of the ship were emitting beams of red and yellow light that looked to Jake like they were scanning the tarmac. The intense white light slowly faded to be replaced by a less harsh blue light. The red and yellow lights converged on the two saucers sitting on the runway, then blinked off. The four people standing next to the helicopter watched in awe as a large hatch on the bottom of the ship slowly slid open revealing a gaping hole.

Jake turned toward Griggs while keeping his eyes firmly glued to the ship. "Is that the same ship that crashed not far from here?"

Griggs assessed the craft. "It's hard to tell, but it looks very similar."

Everyone took a nervous step backward as the two saucers shuddered to life and slowly lifted skyward. The two crafts floated silently upward until they entered the bay of the giant ship hovering above them. The red and yellow lights reappeared. They shone directly into the hangar past the group hitting the large metal door at the rear.

Griggs pointed at the door. "That's where the other saucers are. It's locked up tighter that Fort Knox, though."

As the final words were leaving Griggs' mouth, the giant door began to slowly slide open. Jake smiled. "Guess you spoke too soon."

The door groaned as it stopped. Single file, the remaining saucers hovered out of the door toward the mighty ship waiting outside. The group watched in awe as the large saucers floated past them out of the hangar. Rising up, the saucers slowly made their way into the bay of the awaiting ship. Once they were all inside, the hatch slowly sealed shut. They all watched as the silver ship pulled slightly back from the hangar and stopped.

Jake felt a wave of fear roll through him for the first time as the ship angled itself toward the hangar. A small door opened at the front of the ship and a long slender tube extended out of it.

Grabbing Christina, Jake yelled for Griggs to grab Alex. "Run!" The four sprinted away from the hangar as quickly as they could.

The tube pulsed with energy as it heated up. Arcs of blue electricity flew off the tube in all directions. Suddenly, a green bolt of energy discharged with a deafening roar toward the hangar hitting it dead center. It exploded in a giant ball of red and green flames sending shards of wood, steel and rock sailing through the air in all directions. The shockwave from the explosion tore along the ground like a ripple in a pond knocking the four down onto the tarmac. Jake quickly threw himself on top of Christina and Griggs did the same for Alex to shield them from flying debris and shrapnel.

Jake turned his head around to see what happened. Flames arced high into the sky and black clouds of smoke billowed away from the demolished hangar. The large silvery ship hung overhead in a moment of silence as it retracted its weapon. It paused above the four.

A slim blue beam shot out the bottom of the ship and slammed into Jake's head. Flashes of images throughout the machine race's evolution cycled through his mind's eye. He closed his eyes tightly to try and block out the visions racing through his brain. His head throbbed from the mass of images flooding though it. Writhing on the ground, he slammed his hands to his temples trying to stop the pain. Slowly opening his eyes, he felt the pain pass.

He watched as the large sliver ship slowly turned around and immediately shot into the sky, then out of sight at an incredible speed. He rolled off Christina and laid flat on his back on the tarmac staring up at the sky. It had become a cloudy morning as the sun slowly rose through the clouds in the eastern sky giving everything a pink and orange color. He listened as thunder clapped and rain began to fall.

The large raindrops fell loudly on the tarmac next to them. Christina drew herself up into a sitting position next to Jake and lifted her head to the sky. She allowed the rain to fall on her face and run down her neck. It felt cleansing to her.

Griggs and Alex lifted themselves off the wet ground. She smiled and opened her arms palms to the sky. The rain fell heavily on her face and hands. "We made it."

Jake stood and quickly helped Christina off the ground. "I'm not sure about that yet. We still need to get out of here." He looked over at the charred wreckage of the helicopter. "It seems we've lost our ride."

Griggs pointed across the runway into the Nevada desert. "I think our best bet right now is just to walk out of here. All staff personnel will be busy dealing with the destruction."

Alex lowered her hands and stepped in front of Griggs. "I really don't feel up to walking all that way."

Christina glanced around the tarmac. "Why don't we just use one of those?" She pointed at several white Jeep Cherokees sitting on the far side of the runway.

Jake smiled and started walking toward them. "We're back in business."

The four climbed into the Jeep with the two women in the back and Jake and Griggs in the front. Jake slid behind the wheel and looked down at the ignition. "There's no key." He glanced over at Griggs and caught sight of a knife on his belt. Reaching over, he yanked the knife free and jammed it into the ignition. He twisted hard and the lock turned over starting the vehicle.

Alex laughed at Jake. "Where did you learn to do that?"

"I spent a summer in juvenile detention for stealing cars." He laughed. "Long story. Let's get out of here."

Stepping on the clutch, he pushed the gear shifter into reverse and slowly pulled the vehicle away from the building. Popping it into first gear, he hit the accelerator and sent the vehicle careening off into the desert away from the burning ruins of Area 51.

CHAPTER NINETEEN

The journey back to Las Vegas was an uneventful one to the satisfaction of the group in the white Jeep Cherokee. No words had been spoken between them as they had all retreated into their own minds in an effort to deal with everything they had just been through.

Jake guided the vehicle down a back street and parked it in front of a small dirty coffee shop. Turning around, he glanced over the other passengers in the vehicle. Griggs had fallen asleep in the passenger seat with his head laid back on the headrest. He had just started to wake up when Jake stopped. Alex had wrapped herself tighter in her robe and was biting her nails. Christina had been staring out the window the entire trip with her elbow resting on the edge of the door and her hand holding her head up. Jake knew she was taking it the hardest.

"Let's get a cup of coffee. I think we all need it."

Griggs nodded and got out of the Jeep and stretched. Alex slowly reached for the door handle and opened it. Christina didn't move.

He looked at Griggs and Alex. "You two go ahead. We'll join you in a minute." The two went on ahead. Climbing into the back seat with Christina, he closed the door. "Are you okay?"

She shook her head. "No."

"You can talk about it. It'll make you feel better."

She turned to him with tears in her eyes. "I miss my dad."

He slowly rubbed his hand up and down her back. "I lost my father when I was a little younger than you." He was trying to be as comforting as possible. "I can only tell you this, the pain never goes away, but you eventually learn to deal with it. I just want you to remember one thing. He gave his life to save yours. He loved you very much."

"I know he loved me. I just wish I could've told him that I loved him, too." "He already knew."

She smiled as the tears rolled down her cheeks.

Something occurred to him. Reaching into the back of the Jeep, he grabbed his black duffel bag and unzipped it. He rooted around inside until he found what he was looking for.

"I want you to take this," he opened a small black day planner and removed several large bills.

"I can't take your money."

"It's not mine. It's the fee your parents paid me." He pushed the money toward her.

She slowly took it.

"I want you and your mother to pack up what you can and buy plane tickets to get as far away from here as possible."

She leaned over and wrapped her arms around his neck. "Thank you, Jake." He returned the hug. "You're welcome. Now let's go get a cup of coffee."

Letting go, she reached over and opened the door. Getting out of the Jeep, her bare feet landed on the warm concrete. She turned to the east and stared at the rising sun. It rose through the sky casting shimmering images on the many glass

283

buildings dominating the Las Vegas skyline. Taking a deep breath of the cool morning air, she slowly exhaled it and savored its sweet taste. It was a brand new day for her. Things were going to be better for her from now on. She was going to make sure of that.

***

After dropping off Christina at her mother's house, the three made their way down into the heart of Sin City. They watched the people on the sparsely populated streets head out of the casinos with bleary eyes. Alex wondered if they were going home, or on to the next game. Jake pulled over in front of a massive casino and got out. He had gone back to his usual dress of jeans, a t-shirt and his brown leather jacket. Griggs stepped out next. He had removed the heavy gear he was wearing and had stripped down to a white t-shirt and a pair of jeans he had on under the jump suit. Alex exited the Jeep. She had traded the robe and sandals she was wearing for a plain blue dress Christina's mother had lent her.

Alex looked at Jake. "Why are we here?"

"We need to talk and I wanted to find the most public place I could." Griggs walked past Alex. "Just to be safe."

She stopped. "You think they'll still be after us? After what that ship did to the base?"

"I wouldn't put it past them," Jake answered grimly.

Walking into the casino, Jake was surprised to see a good portion of the tables and slot machines still occupied. He laughed out loud. "Don't these people ever go home?"

"I was just wondering the same thing," Alex replied.

Jake directed them to a small round table at the rear of the bar area. Small candles stood in the center of it, giving off a small amount of light from its flickering flame in the dimly lit bar. Excess light from the casino was filtering in, but it wasn't enough to brighten the place.

Griggs caught the attention of the waitress and ordered a beer. Alex stared at him in amazement. "Isn't it a little early for that?"

He shook his head and smiled. "Nah. I've decided to celebrate a job well done." The waitress returned with his beer and he took a long swallow.

"We're not done."

Griggs set his beer down on the table and looked at Jake in awe. "What do you mean?"

"I mean, we're not done."

"We did everything Davis wanted us to. We rescued his daughter and with the help of our friends from outer space," he pointed his finger upwards, "we destroyed the base."

Jake nodded. "In that aspect, you're right. We did do everything Davis asked us to, but there's still one thing we have to do."

"What?"

Jake shifted in his seat. "When the alien ship was about to leave," he paused, "it somehow beamed the entire history of its civilization into my mind."

Alex's eyes went wide. "You know the history of an alien civilization?" Jake grabbed Griggs' beer and took a big gulp, "Yeah."

"They asked you to do something for them?"

"Yeah. They want us to destroy one final artifact they left here on Earth. They said it was some kind of super energy source capable of destroying this entire planet if used incorrectly." Jake took another sip of Griggs' beer. "From what I can understand, they're a race of machines. They've been capable of exploring the universe even before life began to develop on this planet. They've traversed the universe in search of other sentient beings like themselves."

Alex was totally engaged in the story.

Jake continued. "When this planet was still young, it became sort of an interstellar gas station for this race. They used it to refuel and make repairs on themselves. From what I can piece together, there was a great catastrophe on their home world and all explorers were called back to help. In the confusion, they left several members of their race here, along with some very important pieces of their technology. One of those pieces is still at a place called S-4."

Alex smiled. She felt as if she had hit the jackpot in her career. "You mean all the saucers kept at Area 51 were actually living beings? What about all the little gray men with big black eyes everyone is always talking about?"

Griggs answered. "Oh, they're real."

"But not in the capacity you think," Jake cut in. "They're a biologically engineered species designed for the sole purpose of working for the machines and making in-flight repairs to the ships they couldn't do themselves."

"Incredible." Alex grabbed the beer and took a big swallow. "What's 'S-4'?" "It's basically the place where all the testing and back engineering of extra-terrestrial technology happens," Griggs answered. "Site 4, or better known as S-4, creates the black project aircraft and devices, and Area 51 then takes them and tests them."

Jake tapped his fingers. "Where is it?"

"It's near the eastern border of the Tonopah Test Range, about ten miles south of the Groom Lake Complex. It's another underground base."

"What's the government's obsession with underground bases?"

"Most of these bases started out aboveground. Area 51 and S-4 went underground after the government experimented in Colorado in the mid 60's and created NORAD deep inside Cheyenne Mountain," Griggs explained. "These bases were designed to withstand a Soviet nuclear attack on the country. It's rumored that a vast underground network of tunnels connect all the bases, but I've never actually seen the tubes."

Alex mulled over what Griggs had just said. Her curiosity returned to the artifact. "So what is this piece we're looking for?"

Jake thought for a moment. "I can't really describe it," He grabbed one of the cocktail napkins off the table and removed a pen from his jacket. "But I can draw it."

He roughly sketched a thin object with a large globe on top with four legs extending down from it and some kind of control panel on the front. Alex quickly snatched the paper from him and stared at it. "I found this!"

"What?" Jake was confused.

"Remember I told you that they grabbed me off

of a dig in Egypt?" Jake nodded.

"This is the piece I found underneath the Sphinx!" She looked at the drawing. "When those goons carted me off, they must've picked it up too."

"We have to destroy it." He turned to Griggs. "Do you know *exactly* where S-4 is?"

"Yeah, I did a couple of patrols there when I first arrived at Dreamland. I can get you there." Griggs snatched back his beer and drank down the final gulp. "But I just want to go on record as saying I don't think this is a very good idea."

"Noted." Jake turned to Alex. "Are you in?" Alex smiled. "Let's go."

CHAPTER TWENTY

General Perry lifted himself off the infirmary bed. Pain shot up through his leg as he tried to put pressure on the cast covering his broken limb. The infirmary was a sterile white room with several examination tables and surgical equipment near them. A multitude of doctors were taking care of wounded soldiers scattered throughout the room. Perry ran his left hand along his chest feeling the bandages around his ribs. Looking down at his broken arm, he sighed. Through his entire life, the worst injury he had ever sustained was a sprained ankle he'd received playing high school basketball. One of the doctors lifted Perry's jacket off the desk and handed it to him. Slipping it over his shoulders, he leaned back against the cold metal table.

"How long have I been out?" Perry asked the doctor.

"Several hours at least. We found you under your desk with numerous injuries." Perry rubbed his face. "And the advisors?"

"They're long since gone. They took the morning transport off the base, then caught a plane back to Washington, DC."

"Shit!" He slammed his fist against the table. He walked out the room and slammed the door behind him. Crews of repairmen and engineers were rushing through the halls. Perry grabbed one by the arm and stopped him. "I want a full report."

The man didn't recognize him at first, then saw the stars on his collar and snapped to attention.

"Yes, sir." He thought for a moment. "The base has sustained major damage. The hangar, for all intents and purposes, has been destroyed. The underground portion has lost most of its structural integrity. It looks like we could have a major collapse on our hands if we don't act fast."

Perry patted him on the back. "Good work, son. Get back to work."

The engineer saluted and went about his job. Perry took a right turn down an adjoining hallway. Most of the lights in the ceiling were out. Several portable lights had been placed around the base to provide illumination until the fixtures could be repaired. Taking another right, he found the hall blocked with debris that had fallen away from the walls and the ceiling. Perry spun around and retraced his steps back down the hall.

He grabbed another worker passing by. "How do I get to the command room from here?"

The man thought for a moment. "You can't take the way through the hangar, because it's been blocked. You'll have to go through the research bay. It was one of the few areas not damaged by the blast."

"Dismissed." Perry turned around and started to walk the opposite way down the hall. Passing the infirmary, he was stopped abruptly by Anne.

"General Perry. Just the man I was looking for." "Why is that?"

"I have bad news. Colonel Hunter is dead."

"Dear God." Perry tried to sound concerned. "What happened?"

"From what we can pull together, either Griggs or Silver shot him. He was found next to the dead body of General Davis."

"Well, at least we won't have to worry about Davis anymore. Hunter is just going to have to be counted as a casualty of war." He started walking toward the control room. "What happened to Silver and Griggs?"

"At last report, our security system tracked them leaving the base in a white Jeep Cherokee. One of our operatives located them with Doctor Robinson at a casino in downtown Las Vegas. They couldn't make a move because the place was so crowded, but we do have people following them."

"Do we have any indication of where they're going next?" "Our operative reports they were discussing S-4."

Perry slammed his fist into his open hand, then cringed. "Damn broken arm." He rubbed his arm. "This could be very good for us. I want all available soldiers transferred to S-4 immediately. That includes you and our man in black."

Anne looked down at her feet. "He was killed in the explosion. I narrowly escaped being trapped in the explosion myself."

"Damn. He was a good man."

"We have other men in black, sir."

"Not any as good as him." They stopped at a door. Perry removed his key card and slid it through the control box. The door slowly began to slide open. "Why's the door taking so long?"

"The base's main power generators were damaged. We're operating on reserve power, and there's not a lot to go around."

The two stepped through the now open door. "I will be joining you at S-4 shortly. I just need to take

291

care of a few things here first." "Like what?"

"First off, I need to promote a new colonel. Then I need to check in with Washington." The two went by another hallway damaged in the blast. He stopped and turned to face her. "Major Carroll, I'm giving you a field promotion to Lieutenant Colonel. Stop these men, Anne. I don't have time for another mistake like the last one."

She nodded and ran her hand through her long brown hair. Her green eyes sparkled with a hint of evil, "Yes, sir."

* * *

The three were stocked with supplies and on the road again by dusk. Jake had stretched out in the backseat and was taking a short nap. Griggs was driving and Alex was riding shotgun. Both were watching the sun set on the horizon.

Alex turned to Griggs. "If there's one thing you can say about Nevada, it does have the best sunsets."

Griggs agreed.

"You know, I don't know your first name. All I've ever heard Jake call you is Griggs or Major."

He smiled. "My name is Jason. During the plan to get you out, I was Silver's commanding officer. That's why he calls me major."

"Makes sense." She stared out the window at the sunset. "Do you mind if I ask you a question?"

"Shoot. We're still about half an hour out of Tonopah. From there, it's only about forty more miles until we reach S-4."

"How did you get caught up in this whole thing?" "You mean rescuing you?"

"No, I mean Area 51 in general."

292

"Oh," he checked his watch. "I was assigned there after I was labeled a 'War Hero' in Desert Storm."

"What did you do?"

"I saved my entire platoon by taking out an entire armored division by myself. Several tanks pinned us down. We didn't have the firepower to bring them down, and our radio had been damaged when our communications officer was killed. I made my way around the rear of the closest tank and forced my way inside. I took control of the tank and destroyed the other three."

"Jesus," Alex softly exclaimed. "What are you? The 'Terminator'?"

Griggs smiled. "Just standing up for what I believed in. I joined the Marines to defend my country and that's what I was doing."

"That still doesn't explain how you got to Area 51."

"The Groom Lake Complex is the United States most Top Secret facility. They only want the 'best of the best' there. They feel that way, there will be less possibility of having a leak."

"What they never counted on, though, is that a lot of the soldiers discover what they're doing at the base is wrong." Alex was starting to get the picture.

"Right."

"So why did you join the marines in the first place?"

"It was really the only thing I could do." He checked his watch. "I'm originally from the Pacific Northwest. I wasn't good in school and the only job I could get in my hometown was work at my father's sawmill. So I didn't have many options."

"You can't tell me that a big man like you didn't get any kind of sports scholarship. You didn't play football?"

"Yeah, I played some high school football, but I decided to pursue a different goal my senior year."

"Which was?"

He grinned at her. "Women."

"Very nice. So you were the average hormonally-driven teenage male."

"Yeah. Blew my chance at a football scholarship to the University of Oklahoma all for a couple of parties and some wild sex."

"I guess everyone goes through that phase in school. I know I did. I'm glad I got it out of my system before I went to college, though. When I went up for my Ph.D., I needed to study hard. I didn't have any time for parties or men."

"Sometimes I wish I had gone to college." He guided the white Jeep smoothly around a bend in the road. "I could've been more than just some grunt in the military. You know what I always wanted to be?"

She looked at him and smiled. "What?" "I always wanted to be a teacher." "What kind of teacher?"

"It didn't matter. I always thought it would be incredible to shape young people's minds, ya know? To be the person they went to when they wanted to learn."

"I like that," she said softly to him.

The sun had now settled down behind the horizon allowing the stars to slowly rise above it into a clear night sky. "We're almost there. You might want to wake Mr. Snooze up." He pointed with his thumb into the backseat.

Alex shifted in her seat so she could reach back and wake Jake. "I had a nice talk. Thanks, Jason."

He smiled and nodded. "I did, too."

She reached back and shook Jake. Slowly, he rolled off his side and onto his back. Opening his eyes, he started to rub the sleep out of them. He cleared his throat and sat up. "Are we there yet?"

"I'm just about to take the turnoff that leads there. It should only be another ten minutes or so."

"Do we have a plan?" he asked groggily. "Not yet," Alex replied.

"We better come up with one in a hurry then."

CHAPTER TWENTY-ONE

Anne stepped out of the helicopter wearing full black army fatigues, her brown hair up in a ponytail. Several soldiers accompanying her also stepped off the chopper. The team moved away from the helicopter as it slowly lifted off the pad into the night sky.

The helicopter pad was just an area of leveled dirt on the left side of the road near the entrance. The road leading down into the base was very winding and treacherous and went through several sheer walls that dropped off hundreds of feet into the canyon below.

Anne looked around the terrain. S-4 was a very different place than Area 51. Unlike Area 51, S-4 had no real outstanding features. It had no hangars or runways and only a few communication towers littered the barren landscape. The base had been moved totally underground several years ago. The only major landmark that remained aboveground was the entrance. It was a huge archway built into the side of the mountain. There was a guard shack built on the right side of the archway that housed at least four guards and two white Jeep Cherokees.

Anne stood in front of her ten-man strike force. The men were standing at attention side-by-side near the entrance. She walked down the line and inspected each man. "Welcome to Site 4, gentlemen," she said in her most commanding voice. "I know many of you have never been assigned here, so the base will be very unfamiliar to you, but we are here for a very specific reason." She paced back and forth in front of them with her hands clasped behind her back. "We are here to stop an assault on this facility. You are to use every means necessary to stop these men." She stopped in the center of the men. "Deadly force is authorized."

The men briefly broke formation when they heard that, but quickly recomposed themselves and snapped to attention.

"You will report only to me," she continued. "If another officer tries to pull you off what you are doing, tell them no and if they have any questions, tell them to find me or General Perry." She looked at her group. "Understood?"

"Yes, Colonel!" they shouted in unison.

"All right, everyone inside. Split up. I want regular reports every fifteen minutes." She started to walk away. "Dismissed."

The men made their way toward the entrance and walked inside. Anne made her way over to the guard shack and opened the door. Four men dressed in standard green army fatigues stood inside going about their normal duties. They quickly turned and saluted as she walked in. "At ease."

"What can we do for you, Colonel?"

"How many vehicles pass through these gates every day?"

The nearest man answered. "Probably between forty and fifty." "And what's the standard procedure for checking them?"

"We have every passenger in the vehicle show their ID, then we check for possible stowaways inside the vehicle or in the trunk. If they pass, we let them through."

Anne nodded. She glanced over at the entrance. "Is that the only thing keeping vehicles from going in?" She pointed at a black and yellow striped bar crossing in front of the entrance.

"Yeah. When a vehicle checks out, we raise the bar and let them through." "That's it?"

"Colonel, this facility is not as well-known as Area 51. The need for security around here is not as important. Added to the fact our location is very well-hidden deep inside this canyon makes this base very, if not extremely, difficult to infiltrate."

"Not as important? This base houses some of the most Top Secret devices in the world." She got in the face of the man talking to her. "I want security doubled at the gate for the next forty-eight hours," she yelled. "I don't care if you bring the cook up to stand at the front door. Do you understand me?"

The man brought himself to attention. "Yes, Colonel."

"Very good."

***

They had jettisoned the Jeep about five miles outside the base perimeter. All three were now dressed in black fatigues with combat boots and full armaments.

Moving single file across the desert, they moved back and forth between the sagebrush under the light of the full moon.

Griggs was in the lead. He stopped and turned back to the others. "This full moon is really going to hinder our mission. It's too bright out here."

Jake looked around. "We've got no choice. We have to complete this mission." "We need to get in there before they do any tests on the device." Alex was standing between the two.

"Agreed." Griggs looked around. "I have no idea what kind of security they have surrounding the base. If it's anything like what we have at Groom Lake, then they probably already know we're coming."

"Great," Jake moaned.

"We want to get in there and get out as quickly and as quietly as possible," Griggs stated. "Here's my plan. S-4 only has one entrance. We need to get in there."

Jake chuckled to himself. "Very good, Major. Did you come up with that all by yourself?"

Griggs got defensive. "I don't see you coming up with anything better." Alex stepped between them. "All right, break it up. We have a mission to complete."

Jake thought for a moment. "That can't be the only entrance into the base. I'm betting the facility has to have some kind of ventilation system we can get in through."

"It probably doesn't. You have to remember, Jake, these bases were designed to survive a direct nuclear assault. They can operate completely independently within themselves. A ventilation system sucking in contaminated air probably isn't the best idea."

"I see your point." Jake scanned the horizon. "How about those?" Jake pointed to several towers in the distance.

Griggs stared for a moment. "It's possible there's a passage into the base from there."

Alex started walking away. "Let's go then."

A black military helicopter skimmed low over the hills and sagebrush of the Nevada desert on its way to the Site 4 complex, having taken off from Area 51 only moments before. The motors of the rotor blades chugged loudly inside the cockpit.

Perry looked out through the side window at the shadow of the helicopter on the ground. He quickly adjusted his black helmet and tightened his seatbelt. He had never liked riding in a helicopter. He turned and looked at the pilot. "What's our ETA?" "About ten minutes, sir," the pilot yelled over the noise.

"Good." Perry turned around and looked at the group of soldiers seated in the rear. "Do you understand what your mission objective is?"

The CO of the men answered. "To eliminate the conspirators, sir!" "Affirmative." He handed back several photos of Jake and Griggs. The CO grabbed them and began handing them out. "Take a good look at these men. The next time I see them, I want to be identifying their bodies in the morgue."

"Yes, sir."

***

Using the shadows and moving quickly around the rocks and sagebrush, they promptly reached one of the nearest communication towers. It was a tall, slim building painted in standard desert camouflage. The several tones of brown hid the tower very well in the stark desert environment. The top of the tower was littered with satellite dishes of all shapes and sizes.

Griggs motioned with his hand for Jake and Alex to spread out and look for a door. Griggs

300

turned his back to the tower and scanned the horizon for troops. Even though the full moon was shining brightly, it was still very difficult for him to see. Reaching around, he removed a pair of night vision goggles from a small pack he had slung over his shoulder.

Slipping them on over his eyes, the nightscape was turned from black into a bright green. He adjusted a small knob on the bottom of the goggles to increase their light sensitivity. He quickly crouched down behind a bush as he spotted a black helicopter approaching from the northwest.

"Get down!" he shouted to the other two.

Jake dropped to the ground and flattened himself against it. Alex dropped down to her knees and rolled behind a large patch of sagebrush near her. They all watched silently as the helicopter roared overhead toward the landing pad.

Jake lifted himself off the ground and dusted himself off. He shouted to the others. "I found the door!" Alex and Griggs trotted around the corner of the tower and stopped next to Jake. "It looks like a service hatch. But it's screwed down."

Griggs knelt down next to the hatch and pulled a compact electric screwdriver out of his pouch. "No problem." He went to work removing the screws.

"What else do you have in that pouch?" Alex pointed at his pack.

"Just what I thought I might need." He removed the final screw and pulled off the panel. "It looks like a tight fit, but I think we can make it." Placing the screwdriver back in his pack, he took his weapon off his shoulder and handed it to Alex.

Slowly, he began to crawl inside.

"What's in there?"

"There's a shaft that leads down into the base," Griggs replied. "How do we get down it?" Jake asked.

"There's a ladder heading down. I'll start down and then you two follow me. Hand me my weapon."

Jake pushed the gun through the hatch. "You go next, Alex." She nodded and gracefully slid into the hatch. Jake took another quick glance around. Stepping into the hatch, he grabbed the panel and pulled it back into place behind him. Flipping on a small flashlight he retrieved from his belt, he examined the tube. Several pipes ran the length of the tower along with numerous dark gray power cords. Multi-colored wires worked their way across and around the tube like a spider's web. He turned around and looked down at the shaft leading down. It was barely wide enough for him to fit. Going feet first, he climbed down into the shaft. Shining the light down below him, he saw Alex and Griggs climbing swiftly down the ladder. Jake began to feel claustrophobic in the tube. Closing his eyes for a moment, he took a deep breath, then started down the ladder.

***

"Report!" Anne stood just outside the entrance with her hand on her earpiece. Looking up into the sky, she saw General Perry's helicopter approaching.

A voice erupted in her ear. "Nothing to report, sir. The area is clear." "Very good. Carry on, Major." She strode slowly toward the landing pad.

The helicopter hovered above. The rotors were

kicking up a lot of dust on the landing pad, sending thick clouds of it in all directions. Anne closed her mouth and squinted through the flying dirt trying to keep her eyes on the helicopter. It touched down gracefully on the pad and the rotors began to slow. The cargo door slid open and several soldiers in black fatigues poured out and formed up in front of the helicopter. Opening the passenger door, Perry stepped out and adjusted his uniform. Beside the sling on his arm, the only visible remnant of his injuries was a cane he used to help him walk.

Anne immediately stepped up and saluted him. "How are you feeling, sir?"

"Like a desk landed on me." He returned the salute and began walking toward his men. They were standing at attention near the entrance. "I want an update, Colonel."

She snapped to attention. "The area is clear, sir. No sign of them yet." "They're here."

"How do you know that, sir?"

"When we were flying in, we saw a white Jeep abandoned just off the access road. They're here all right." He looked around hoping to catch a glimpse of them.

"I've had my men sweeping the base for forty-five minutes now and they haven't turned up anything so far."

"Keep looking, Colonel. I want those men dead by sunrise. Dismissed." He started toward his men.

Anne turned around and walked back toward the entrance to the base. She checked her watch. It was twenty-one hundred hours. The sun rose here about six hundred hours. That meant she had about nine hours to find these men.

Emerging from the tube, the three found themselves in a long, narrow hallway. Black and silver tubes ran the length of it, accompanied by wave after wave of multi- colored wire. It was dark except for small lights affixed to the left wall about every ten feet. Walking in single file, they cautiously made their way down the hall. Griggs held his weapon at the ready as he rounded a small bend.

Quickly stopping, he waved Jake and Alex back. The hall came to an abrupt end just ahead of them. Griggs spotted two soldiers in green army fatigues leaning against the wall opposite the exit. He pulled himself back around the corner and faced the other two. "Two soldiers just ahead," he whispered. "What are you planning to do?" Alex asked.

He shook his head. "Stay here. Jake." Griggs looked over at him. "Come with me." Jake stepped up next to Griggs. "Follow my lead."

He removed a rock he had picked up off the desert floor from his pouch. He tossed it behind him. It made a loud clunk as it hit the wall, then the floor, catching the guards' attention. They slowly walked toward the service entrance to investigate. The first guard peeked his head inside the darkened hall followed by the other. Both shrugged and turned around to walk back to their resting spot. With speed and accuracy, Jake and Griggs leapt out of the shadows and grabbed the two men around the neck and the mouth. Pulling the two back around the corner, Griggs removed his knife and slit the man's throat. Jake twisted hard and snapped the other man's neck.

They grabbed the bodies under the arms and pulled them down the hall, arranging them in a heap near the entrance to the communication tower.

The two men jogged back to where Alex was waiting. Jake poked his head around the corner. Nothing. Griggs stepped around him toward the mouth of the hallway. Stepping into the bright artificial lights, he scanned the room they were standing in. It was large and vaguely reminded him of a nurse's station in a hospital.

Two hallways stretched out from either side of the room. On the opposite side just to the left of the service door was a short wall with desks sitting behind it. He motioned for the other two to join him.

Jake stepped out into the light and squinted a little bit. It was brighter than he was used to. Alex stood at his right looking down the long hallway. She tapped Griggs on the shoulder. "Which way?"

He shrugged. "I don't know. This place is set up entirely different than Area 51." Jake pulled a coin out of his pocket and flipped it into the air. "Heads we go left, tails we go right." Catching it, he placed it on the back of his hand. "Very scientific," Alex commented.

He lifted his hand off the coin. "Heads. We go left." The three carefully started walking to their left.

***

Perry knocked on the door and then opened it into the small office. A younger man with dark brown hair was sitting behind a small wooden desk and rifling through a small stack of papers sitting in

305

front of him. His blue uniform jacket was draped over the back of his tall gray padded chair, while his sleeves were rolled up to his elbows. Lifting a black ballpoint pen off the desk, he quickly signed his name to the bottom of the sheet and finally looked up.

He immediately jumped to his feet and saluted. "Sorry, sir. I hadn't been informed of your arrival." He adjusted his large black-rimmed glasses.

"At ease, Colonel Lucas." He returned the salute.

Lucas held out his hand to a chair sitting in front of his desk. "Please, General, have a seat." Lucas waited until after Perry took his seat to sit down. He folded his hands in front of him. "What can I do for you, General Perry?"

"I need you to put this facility on full alert." Lucas looked alarmed. "Why is that, sir?"

"We have reason to believe that the two men who blew up the hangar at Area 51 are trying to infiltrate your base. I need your help in finding these men and destroying them."

"You have it, General," the young Colonel stuttered.

Perry studied the younger man for a moment. "How long have you been in the Air Force, Colonel?"

"About five years, General. I transferred here directly from Nellis." "And you're already a Colonel?"

"Yes, sir. Graduated top of my class at the academy."

Perry muttered under his breath. "Colonel Lucas, I have no idea how you got assigned to such

306

a sensitive position when it's obvious you're an idiot."

"Sir?"

Perry looked at his watch. "As of twenty-one hundred hours, I am relieving you of duty. I need everyone operating at one hundred and ten percent, and you're obviously not capable of that."

"I really don't understand—"

"These men destroyed a good portion of Area 51, and killed several of my best soldiers. I want these men dead and I don't want any mistakes. I've brought in several of my own teams and officers to oversee this operation. I just want you out of the way until we're done."

Lucas hung his head. "Yes, sir."

***

Jake slung his weapon over his shoulder and pulled his pistol out of its holster. With his back against the wall, he carefully peeked around the corner. Two guards were standing in front of a large door with a black and yellow 'restricted' sign on it. He pulled a silencer out of his pouch and carefully screwed it onto the pistol. Swiftly moving around the corner, he fired off two shots hitting both guards in the chest. They quickly slumped to the floor.

Alex and Griggs followed Jake around the corner. "Maybe your guess was right, Jake."

Holding the pistol at his side, Jake stepped closer to the door. "There's no control box next to the door."

Griggs moved up next to Jake. "S-4 isn't as heavily guarded as Area 51 because this base is less well-known and better hidden from spy satellites." Griggs grabbed the handle of the door and twisted it. The door smoothly opened. "Thus, no ID boxes next to the doors."

Alex had a perplexed look on her face. "Doesn't that seem strange to you? A secret base used in the research and development of extra-terrestrial technology has less security than your average Air Force base."

Griggs stepped through the door. "This base is like the ugly stepchild nobody wants to watch over. Being assigned at Area 51, you get to watch alien ships get tested and new kinds of weapons used. Here at S-4, you get to protect a bunch of egghead scientists trying to figure this alien shit out. Not real exciting."

"Okay." Jake smiled as he followed Jake through the door. "That's the strangest explanation I have ever heard."

Both men stopped in their tracks when they entered the next room. The white sterilized look of the rest of the base was replaced with flat gray concrete floors and walls. It was lined with tall wooden racks filled with what looked to Jake like junk.

Jake walked over to the nearest shelf and lifted a small hunk of metal off it. He turned it over in his hand to examine it. It was a solid piece of metal about the size of a softball but weighed almost nothing at all. Its silvery skin glistened in the low light of the room. He reached over and placed it back on the shelf.

He turned back to Griggs. "What is this place?"

Alex pushed past the two men and began to explore the room. "This must be where they keep the recovered extra-terrestrial artifacts!" She was giddy with excitement.

"You mean the device we're looking for could be in this room?"

"Probably not. This all looks like small stuff. The device we're looking for is about four feet tall and three feet wide."

"Where do you think it would be, Major?" Jake asked.

"I'm not sure. When I was here, I was never allowed to be this far into the base." "Well, let's keep looking," Jake sighed. Griggs started walking past the two toward the exit on the other side of the room. Jake turned around and grabbed Alex by the arm. "Come on, Doctor." She followed reluctantly.

CHAPTER TWENTY-TWO

"Sir, we've found several bodies inside the service tube of communication tower number three."

Anne pressed her earpiece tightly in her ear. "Very good, Major. They must be around there somewhere. Find them."

"Yes, Colonel."

She reached down and clicked a knob on her portable radio. "General Perry, are you there?"

Her earpiece crackled to life. "Yes, Colonel. Go ahead."

"General, we've found several bodies inside the service tube to one of the communication towers. They've obviously entered the base through there."

"Good work, Colonel. Have you got a bead on them yet?"

"No, sir, but at least we know what level they're on now. I have my men combing that level right now."

Her radio began to beep. She switched it back to the previous channel. "Carroll here."

The excited voice of her major filled her earpiece. "Colonel, we have them!"

***

Machine gun fire slammed against the frame of the large steel door in front of them. Griggs ducked around the corner and pressed his back to the wall. Glancing across the room, he saw several soldiers taking up positions in front of the other door. He charged the door, gun blazing. The soldiers swiftly

310

pulled back out of the way to avoid the barrage. Griggs reached the door and slammed it closed with his outstretched hand. He looked across the way to see Jake doing the same at the other door.

He shouted across the room. "We've got to find another way." He pointed to his left and began to run.

Jake grabbed Alex by the hand and led her to the opposite side of the room where they met up with Griggs. The three searched for another exit. Alex was panting. "Now what?"

"They're going to be through those doors any minute now."

"Shit," Griggs muttered to himself. "So much for our quiet operation." Jake leaned back against the wall and let his head fall back against it accidentally catching sight of a large vent on the ceiling. "Look there!" Alex looked up. "It's too high!"

"No it's not," Griggs replied. "Follow me." Slinging his gun over his shoulder, he started to climb the nearest rack of shelves.

Jake assessed the rack. "Are you sure that's going to hold?"

"Only one way to find out." Griggs quickly traversed the shelf. Once on top, he used the butt of his gun to knock the screen loose. Grabbing it with both hands, he wrenched it off and dropped it to the floor. Kneeling down, he lowered a hand to Alex. "Come on."

Alex slowly made her way up to the top of the shelf. With a boost from Griggs, she was able to pull herself up into the ventilation shaft. Jake quickly followed suit and climbed up onto the shelf.

Leaning over precariously, Griggs grabbed the edge of the vent and pulled himself in.

Jake carefully reached over and grabbed the lip of the vent and started to pull himself inside when the two doors exploded off their hinges sending them flying into the room, along with smoke and hundreds of shards from the wall and door frames. The shockwave from the explosion sent Jake falling to the concrete floor. He landed flat on his back knocking the wind out of himself.

Gasping for air, he rolled over onto his stomach and lifted himself up. Looking up into the open shaft, he saw Griggs waving him up frantically. Jake scanned the room. On the far side, several soldiers made their way in with weapons drawn.

He knew he only had one chance. Leaping at the shelf, he climbed up as fast as he could. Bullets ricocheted off the shelves and artifacts around him. One of the armed soldiers ran around the corner and drew a quick bead on him. Before he could fire, Jake grabbed one of the chunks of metal off the shelves and tossed it at him with all his strength. The piece of metal hit the man in the head and knocked him down.

Reaching the top of the shelf, Jake leapt into the shaft. He pulled himself up as bullets strafed the ceiling around him. Both Griggs and Alex were sitting in the tunnel staring at him. "What are you two waiting for? Go!"

All three started crawling away from the hole as fast as possible, when Jake heard something heavy hit the floor behind him. Stopping, he carefully turned around to see a grenade sitting behind him. "Shit!" He kicked it as hard as he could, sending it skittering along the shaft until it fell through the hole. "Get down!"

The three dropped to their bellies as an explosion rocked the room they were just in. A plume of flame shot into the shaft and scorched the top of it. Jake felt the flames burning the top of the shaft just above him. Staying on his stomach, he quickly crawled away from the heat. Stopping at an intersection in the vent, they tried to catch their breath.

"Now what?" Alex asked.

***

Anne stood against one of the walls in the dimly lit hallway outside the main research facility. Her arms were crossed while she was biting her nails on her right hand. She stopped when she heard the door next to her begin to open. Brushing an errant lock of hair out of her face, she snapped to attention.

Perry quickly stepped out the door. "At ease, Colonel."

He held it open and waved her inside. Anne stared around the room. It was small and white with observation windows in the ceiling. The banks of computers were destroyed and there were huge black char marks on the walls and floors. She stared at the large object in the middle of the room. The large orb in the center of the device was glowing a bright white light.

She stepped closer to it. "What is this?" She reached her hands toward the device.

"Don't touch it!" He grabbed her hands and ripped them away from the device. "We have no idea what would happen if it came into human

313

contact."

She took a step back from the device. "What is it?"

"We have no idea. It was found buried under the Sphinx in Egypt. They estimated it to be thousands of years old." He stared at the glowing orb. "It's been continuously working for all that time."

"That's incredible. What kind of power source does it run on?"

"Again, we have no idea. That's what our men were trying to find out when they blew up this room. Our main researcher was killed in that explosion." "Why are you showing this to me?"

"I think this is what they're after." "What makes you think that?"

"This device was discovered by Doctor Alex Robinson."

Anne laughed to herself. "She brought Silver and Griggs here to get her discovery back?"

"That's one possibility. The other is that she knows something about the device we don't."

"What could she know?"

He quickly stepped up to her. "Never underestimate your enemies." She snapped to attention. "Yes, sir. Sorry, sir."

He backed down. Walking around the object, he stood on the other side of it and continued to address her. "I'm altering my orders, Colonel. I want the three of them alive."

"Sir?"

"I want to know what Doctor Robinson knows about this device." "Yes, sir."

"Dismissed."

314

He watched as she snapped around and walked out the door, closing it behind her. He shifted his attention to the device. He stared at the control panel located at the base of the device. It had a line of several characters that reminded him of hieroglyphics along the bottom. A recessed handprint occupied the center of the control panel. He knew no human had designed this device. The handprint had four long fingers and a thumb on each side.

The glowing orb filled his eyes. He felt a wave of calm flow over him. Kneeling down next to the control panel, he opened his hand and slowly reached toward it. He heard its song in his head. It was calling to him. His hand moved closer to the panel. Sweat rolled down his forehead. He ran his fingers over the recessed handprint. Every line in the print was copied, right down to the wrinkles in the joints of the fingers.

The song grew louder in his ears. Flattening his hand, he moved it closer. He closed his eyes and tried to block out its voice. Pulling his hand away, he covered both ears. Stumbling backward, he fell into one of the computer banks.

The voices suddenly stopped. His hands came off his ears and went loosely to his sides. Wiping the sweat off his brow, he quickly moved past the device toward the door. Throwing it open, he stepped outside into the seemingly cooler air of the rest of the facility. A group of soldiers were walking down the hallway next to him. He stepped in front of the last three in line. Grabbing one by the arm, he pulled him aside.

"I need you to guard this door with your life,

soldier!" The soldier nodded. "Yes, sir!"

"I don't want anyone in this room without my expressed consent. Do you understand?"

"Yes, sir!"

"Very good." Perry grabbed the other two soldiers, turned around, and began to walk away.

***

The ventilation shaft had come to a dead end. Turning around, Jake crawled back toward a vent on the bottom of the shaft. He peered through the grate at the hallway below. He watched as General Perry and two soldiers strode briskly under the vent. Looking to the left, he saw a large door. He waved for Alex and Griggs to come look.

"I just saw General Perry walk by."

"Damn," Griggs muttered as he looked through the vent. "What's he doing here?" "I wish I knew."

Alex cringed. "He has to be on to us. He knows we're here to destroy the artifact."

"How would he know that?" Jake asked.

"They do keep files, you know. They are aware that I was the one who found the device in the first place."

Griggs smiled. "She's right, Jake."

"Well, whatever the case, we need to get down there. Hand me your screwdriver, Major."

Griggs reached into his pack and fished it out. "Here."

Grabbing the screwdriver, Jake immediately went to work removing the screws in the vent cover. Removing the final screw, he handed the screwdriver back to Griggs, then slowly lifted the cover off the vent. Sliding it in front of the hole, he lowered his head down and took a look around. The hallway below was empty except for a single soldier standing guard next to the large door.

He pulled his head back up. "There's one guard standing next to the door. Otherwise, the hall's empty."

"That shouldn't be much of a problem," Griggs concluded. Moving over to the vent, he lowered his feet.

"No, wait!"

Before the words had left Jake's mouth, Griggs had pushed off the edge and was on the ground below. He lifted his arm to swing at the soldier but before he could, the guard had raised his gun.

"Shit," Jake muttered to himself.

The soldier stepped closer to Griggs. "Turn around and put your hands up against the wall." With a sigh, Griggs complied.

Jake and Alex watched as the soldier pressed the barrel of the gun into Griggs' back as he moved him closer to the wall. Lowering his weapon, he began to pat Griggs down looking for weapons. Alex looked over to Jake and nodded. "It's now or never."

Positioning himself over the vent, Jake took a deep breath, then pushed himself through the vent. It was less than a second later when Jake's boots slammed into the soldier's head knocking him down. They lay in a heap on the floor. His spine was broken, leaving his body twisted in an unnatural position.

"Jesus, Jake, what took you so long?"

Jake pointed up to the vent. "What I just did is not easy!" "Hey!" Alex waved at the two. "How am I going to get down?" Both men looked up at her.

"Jump."

"All right." She lowered her body into the vent. "Here we go!" She swung down and let go falling to the ground. She landed with a thud next to Griggs.

Jake patted her on the back. "See, that wasn't so hard, was it?"

She quickly reached around and smacked Jake on the back of the head. "Do you think before you talk?"

Griggs laughed. "All right, you two, knock it off."

Jake turned around and walked toward the door. "Let's see what they were guarding behind this door." Griggs and Alex followed him. He reached down and grabbed the handle. Turning around, he looked at his companions. "Ready?"

They both nodded.

Twisting the knob, he slowly pulled open the door. "Jesus." Alex moved past him into the room. "This is it!"

Griggs and Jake joined her in the scorched room. The device was standing in the center surrounded by banks of burnt out computers. "That's exactly how I saw it in my mind." Jake walked closer to it. "It's incredible."

"Don't touch it!" Alex jumped between Jake and the device. "We don't know what will happen."

Jake took a step back and shook his head. "You're right. It just kind of drew me toward it."

Griggs took a step toward it. "Yeah, as soon as I saw it, I wanted to touch it. I heard something, too." He thought for a moment. "It sounded like...singing." "That's what I heard, too."

Alex turned around and stared at the device. "I

didn't feel or hear anything." Griggs rubbed his chin. "That's damn strange."

"Maybe it has something to with the 'Y' chromosome," Alex theorized. "I don't understand." Jake confessed.

"It's just a guess, but maybe the reason I didn't hear anything is because I don't have a 'Y' chromosome. Women are 'XX', while men are 'XY'. Maybe it can only communicate with a 'Y' chromosome."

Griggs rubbed his chin. "Sounds kind of far-fetched to me, Alex."

"It's just a theory. I'd need to have a lot of research time to prove it."

"How are we supposed to destroy this thing?" The three surrounded the object studying it. Jake holstered his weapon. "We can't just gun it down. We don't know what it would do. It could cause some kind of explosion. We've gotta do this the right way."

Alex suggested.

"What would be the right way, Doctor?" Jake asked.

She thought about it for a moment. "I have no idea. First, I need to know what it is. Look around for any kind of notes or data."

Jake spun around. "How are we supposed to find anything in this room? It's all burned to hell."

"Dig through the rubble."

"Shit." Griggs knelt down and started sifting through some of the debris. Jake lifted up a small sheet of metal, then stopped. "Come look at this." Alex and Griggs made their way over to Jake. Alex gasped. "What is that?"

Jake flipped the sheet of metal out of the way revealing a white chalk outline of a body. "This is the last guy that tried messing with that thing."

Griggs assessed the outline. "Why isn't the inside charred?"

Jake stood up. "That indicates the body was already lying there when the rest of the room was burning."

"How do you know that?" Alex wondered.

"FBI agent for twelve years." He continued to study the outline. "This could mean one of two things. Either he burned to death in the fire, or he was already dead and the fire consumed him."

"How could we tell?" Griggs asked.

"I would need to see the body to be positive, but I don't think that's important now. What we need to find out now is what they were trying to do with the device."

"I'll tell you." All three spun around to see General Perry and two other soldiers standing in the doorway with their weapons trained on them. "If you'll all be so kind as to drop your weapons on the floor." Jake slowly complied. Kneeling down, he laid his pistol on the floor. Alex and Griggs followed suit.

Walking into the room, Perry kicked their weapons away from them. His two men took up positions on either side of the door. "It's so good to see you three again." He walked around behind Griggs. "You made a real mess of my base; killed my colonel, and several of my best men. You were also instrumental in the loss of all the recovered saucers." He delivered a savage blow to Griggs' lower back. Griggs let out a moan and dropped to the floor.

Perry stepped around behind Jake. Adjusting the sling around his arm, he held up his pistol to the back of Jake's head. "Mr. Silver, it's so very nice to see you again." He cocked the hammer back on his gun. "I'm going to enjoy killing you." He slowly dropped his weapon down to his side, "But not yet. First I need to ask the good doctor some questions."

"What do you want from me?" Alex asked in a hateful tone.

Perry lifted his pistol and held it up to her temple. "I want everything you know about the device."

"I don't know anything."

"That's very unfortunate for you. That means I don't need you anymore." He pressed the gun harder into her temple.

"You better get out of her face." Griggs had risen to his feet.

Griggs smiled. Lowering the gun, he walked over to Griggs. "Or what, Major?" "I'll kill you where you stand," Griggs sneered.

Perry lifted his weapon and held it into Griggs' stomach. "Are you threatening me?"

"I am."

"Again, that is very unfortunate." Perry pulled the trigger sending Griggs back to the floor.

"You son of a bitch!" Jake charged Perry. Leaping, he knocked Perry down. Once down, Jake delivered several rapid jabs to his face. From behind him, the two soldiers grabbed him and threw him off Perry. Using the butts of their rifles, they started to beat Jake.

Perry jumped to his feet. "Stop! I want him

alive for now. Take them all to the brig."

The soldiers lifted Jake and Griggs off the floor. After rounding up Alex, they escorted the three of them out. Perry stood alone in the room. The song slowly started in his head again. Holding his hands over his ears, he ran out of the room.

CHAPTER TWENTY-THREE

Jake came to lying flat on his back on the floor of the cell. Slowly sitting up, he glanced around. It was painted a flat gray with a red stripe running around the room about a foot below the ceiling. Black steel bars crossed the front of the cell. Rubbing his face, he glanced over at the only cot in the room. Standing, he moved over to the cot and sat down on the edge.

"How is he?"

Alex was sitting with her back against the wall with Griggs' head resting on her lap. His arms were crossed over the bullet hole in his stomach. His clothes were soaked with blood. "He keeps drifting in and out of consciousness. I'm keeping pressure on the wound, but he's still bleeding very badly."

"We need to get him out of here and to a hospital." He rubbed his face. "How long have I been out?"

"I'd say only about half an hour."

Jake walked over and grabbed the cell bars shaking them vigorously. A huge black guard stepped around the corner. "Knock that shit off," he warned Jake in a deep booming tone. "General Perry gave me full authority to kill you."

Jake let go of the bars and stepped back. "Hey, take it easy."

The guard slammed his huge hand against the bars. "If I have to come back here again, I will kill you."

He watched as the guard slowly walked away

from the cell. Turning around, he walked over and leaned over Alex. "Do we have any weapons left?"

"No," she whispered. "They took everything when they put us in the cell." "Damn." He rubbed his chin. "I'll just have to improvise." He walked back over to the cell and grabbed the bars. Shaking them wildly, he yelled for the guard.

He watched as the guard slowly made his way back to the cell. "What the hell do you want now?"

Jake pointed at Griggs. "He's dying! He needs medical attention right now!" "You're gonna need medical attention if you don't shut up."

"Please."

The guard waved a hand at Jake dismissing him. Turning around, he started to walk away. Quickly stepping up to the bars, Jake reached through them grabbing the guard around the neck. Pulling with all his strength, he slammed the huge man back against the bars. Wrapping his arm around the man's throat, Jake used his other hand to repeatedly whack his head against them.

The guard let out a yell as he tried to break free. Latching onto Jake's arm, the guard pulled in an effort to break free as the blood flow to his brain slowed. Rearing back, Jake slammed his balled fist into the back of the guard's head. The guard started making a gurgling sound as his body went limp. Still holding him around the neck, Jake reached down to his belt and unhooked the keys on his belt. Letting go, the man slumped to the floor.

Sifting through the keys on the ring, he reached around and tried key after key until he heard the tumblers turn in the lock. "Got it." He turned around to Alex. "Stay here. I've got to take care of something." Alex nodded. "When I come back, I need him ready to move."

"Be careful." He nodded as he pushed open the door and stepped out.

***

General Perry paced uneasily back and forth outside the main control room. The hall outside was a maze of pipes and steel girders. Perry knew a good portion of the interiors in this base had never been completed due to budget cutbacks in the early seventies. The government felt as long as the outer shell was complete, the innards could wait until more revenue was generated. Leaning up against one of the pipes, he watched as the door slowly opened.

A young female with short brown hair stepped out of the door. "General Perry?" "Yes, Private?"

"I have the President on the phone as you requested. He wants to speak with you."

"Thank you, Private. That will be all."

The young girl turned and strode away. Reaching down, he grabbed the doorknob and slowly opened the door. Stepping inside, he saw a large round wooden conference table. The walls and floor were the standard gray cement. Pipes and tubes dominated the ceiling. A lone red phone sat in the middle of the table. A yellow button on the base of the phone flashed rapidly.

Taking a deep breath, he slowly picked up the receiver and pressed the button. "Yes, Mr. President?"

"I'm holding a report in my hand my advisors filed this morning. It paints a very unflattering picture of you and your actions recently at the base.

I want an explanation and I want it now!" the President's voice roared over the telephone.

"I took the action I deemed necessary. If I had to do it all over again, I'm confident I would make the same choices."

"That still doesn't explain why the hangar of the most Top Secret base in the world is blown to hell. That's a multi-billion dollar installation you helped destroy. I need answers. Congress is breathing down my throat."

"We had two men infiltrate the base and—"

"God dammit, General. I don't want to hear that. I sent you down there to evaluate and fix the problems the base had, not destroy the damned thing."

"Mr. President, I—" Perry was trying hard to defend himself the best he could. "General, it pains me to do this," the President let out a long sigh, "I am relieving you of your command. I want you on the next transport back to Washington so you can explain your actions to Congress."

"Yes, Mr. President. I understand."

"As of right now, I want you to turn yourself over to base security to be detained until your flight leaves. Is that understood?"

The line went dead. Perry slammed the phone down. "The hell I will. If I'm going down, I'm taking Griggs and Silver with me."

***

Jake jogged around the corner. Stopping, he saw the door just up ahead. Accelerating to full speed, he sprinted down the remaining few feet of the corridor. Stopping at the door, he reached for the handle. Out of the corner of his eye, he saw several long shadows creep into the hallway.

He turned the door handle. "Shit. Locked."

Frantically, he twisted it hard back and forth. The shadows were growing longer.

Lowering a shoulder, he slammed into the door. He did it again. The footsteps were growing louder. Taking several steps back, he charged the door. Dropping his shoulder, he hit it with a thud. It broke open sending him spilling onto the floor. Quickly getting up, he slammed the door shut and stood with his back against it.

He took a moment to catch his breath. Turning to his side, he pressed his ear up against the door and listened as the sound of footsteps went by him. He waited a moment longer to move. Slowly turning around, he came face to face with the device. He walked around it, carefully surveying it from each side. Then he found it. The handprint in the middle of the control panel had an odd green glow to it. He had never seen it look this way before. It was casting a hazy green shadow on the ground and debris around it. Kneeling down, he wiped the sweat off his palms on his jeans. Reaching, he began to slowly extend his hand toward the panel. A bullet slammed into the dead bank of computers behind him. He dove to the floor covering his head.

"Come on out of there, Silver. We need to have a little talk."

Jake slowly stood. "General Perry. Somehow I knew you'd show up here."

Perry walked slowly into the room with his weapon pointed at Jake. "I just thought I would let you know I've been relieved of duty because of you, and I've come here to kill you."

"Even if you do, my companions are already on their way out of the base." "You mean poor Major Griggs and Doctor Robinson?"

Jake's eyes grew wide.

"I've already taken care of them."

Jake started to charge Perry. "You son of a bitch!"

Perry lifted his weapon and shoved it in Jake's face. "I wouldn't do that, if I were you. One more stupid stunt like that, and I'll have to punch a couple holes in you."

"I'd really prefer that you didn't." In a flash, Jake had knocked the gun out of Perry's hand and sent a punch flying into his jaw.

The older man staggered back hitting the wall. "You son of a bitch." He charged Jake hitting him in the gut.

The two men went sprawling to the ground with Perry on top. Lifting to his knees, Perry threw several more punches into Jake's midsection. Recovering, Jake tossed a jab into Perry's nose knocking the general off him. Flipping over, Jake crawled toward the control panel and stretched out his hand.

From behind, Perry jumped on him, flattening them both to the ground. Grabbing Jake's hand, he slammed it to the ground. Lifting, Perry sent punch after punch into Jake's kidney.

Trying to break free, Jake started to writhe. Grabbing Perry's arm, he twisted the older man off him. Rolling over, Jake sent his knee flying into Perry's midsection. The old man groaned. Lifting up, he grabbed Perry's broken arm and twisted it as hard as he could.

Perry screamed in pain as Jake rebroke the bones in his arm. Quickly standing, he kicked the old man in the ribs. Swiftly turning around, he threw himself toward the device. Landing on his knees, he reached toward the device, just barely missing. Reaching again, he quickly pressed his fingers into the recessed handprint.

Before he could touch his palm, Perry sprang up behind him and ripped him away from the device. "Don't touch that!"

Rolling over, Jake raised his booted foot up and sent Perry careening away from him. Perry slammed into one of the dead banks of computers.

Lifting to his knees, Jake jabbed his hand into the print. From behind him, he heard Perry screaming. Standing, he took several steps away from the device.

Jake watched as the control box slowly transformed into a solid block of metal. The legs slowly began to retract as the device lowered itself to the ground. Two panels on the body slid open revealing a mass of wires and blinking lights. Two snakelike coils emerged from the holes and worked their way down to the ground. Two claws extended from the coils and forced themselves into the ground. The orb on top started glowing a bright red and a high-pitched squealing began emanating from the device.

Bolts of lightning began to shoot off the orb in all directions hitting everything in the room. Small fires broke out where the bolts of electricity hit.

The solid red light of the orb started to blink on and off rapidly as the device began to shudder. "Oh, shit," Jake muttered.

Perry's eyes widened as he stared at the device. "What the hell is going on?"

"I think we're in trouble here." The ground around them began to shake. "Run!"

The two men charged for the door. Kicking a foot out, Perry tripped Jake sending him to the floor with a thud. Looking up, Jake watched Perry run out of the room.

Muttering under his breath as he lifted himself, he charged out of the room after Perry. Looking back, he saw a huge ball of flame shoot out of the room into the hall. Turning his attention back ahead, he caught Perry skittering around a corner.

Skidding to a stop, he watched Perry bolt out of sight. "Shit." He kicked the wall as hard as he could. Turning around, he started to make his way back toward Alex and Griggs.

***

Rounding the corner, Perry stopped short as a large girder fell from the ceiling, just narrowly missing him. The base was shaking violently now. Large chunks of plaster were falling down and shattering on the floor around him. Ducking around the corner, he stepped over the girder and proceeded on his way.

Reaching the control room, he raced through the door. Moving past the large conference table, he raced for the door on the opposite side of the room. Grabbing the handle, he opened it just as another tremor shook the base.

Losing his footing, Perry fell to the floor. Lifting himself, he stared around the empty room. The banks of computers whirred and beeped warnings of the impending doom of the base. He grabbed for the phone on the wall next to the door. Picking up the receiver, he keyed the intercom button. "This is General Perry," his voice echoed through the halls of the base. "The base is about to suffer a major meltdown. I'm ordering a total evacuation immediately!"

Dropping the phone, he took a step back into the conference room. Laying his hands on the table, he gritted his teeth. "Two bases destroyed in two days." He slammed his fist down. "I'll have your head, Silver."

CHAPTER TWENTY-FOUR

"Is he ready to go?"

"No! He's lost a lot of blood. I don't think he's going to make it." Alex was cradling Griggs in her arms on the cot.

"We need to get out of here now!" The base shuddered again. Jake grabbed onto the cell bars trying to maintain his balance.

Alex ran her hand across Griggs' sweaty forehead. "If we move him, we run the risk of losing him," her eyes were pleading with Jake.

"If we don't move him, we're all going to die." Another tremor ran through the base. Keeping his footing, Jake walked over to the cot and knelt down. He slowly reached over and took Alex's hand. "We need to go, Alex."

She nodded.

Reaching over, he slipped his arm under Griggs and helped him sit up. Grabbing Griggs' face, he turned it toward him. "Are you with us, Major?" Griggs moaned and his eyes started to roll back in his head. Jake shook him. "Come on, Major, stay with us!"

"Yeah," his voice was weak. "We need to move you."

He nodded. "I can make it." Slowly, he twisted on the cot and lowered his feet to the ground.

Alex stood next to him. "Put your hand on my shoulder. I'll help you up."

Klaxons all over the base started to sound as another shockwave rumbled. Jake lifted Griggs' arm over his shoulder and helped him to his feet. Griggs let out a moan of pain as they hobbled toward the cell door.

Jake and Alex helped their injured friend through the door and into the hallway. The three stumbled toward the wall as another tremor rocked the base.

Jake frowned. "We need to pick up the pace."

Griggs moaned again. "I'm going as fast as I can here."

The three scooted around the corner, narrowly missing the ceiling panels and lights crashing down around them. Reaching forward, Jake opened the door in front of them, then stepped back with wide eyes.

"We're not going this way." Rubble from the collapsed walls and ceiling filled the hallway making it impassable. Dust from the collapse flowed out filling the hallway.

Turning around, Jake looked behind them. "Shit! The hall behind us collapsed!" Alex pointed to a door partially buried behind a pile of debris. "That looks like our only choice."

Jake nodded. Moving Griggs over to the nearest wall, they leaned him against it. "Stay here, Major."

He tried to laugh. "I don't think I'm going anywhere."

Jake and Alex quickly moved over to the door and began throwing the debris out of the way. Piece by piece, they moved it. Finally opening the door, they found the hallway empty. Alex let out a sigh of relief. Running back over to Griggs, they grabbed him and swiftly started through the exit. Halfway down the hall, another shockwave slammed into the base. Griggs lost his footing and fell hard to the ground.

Kneeling down next to him, Jake slipped an arm around his midsection and began to lift him up. Once back on his feet, Jake quickly pulled his arm away. Looking down, he saw that blood had soaked his shirtsleeve and hand.

"Damn." He tried to wipe some of the blood off on his pants. "Turn around, Major." Griggs slowly spun around. Running his hand across Griggs' wound, Jake stared at the blood that had accumulated on his hand. "When you fell, you must've exacerbated your injury. Are you okay?"

Griggs thought for a moment. "Yeah, I feel fi—" His eyes rolled back and he began to fall to the floor.

Quickly, Jake reached out, catching Griggs before he could hit the ground. Doing his best to support Griggs, he slowly lowered his friend to the floor. "Major!"

Alex fell to her knees next to him. "Jason!" She gently touched his face with both hands and drew her mouth close to his ear. "Don't leave me."

"I think it would be best if you stepped away from the major." Jake and Alex looked up to see Anne standing in front of them with her weapon drawn.

"Anne," Jake groaned. "How did you get here?"

Walking toward Jake, she began to wave her gun in his face. "I told you that I worked at Area 51, I just lied about what I did." She ran her gloved hand across his face. "It's nice to see you again."

He forcefully pushed her hand away from his

face. "Don't touch me," he said in an icy tone. "You had Christina's father killed for talking to me."

"I did nothing of the sort." She smirked. "I merely informed my commanding officer that one of his main researchers was imparting Top Secret material to a civilian. He made the call after that."

Rage filled Jake. "You cold-hearted bitch. He had a wife and daughter to support. Did you ever think about that?"

"My only concern was national security." "And yourself."

"Well," she pushed her gun into his gut, "someone's in a pissy mood today."

"I'm not in the mood for your shit, Anne. Either kill me or get the fuck out of my way."

Stepping back, she cocked the hammer back on her pistol. "Fine, if that's the way you want it." She started to squeeze the trigger.

"I don't think so." Jumping at that moment, Alex kicked Anne, knocking the gun out of her hand.

Anne grabbed her throbbing hand. "You bitch!" Taking several steps forward, she leaped at Alex knocking her down. In a flurry, she was sending her fists into Alex's face, scratching and tearing at her hair. Quickly reaching down, Jake pulled Anne off Alex and threw her across the room.

Anne recovered and charged Jake. Leaping off her feet, she sent a high kick into Jake's chest knocking the wind out of him. He fell to the ground and rolled to his left, just as she was about to stomp on his face. Grabbing her leg, he tossed her to the ground.

Alex lifted herself onto her feet and brushed a

mess of hair out of her face. Turning around, she bent down and picked up Anne's gun.

Anne smirked. "Even if you kill me, you'll never make it out of here alive."

"I'll take my chances." Alex pulled the trigger. Anne's body slumped to the ground as blood oozed from the wound in her midsection. Slipping the pistol into her holster, she knelt down next to Griggs. "We need to get him out of here."

Jake knelt down beside her. Reaching over, he placed his fingers on Griggs' neck and pressed down. An odd expression passed over his face as he moved his fingers across Griggs' throat. "I can't find a pulse."

Tears welled up in her eyes as she lowered her head to his chest and tried to listen for breathing. "He's not breathing either." She straddled him and laid her hands in the middle of his chest. She quickly began administering CPR. She pumped hard feeling his ribs crack under her hands. Lowering down, she leaned his head back and pushed two long puffs of air into his lungs. Lifting, she pumped hard again.

"Come on!" she screamed. She continued to breathe for him and pump on his chest.

Jake laid a hand on her shoulder, "He's gone, Alex."

"No!" she cried. Pushing Jake away, she continued with the CPR. She was determined to save him.

Grabbing her, Jake pulled her off Griggs. "He's gone!" She struggled in his arms. "No! I can save him!"

"You can't. Let him go," he said in a low soft

voice. "We need to get out of here." Tears rolled down her face.

"He would've wanted it that way."

"I know," she said in a weak voice.

Kneeling down next to their fallen comrade, Jake laid his hand on his friend's chest. "Thank you, Major Griggs. God speed on your way." Carefully, he closed his friend's eyes.

***

Perry stepped out of the conference room into the hallway. The pipes running along the ceiling had cracked and fallen to the floor in a large heap. Trying to navigate around them, he stepped on one and slipped. Falling down hard, his head slammed into one of the broken pipes cutting a long laceration in his forehead. Rolling off it, he held his hand on the cut trying to stop the blood streaming down his face. Lifting himself out of the rubble, he cautiously made his way to the end of the hall.

Four soldiers, oblivious to everything except their own safety, sprinted past him nearly knocking him down on their way toward the exit. Catching himself on the nearby wall, he cursed them under his breath.

Cradling his broken arm, he walked unsteadily down the hall. Turning the corner, he found himself confronted by the room that held the device. Moving cautiously closer, he poked his head around the edge of the door to take a look inside. A huge ball of flame shot past him as he pulled his head back from the door.

Flattening himself against the wall, he tried to think. He needed to find a way to shut the device down. He wasn't about to have the two most Top

337

Secret bases in the United States destroyed while they were under his command.

Taking a deep breath, he jumped around the corner and spotted the object. It had now completely cocooned the room in a mass of wires and cable. He watched in horror as several more coils shot out from the device and adhered themselves to the walls and ceiling. Surges of blue electricity shot along the cables toward the nest around it heating the wires and cables until it became one solid mass.

"Jesus," Perry muttered to himself. Just then, a bright beam of red light shot out of the glowing orb atop the device and slammed into his head. He knew in that instant this was no 'power source' as they had once believed, but a doomsday weapon. Through the mind link, he realized the aliens who created it to destroy their enemies used it, sometimes, on members of their own race who didn't conform to their society. This particular device had been left on Earth to destroy the colonists in case they stepped out of line. Perry came to another realization. It was alive.

The red beam of light suddenly died. Several coils snaked their way toward him, wrapping themselves around his legs and arms. They crawled up his body until they had him entirely wrapped up. The coils began to retract pulling him to the ground. He cried out in terror, only to be silenced by one of the chords which worked its way up into his throat. He immediately started to gag and choke. It was cutting off his oxygen.

The device carefully maneuvered him into the web of wires. Once he was in place, the coils holding him broke off from the device keeping him immobile. He was trying to breathe, but failing. He watched another surge of energy blaze out from the device toward him. In horror, he saw the cables around him solidify in place. He knew he was going to die.

***

Jake and Alex rounded another corner and came face-to-face with several soldiers. Jake thought quickly. "General Perry has ordered an evacuation. What's the quickest way out of here?"

The soldiers looked at each other, then back at Jake and Alex. A long silence past before they answered. "Why don't you know the way?"

Alex answered. "We were part of the team General Perry brought over here from Area 51. We're not familiar with the layout of this base."

The lead soldier nodded. "Go back the way you came. Take the first right; follow that hall until you can take another right. That should lead straight to the main exit."

Jake smiled. "Thank you."

As they turned to leave, one of the soldiers grabbed Jake's shoulder. "Aren't you forgetting something, Lieutenant?"

Jake spun around. He had no idea what he meant. Then he caught sight of the rank on his collar. He was a major. "Sorry, sir." Jake snapped to attention and saluted. Alex understood and followed suit. The major returned the salute.

The two turned around again and made their way back down the hall. Taking the first right, they found themselves back in front of the room that housed the device.

339

"Shit. I really don't want to be back here again," Alex moaned. "I'm with you on that one," Jake agreed.

The two started to walk past the room when Alex heard a moan. "Did you hear that, Jake?"

"Nope. Keep going."

Alex stopped. "I've got to know what the device is doing, Jake. I'm a researcher after all."

"No. Let's get the hell out of here while we still can."

It was too late, Alex had already stepped in front of the door. She gasped. "Oh my God, come look at this, Jake."

Reluctantly, Jake moved next to her. His eyes went wide. "Jesus. What the hell is it doing in there?"

"I have no idea." She began to move closer, but Jake grabbed her and pulled her back.

"Look over there." He pointed toward what appeared to be a body mummified in the cables. "I don't think you want to end up like that poor bastard."

She nodded.

"Let's get the hell out of here."

The base began to shake again. Dodging the falling ceiling tiles and pipes, they made their way down the hallway and took the next right. At the end of the corridor, they found themselves standing in the middle of a cavernous room that appeared to be carved directly out of the mountain. Several white Jeeps were parked there, along with an assortment of other vehicles. Grabbing Alex by the arm, Jake led her to one of the parked white Jeeps.

Climbing inside, Jake reached down and

grabbed at the ignition. "Shit. No keys." Another shockwave rattled through the base. A large rock came loose from the roof and smashed through the windshield of their Jeep. Jake and Alex stared at each other, then quickly jumped out.

Jake pointed at a black SUV parked across from them. "Let's try that one." They weaved their way through the falling debris toward the vehicle. Grabbing the door handle, Jake opened the door and jumped inside. Reaching down, he found the keys still in the ignition.

"We're in business here." Twisting the keys hard, he listened to the powerful engine roar to life. Grabbing the stick shift, he pushed the clutch to the floor and popped it into reverse. Looking behind him, he swiftly guided the vehicle out of the parking spot and turned it around.

He pressed down on the clutch and put the vehicle into first. He glanced over at Alex. "Ready?"

She nodded.

Jake stomped on the accelerator. The rear wheels peeled out and began to smoke. Finally catching, they sent the vehicle screaming toward the main gate. Popping it into second gear, they moved faster. Hitting the ramp that led to the main gate, the SUV became airborne.

Jake gunned the accelerator as they landed, smashing through the guardrail. Two of the men in the guard shack jumped out and tried to squeeze off several rounds, but it was too late. The black SUV had already sped around the corner.

***

Perry stared at the glowing device. He knew

this was it. It changed from a bright red color to a deep green and began to spin on its axis. It began to emit a high-pitched whine, then suddenly stopped. The orb went black and everything fell silent. For a brief instant, Perry could actually hear his heart beating.

Seconds later, it exploded. Fire engulfed the room and Perry was killed instantly. The explosion came in two waves. The first wave was fire. It moved through the base like a flood of water obliterating everything in its path. Soldiers ran frantically through the base trying to escape the flames, only to be caught and burned to death. Several men on fire ran screaming through the halls.

The second wave followed with the force of hundreds of nuclear missiles. It immediately knocked down the inner structures of the base causing it to implode. The mountain above the base crashed down burying all the men still inside under tons of rock and debris. Those who weren't burned to death by the fires were crushed to death.

Then as quickly as it began, it was over. The dust slowly began to settle back down. The screams of men trapped in the rocks slowly faded as they suffocated. It was a horrible way to die.

***

Jake and Alex felt the explosion. Turning to look behind them, they saw a huge plume of flames and debris reaching high into the morning sky. Jake tightened his grip on the wheel as Alex pulled her seatbelt over her chest and buckled it.

"Drive!" she said without looking back at Jake.

Jake complied, swiftly making his way through the gears until he hit fifth. Still staring behind them,

Alex watched as the second wave of the explosion neared them.

"Drive faster!"

"I'm going as fast as I can!"

The wave of dust and debris caught them and tossed them into the air. Small rocks whizzed past them with the speed of a bullet. A giant rock smashed through the rear window sending shards of glass hurtling through the vehicle. Alex ducked down and covered her head as several of the glass shards sliced at her arms. The vehicle slammed back into the desert floor front first. Jake tried to regain control of the vehicle as it skidded through the soft desert soil. Twisting the wheel hard in his hands, he skillfully steered the Jeep away from the wave.

CHAPTER TWENTY-FIVE

Several days had passed since they had escaped from Area 51 and finished their assault on S-4. They hadn't stopped when they reached Las Vegas. They both wanted to get as far away from there as they possibly could. They drove straight through central Utah, only stopping for gas in a small town in the middle of nowhere.

Finally passing over the state line into Colorado, Jake finally breathed a sigh of relief. Alex had fallen asleep in the seat next to him. As far as he knew, this was the first decent rest she had in days. He knew he hadn't the chance to rest since he took this case.

Nearly an hour later, they began passing through Grand Junction. The stepped mountains around them were stark in comparison to the luscious trees and greens of the orchards on either side of the highway.

Rolling down the window, he felt the warm dry air on his face and took a deep breath of the sweet fragrance of the peaches and other fruit growing on the trees all around him.

He needed to rest. He had been driving straight for ten hours. Clicking on the turn signal, he slowly pulled the SUV onto the off-ramp and made his way downtown. The city was lush with trees and buildings. The streets were busy with cars and people making their way back and forth during their normal lives. He wondered if any of them even suspected what they had just been through.

Pulling onto the main street, he stared at the small shops and the people moving on the sidewalks. Taking a left, he followed another street until it connected with Lincoln Avenue. Guiding the large black vehicle to the right, he followed the road until he saw a large hotel to his left.

Pulling into the turn lane, he waited patiently until he could drive into the hotel's parking lot. He watched the parade of cars pass by him as his mind started to wander back to what they had done. Shaking it off, he saw an opening in the traffic and carefully pulled into the hotel's parking lot.

Finding a spot in the front, he turned off the ignition and stepped out. Stretching his legs, he walked in the front doors and up to the empty registration desk. Everything in the room was a dark shade of brown, from the wooden chairs to the rugs on the floor. He scanned the large room for the clerk, finally deciding to ring the bell.

A door behind the desk opened and a small balding man stepped up to the counter. "Can I help you?"

"I need a room for the night with twin beds."

The man reached behind the desk and pulled out a small card and pen and handed them to Jake. "Please fill this out."

Leaning over on the counter, Jake carefully filled out the card. Signing it at the bottom, he handed it back to the clerk. "Here you go."

The clerk scooped up the card and looked it over. "Very good. That'll be sixty- three dollars."

Jake fished a wad of cash out of his pocket and flipped out four twenty-dollar bills.

The man graciously accepted the bills and

345

handed Jake a key. He pointed over the desk to the back of the room. "You'll be on the third floor. Take the elevator, it's easier." He opened the cash drawer and counted out the change.

"Thanks." Jake took the change and deposited it in his pocket. Turning around, he walked outside to wake Alex. Moving over to the passenger door, he leaned into the window and gently shook her. "Wake up, Alex."

She slowly lifted her head and smiled. "Are we there yet?"

"Yeah, we're there." He returned the smile. Opening her door, he helped her out. "I got us a room so we can get cleaned up and get some rest."

***

The warm water felt good on her aching body. She stood in the center of the shower and just let the water wash over her. She lifted her arms and ran her hands through her long brown hair letting the water hit her on the neck and shoulders. Reaching down, she twisted the shower knobs and turned the water off.

Pushing aside the shower curtain, she stepped out and grabbed a towel off the rack near her. Wrapping it around her body, she went over to the mirror and retrieved a small brush off the sink. Wiping the steam off the mirror with her hand, she ran the brush carefully through her hair several times before replacing it on the sink. Reaching over for a small black travel bag, she unzipped it and pulled out a pair of boxers and a white tank top. Dropping the towel, she slowly pulled on the clean clothes.

Opening the door, she stepped into the room to

346

find Jake stretched out on one of the beds watching TV. Making her way over to the other bed, she slumped down on it and laid her head on the pillows.

Rolling onto her side, she looked at Jake. "You'll feel a little better if you take a shower."

"I know. I just don't have the strength to get up right now."

They both laughed for a moment. A serious look then washed over Alex's face. "Do you think they'll come after us?"

Clicking off the TV, he rose to a sitting position facing her. "I'm sure of it." Alex didn't like that answer. "But it'll take them awhile. They'll have to figure out what happened first."

"I don't want to spend the rest of my life running away."

"Neither do I." He snapped his fingers. "Look at it this way. The only two people that could really identify us, namely General Perry and Colonel Hunter, are dead."

She nodded. "Do you think we did the right thing?" Jake thought for a moment. "I believe we did."

She ran her fingers through her wet hair. "I miss Griggs."

"I do, too. He was a good man and he stood up for what he believed in. He will be missed."

Alex sat silently for a moment. Laying back down, she smiled at Jake. "Let's not think about this anymore right now. I want to watch some TV."

Jake nodded and turned it back on. He surfed through the channels past the talk shows and infomercials until he found a show he liked. Placing the remote next to him he settled back into the bed.

The screen went blank for a moment, but was replaced by a blue screen with the presidential logo on it. That faded into a shot of an empty podium in front of some blue curtains. A man in a dark blue suit and tie stepped up to the podium and cleared his throat. Jake instantly recognized him as the President's Chief of Staff. *"Ladies and gentlemen of the press, the President of the United States."*

The room was quiet as the president took the podium. *"I've called you here today for a very important reason."* He took a deep breath and continued. *"We have lost a great man and a good friend today. My main military advisor General Joshua Perry died in an accident earlier this morning."*

Jake turned to Alex. "Are you listening to this?"

She nodded as she stared at the television. "I can't believe it."

The President cleared his throat and continued. *"He was attending the test flight of one of our newest aircraft at Nellis Air Force Base when the plane crashed shortly after takeoff and killed several of our top men, including General Perry."* He held his hand over his mouth as he coughed. *"Excuse me."* He adjusted his papers on the podium in front of him. *"He was a great man and will be missed."*

The press corps started shouting questions at him. Slowly, he moved away from the podium and was replaced by his Chief of Staff. *"No questions, please. The White House will issue a press release later this evening. Thank you for attending."*

The image faded back to the Presidential logo, then to a local anchorman back in the studio. *"The President has just announced the death of General Josh Perry."* Perry's picture flashed up in the corner of the screen. *"We'll have more details on this tragic story as soon as they become available."* He quickly shifted the notes in front of him, then faced the camera again. *"Later, on 'News 5' at five, a major earthquake rocked the Southwestern United States this morning. Officials say the epicenter was just outside Las Vegas, Nevada. We'll have further details tonight. We now return you to your regularly scheduled programming."*

THE END